Louise Allen has been in... history for as long as she... landscapes and places ev... the past. Venice, Burgundy and the Greek islands are favourites. Louise lives on the Norfolk coast and spends her spare time gardening, researching family history or travelling. Please visit Louise's website, www.louiseallenregency.com, her blog, janeaustenslondon.com, or find her on X, @LouiseRegency, and on Facebook.

Also by Louise Allen

His Convenient Duchess
A Rogue for the Dutiful Duchess
Becoming the Earl's Convenient Wife
How Not to Propose to a Duke
Tempted by Her Enemy Marquis
The Lady Who Said No to the Duke

Liberated Ladies miniseries

Least Likely to Marry a Duke
The Earl's Marriage Bargain
A Marquis in Want of a Wife
The Earl's Reluctant Proposal
A Proposal to Risk Their Friendship

Discover more at millsandboon.co.uk.

THE DANGERS OF DECEIVING A DUKE

Louise Allen

MILLS & BOON

All rights reserved including the right of reproduction in whole or in part in any form. This edition is published by arrangement with Harlequin Enterprises ULC.

This is a work of fiction. Names, characters, places, locations and incidents are purely fictional and bear no relationship to any real life individuals, living or dead, or to any actual places, business establishments, locations, events or incidents. Any resemblance is entirely coincidental.

Without limiting the exclusive rights of any author, contributor or the publisher of this publication, any unauthorised use of this publication to train generative artificial intelligence (AI) technologies is expressly prohibited. HarperCollins also exercise their rights under Article 4(3) of the Digital Single Market Directive 2019/790 and expressly reserve this publication from the text and data mining exception.

® and TM are trademarks owned and used by the trademark owner and/or its licensee. Trademarks marked with ® are registered with the United Kingdom Patent Office and/or the Office for Harmonisation in the Internal Market and in other countries.

First published in Great Britain 2026
by Mills & Boon, an imprint of HarperCollins*Publishers* Ltd,
1 London Bridge Street, London, SE1 9GF

www.harpercollins.co.uk

HarperCollins*Publishers*, Macken House, 39/40 Mayor Street Upper, Dublin 1, D01 C9W8, Ireland

The Dangers of Deceiving a Duke © 2026 Melanie Hilton

ISBN: 978-0-263-41868-2

02/26

Printed and Bound in the UK using 100% Renewable Electricity at CPI Group (UK) Ltd, Croydon, CR0 4YY

This is my 75th story for Harlequin Mills & Boon and I would never have gotten here if it wasn't for AJH. Much love and thanks.

Prologue

Oxfordshire, June 1809.

'Wake up, Miss. This is as far as you can go.'

The voice was rough but kindly, and Caitlin, roused from her uneasy sleep, wondered vaguely who the young lady he was addressing was.

'Come on, Miss, you'll put us all behind.' Something touched her gloved hand and she blinked into consciousness.

She was in a stagecoach. Yes, of course she was. In a stagecoach with a thin man who looked like a clerk and had been sucking peppermint drops the entire time, a plump woman who apparently disapproved of everything and was quite prepared to complain about it, and a lad who announced when he'd boarded that he was being sent home from school because of an outbreak of measles, but they were not to worry because he'd had it already.

And she, of course, was the "Miss". Not "my lady". Not the daughter of an earl any longer.

'Oh. I am sorry. Where are we?' She straightened her bonnet and tried to look alert and intelligent, not half out of her wits with worry and misery. If she was going to survive this, she reminded herself, she was going to have to be in control, to be strong and most definitely not look like a helpless victim.

She was never going to be a victim again. *Never.*

'Duke's Forde, Miss.' The guard was already lifting her valise, her only remaining piece of luggage, down from the coach. 'By rights, with what you paid, we should have put you down at Bishop's Forde, two miles back, but I wouldn't want any decent female having to put up at the Dog and Ferret. Just an alehouse that is, and rough with it. You'll be all right here. These days the Harland Arms isn't what it was, but it's a decent enough place.'

He held out his hand to help her down, and Caitlin dug in her reticule for a sixpenny piece she could ill afford. 'Thank you. I appreciate your consideration. What time is it?'

As if in answer a church clock began to strike. One, two, three, four, five. There was a pause and then *clunk.*

'Is that five or six?'

'Five,' the guard said over his shoulder as he climbed up onto his perch at the back of the coach.

The ostlers had already changed the team. 'It's been doing that for as long as I've been on this route and that's nigh on eight years. Stand clear now, Miss.'

The stage picked up speed and was away in a swirl of dust, leaving Caitlin with her bag at her feet and her reticule with its few precious crowns clutched in her hand. She made herself survey her surroundings calmly. She was on the edge of what seemed to be a market square—or, more accurately, a rectangle with the main road, where she stood, forming one long edge.

At her back was a somewhat down-at-heel inn—The Harland Arms, she supposed. To her left the bottom boundary of the rectangle was formed by the churchyard wall with the church looming up beyond it. The opposite side held a range of almshouses nearest to the churchyard, then the opening of a lane, then some shops. The end opposite the church was a rather dilapidated range of buildings.

The stump of a market cross stood in the centre, and some jackdaws were squabbling over what seemed to be the remains of the market produce—some cabbage leaves or perhaps squashed fruit.

The village—or was it a very small town if it had a market?—was not exactly bustling with activity, she thought. It seemed unlikely to have an employment agency, for example.

As if prompted by the thought of employment and

therefore wages and therefore food, her stomach rumbled. She should go into the inn, ask for a room and a meal and then make a plan.

Caitlin smiled ruefully. That made it sound as though she had any options to choose between when she really had only one. She had made her choice and that was to accept ruin as an exile. But she had to find work. Paid work. Respectable work, which meant she was going to have to forge references.

Great Uncle Alexander was her best option. He had a title, a good—and conveniently very remote—Scottish address and was said to be increasingly vague. If someone enquired whether a Miss Jones, or whatever name she found for herself, had been employed as his late wife's companion, he would hopefully conclude he had forgotten the woman and reply that certainly she had and she had been most satisfactory.

A companion was surely the occupation to try for. It was the most respectable, the least dangerous. Once she set her feet on the slippery slope of domestic service she would never climb back out of it, and besides, an unprotected female was always at risk from amorous employers or their sons.

Although she doubted one could be ruined twice. As she turned towards the inn's entrance Caitlin winced with discomfort. It seemed that losing one's virginity was another thing that women must be punished for with pain, as though the daughters of Eve did not already have enough to put up with. At least Blaine Wykeham had abandoned her before marriage—if he had ever intended that in the first place. She was alone but, mercifully, not tied to him. Society and her parents would say she was ruined, but she was not going to go back and have them make that judgement. She would not allow this to ruin her life.

As she moved, the light breeze shifted direction, bringing with it the scent of fresh bread, of warm sugar and a hint of coffee. Instinctively she turned towards it, crossed the road and set foot on the cobbled surface of the marketplace. The inn held only the prospect of its "ordinary" which was doubtless a greasy mutton stew. That delicious odour sent the promise of some comfort, something badly needed, even if it meant that it would be her only meal for the day.

Caitlin picked her way across the uneven stones and saw that she was approaching a group of three shops that were distinctly better than the rest of those surrounding the market. To the left was some kind of superior leather worker's—*Dangerfield Cordwainer* read the name board in gold on a bottle-green. *Brandon's Fine Fabrics & Haberdashery* came next, in white on deep crimson, and then the source of the tempting aromas, *Duke's Forde Bakery* in brown and white.

To reach it she had to swerve left to avoid a large puddle, and Caitlin gained the pavement just in front of the haberdashery. A shrill yapping made her glance inside as she passed the open door, just as a fluffy white lapdog darted across the shop floor, right in front of a man who must be the proprietor, two rolls of cloth balanced in his arms.

'Pippin! Bad dog!'

'Oh, do look out!'

Pippin dived between the man's feet and he went down with a crash in a tangle of fabric. Caitlin heard the sound of his head hitting the wooden chair at the counter even over the noise the dog was making and the cries of its owner.

The next thing she knew, she was on her knees by his side, holding her entirely inadequate handkerchief against the blood welling from the gash across his forehead. Pressing hard, she looked up. Two middle-aged matrons stood aghast, one of them clutching Pippin to her bosom. A lanky youth in a vast baize apron had frozen in place behind the counter, cutting shears in hand. The only person who appeared to still have their wits about them was a girl of perhaps fifteen, mob cap on head, a white apron around her waist.

'Fetch me clean cold water and soft cotton cloth,' Caitlin ordered her and, as she turned to obey, snapped at the lad, 'And you, don't stand there like a looby. Run and fetch the doctor!'

He dropped the shears and sprinted out of the door.

Caitlin smiled at the two customers. 'Might I suggest that you go next door and take some refreshment for the sake of your nerves, ladies?'

The poor man had suffered a painful injury, and the least she could do was make sure he didn't lose any customers in the process, even if it had been all their fault.

And so, quite by chance, and thanks to a puddle and a lapdog, Lady Caitlin Montgomery changed her name, her very identity and her life forever. Miss Catherine Ransome was going to learn to be a haberdasher.

Chapter One

Duke's Forde, 3 June 1817—eight years later, almost to the day.

'As you will have observed, Your Grace, the place has, sadly, seen better days.'

It took a moment for Quinn Falconer to realise that the steward was addressing him. He was still, after almost two months, unused to being the Duke of Harland. That was his great-uncle Dominic, the seemingly indestructible patriarch of the family. Indestructible, that was, until his heir and only grandson Jordan, Colonel Lord Falconbridge, returned from the battlefield of Waterloo with his left leg amputated and a wound in his side that refused to heal.

A year later Jordan was dead, and his grandfather was left a shattered man who seemed to Quinn to have lost all will to live and who died two months after his heir. And now Quinn was Duke of Harland.

Overnight he had gone from planning improvements to his own modest family estates and growing his small, but promising portfolio of London property to finding his own modest estates and London properties dwarfed by new possessions, new responsibilities managing this vast inheritance with all its demands. He had even reached the point where he had felt secure enough to seek a wife, start a family. There was no time to think about that now, not until the start of the Season, at least.

He had surveyed his new country seat and found, virtually on his own doorstep, the town—or was it a village?—of Duke's Forde.

'This was a prosperous place once, judging by the size of the church and the marketplace and the inn,' he observed to Yorke, sitting beside him in the curricle that he had drawn up at the church end of the market area. 'What happened?' He had driven through the town on his way to Harland Park and an idea had begun to grow in his mind in the days since.

'There was a bad outbreak of some disease, maybe fifty years ago, Your Grace. There were many deaths, the rental income collapsed, as you may imagine, and people began to avoid the place, not to stop at the inn if they could help it. It proved, in the end, to be a pollution of the main wells in the town, but by the time that was discovered and new wells sunk, the damage had been done. The late Duke had only just inherited and had a young wife and child and so he moved to the Norfolk estate for fear for their health. It seems that it was a case of out of sight, out of mind, if I might so phrase it.

'The income continued to fall, His Grace found he preferred the Norfolk estate and then, when he did turn his attention to it, the place seemed too far gone—it had become a large village. The big house was kept up of course, but rarely inhabited by the family. The Colonel used to come now and again.'

'The other estates and the London properties—they are all in good heart, from what I have seen so far,' Quinn said. He was familiar only with Willington Hall in Norfolk and the main London residence, but his study of the account books showed everywhere, including the big house and its lands, just five miles away, to be in a healthy state. 'This place is the only blot on the ledgers and the duchy owns most of the property, does it not? The market still functions?'

'I would say that 80 percent of the property in the parish is the duchy's, Your Grace. The market is held on Wednesdays and that's quite lively still.'

'And we are fifteen miles from Oxford, an ideal stopping place for travellers, you would think. But now they prefer to drive on rather than stay here, which is understandable. If the inn was renovated, the shops and houses put in good order, this place could flourish.

'What it needs is somewhere that is a destination in

itself,' Quinn mused aloud. 'With an assembly room, a circulating library, excellent bedchambers, good food. An hotel. There.' He pointed to the long side of the marketplace. 'With the properties on the short side renovated, and the inn itself, improved…' He narrowed his eyes, assessing it. 'We keep the inn for the stabling and accommodation of a more modest kind. Do the Mails stop here? Yes? Then we could establish a posting house. And there must be room for a livery stables.'

'Er, Your Grace.'

'Yes, Yorke?'

'That all sounds most exciting, Your Grace. Very enterprising. But I should point out that there is just one block of property over there, just where you wish to place your new hotel, that does not belong to the estate. Those three establishments, that I believe you can tell from here are in much better condition, more prosperous.'

'I will buy them out,' Quinn said, amused at his own airy tone. This business of being a duke, with all the power and the resources at his command, must be going to his head. 'Or we can exchange those properties for some on the short side, have them refurbished for the owners. Whatever they are selling, the presence of the new hotel can only be to their benefit in increased trade.'

He clicked his tongue at the bays and winced as

the wheels of the curricle lurched across the uneven stones of the marketplace. 'This all needs re-laying.'

As he halted the pair in front of the first shop, Garnett, his tiger, jumped out and ran to their heads. Quinn flipped the reins around the whip and climbed down, waiting for the steward, who descended with rather more care.

'Dangerfield Cordwainer,' he read, looking up at the restrained gold lettering. 'And very nice too.' The window displayed a pair of driving gauntlets, a pair of boots that would not have looked out of place in Hoby's in St James's and beautifully tooled sets of saddlebags and gun cases. Hanging inside the glass of the upper part of the door was a sign. *Closed.*

'Damn,' Quinn said mildly and strolled along to the next window. '*Mrs Catherine Brandon.* Mrs Brandon appears to be in the haberdashery line. And millinery too. All very elegant and not at all what I would expect in this place,' he added, taking in the tasteful window display of swirls of fabric forming a backdrop to three bonnets, to his eye very much in the mode. 'What have we got next?'

The last of the three shops was the source of the enticing aroma that had been tantalising his nostrils for some minutes. Spices, coffee and warm sugar. '*Madame Madelaine, Confectioner.* And a very feminine establishment indeed. It appears to be full of ladies recovering from spending money next door. I think we will leave this one until last, Yorke. Let us see whether Mrs Brandon is at home.'

She was, he saw as they entered the shop. The arrival of two men caused a flutter amongst the ladies browsing a display of lace on one side and two more apparently discussing ribbons with a neatly dressed female assistant on the other. Behind the counter a young man in a baize apron was cutting cloth from a bolt, under the direction of a woman who must be the owner.

Mid-twenties, Quinn hazarded. Slim, tall and brunette. There was no apron over the elegantly plain gown that covered an equally pleasing figure, and she had a ridiculous confection of lace and ribbon pretending to be a cap—the sign of her married status—perched on her head amidst glossy curls. Mrs Brandon appeared to be as refined as her shop.

As he watched her, she half-turned, alerted by the tinkle of the bell over the door, and smiled, her eyebrows just a little raised at the sight of two men. Her eyes widened for a moment, as though a sudden thought had arrested her, then there was just that faint, polite smile in place.

A memory swept through Quinn, bringing with it the scent of honeysuckle and warmth. But there was no image with the recollection, only that haunting smell of summer. He glanced around, half-expecting to see a vase of honeysuckle somewhere, but the only flowers were in an arrangement of roses.

'Good day, gentlemen. How may I help you?' She came towards them in a subtle rustle of skirts, and Quinn registered that her voice was refined, with no hint that elocution lessons had masked a provincial accent. It would seem she was a lady fallen on hard times and forced to take up the most genteel form of shopkeeping. It was not uncommon.

The scent she brought with her was discreet and herbal. No honeysuckle there either, he must have been imagining it.

'Good morning. I was hoping to speak to the owner.'

'I am Mrs Brandon, and this is my shop.'

'Perhaps we might speak somewhere private?' Quinn kept his voice low, conscious of eyes on them. 'I am Harland.'

The finely drawn brows rose a little higher. She had clearly heard of him. 'Come through to the office, gentlemen,' Mrs Brandon said, turning and leading the way past the end of the counter and towards a closed door. Yorke hurried past and opened it for her and received a slight inclination of her head in acknowledgement.

'Your Grace,' she said when the door was closed. 'Please, take a seat. And Mr—?'

'Yorke, ma'am. I am his Grace's steward.'

She sat, her hands folded on the desk in front of

her. Quinn noticed a plain gold wedding ring and no other jewellery other than pearl studs in her ears and a small gold brooch at the neck of her gown. He was surprised that she did not speak, ask why they were there. Surely she was curious? Dukes in haberdashery shops in obscure market towns must be as rare as hen's teeth.

'You may be aware that I have recently inherited,' he began.

'Indeed I am. My condolences on the loss of your great-uncle and your cousin, Your Grace.'

'Thank you. I have become aware that this town—or perhaps it is a large village?—has been sadly neglected. I believe it has potential for better things, as your establishment and its neighbours show.'

'We like to consider it a town,' she said with that faint smile. 'Many local families find it refreshing not to have to travel into Oxford for what we can provide. If there were more facilities in the town, then I am sure they would be well patronised as well.'

'My feeling exactly.' Quinn was pleased that Mrs Brandon seemed so understanding. He was beginning to warm to the look of intelligence in her hazel eyes, to enjoy the way she was so clearly listening and considering what he had to say. And it was no hardship to look at her either, not that a gentleman would do anything so crass as to openly show that appreciation.

'It is my intention to improve the inn and also to

build an hotel to cater for the carriage trade and to provide an assembly room. Perhaps there would be a circulating library and a billiard room on the premises as well. Throughout the town the properties owned by the estate must be put into good order and more shops of a better class encouraged.'

'An hotel? That would be a very welcome improvement, Your Grace. But what has this to do with me?'

'The ideal location for such a building is here.' He gestured around him. 'Your shop and its two neighbours are right in the middle of where it would best be sited.'

The smile faded from her eyes, leaving them almost green. He thought suddenly of the chill of water under ice. 'These three shops are not part of your estate, Your Grace. Nor are they rented from anyone else.'

'I am aware of that, Mrs Brandon. I am prepared to pay a very good price for them and, in addition, provide other sites in exchange, to be furbished up as you desire at my expense. On the end of the marketplace facing the church would be the right place, I thought.'

'But I have no desire to move. This is my home as well as my business. The area you suggest would be perfectly suitable for the hotel.'

'It has virtually no land behind it. The road turns sharply behind the buildings with the river on the other side.'

'Then build your assembly room over the circulating library and, what was it? Oh, yes, a billiards room, on that site, then the hotel can sit at the end of this side, beyond the confectioner's.'

'The building will not be set off to its best advantage in that position.' Even as he spoke, Quinn could feel the force of her resolve.

'I regret that I am unable to satisfy you in this, Your Grace,' Mrs Brandon said with perfect politeness and without one ounce of regret visible. 'You must forgive me if I find my business interests more important that the ideal aesthetics of a theoretical hotel.'

And if she will not sell, there is no point in my acquiring the two flanking properties. And she knows it.

Time to stop being a gentleman and try a little of that crass appreciation? Quinn met the steady green gaze and allowed his own eyes to widen, just a little, his gaze to grow warm. 'And there is nothing I can say or do that might cause you to change your mind, Mrs Brandon?' he enquired, lowering his voice, letting just a hint of an invitation creep into it.

For a moment he thought he saw a response, a feminine awareness of him as a man, then her lips tightened from a soft bow to a hard line and those eyes remained cold and green.

'Absolutely nothing, Your Grace. Nothing at all.'

That attempt at flirtation had been a major error. He had made an enemy now.

Chapter Two

He thinks he can flirt with me? That I am so empty-headed that I would surrender this building for what? A dalliance? A dalliance with a duke.

Furious with herself for feeling even a momentary attraction, a fleeting weakness, Cat stood up, the two men rising as she did so.

'I do not think there is any point in discussing this further, Your Grace. I wish you well in your endeavours to improve Duke's Forde, and I am certain you will see a good return on your plans. Allow me to see you out.'

The steward opened the door for her and she walked through briskly, aware as she passed the Duke of the scent of leather and citrus. Her skirts brushed his boots, but she did not look down, nor up at him.

Quinn Falconer needs absolutely no encouragement.

Seeing him had brought it all back: the time before, the time when she was Lady Caitlin. She even thought of herself as Cat now, a new name to distance herself from that innocent, trusting girl.

They left and the place was empty except for Ben, her shopman, and Helen, her assistant and maid. They were far too well-trained to blurt out questions, but they were both clearly agog with curiosity.

'That was the new Duke of Harland and his steward, Mr Yorke,' she informed them crisply. 'His Grace wishes to buy the shop as part of his plans to improve the town.'

Ben's jaw dropped and the shears hit the counter with a thud.

'What on earth would a duke want with a haberdashery shop?' Helen asked.

'He only wants the buildings. These three.' She waved a hand to indicate their neighbours. 'He intends to build an hotel.'

'Gawd,' Ben said, then, 'I mean, goodness me, Mrs Brandon.'

'Naturally, I have no intention of selling or moving, but I am sure his plans will be good for business in the long run,' she assured them. 'He has the rest of the marketplace to choose from to locate his new hotel.

'Now, let us unpack the latest consignment from London. With this fine weather many of our ladies are venturing out for carriage rides, and I want to be able to show them the very latest arrivals.'

* * *

Checking the contents of parcels and boxes against orders and deciding on prices and the best way to display the new items was reasonably successful in holding off thoughts of the Duke of Harland.

There was really no reason to dwell on the encounter in any case, Cat told herself when she finished dealing with Mrs Allsop, the Squire's wife. She had heard from her maid, who had got it from the post boy, that Mrs Brandon had received a large consignment on the London goods wagon, and she clearly wanted to be before all her acquaintance in inspecting what it held.

Cat had known who her visitor was after just one glance, even though it must be almost nine years since she had last seen the Honourable Quinn Falconer. She had been almost sixteen and he, she supposed, perhaps twenty. It had been a summer's day, and Mama was holding a picnic luncheon in the garden as part of Anna's come-out.

Caitlin, who was only just beginning to put up her hair and let down her hems, was most definitely not "out" and was forbidden to join the guests who, as Mama had said, did not want to be bothered with gawky girls when all eyes should be on her sister.

Anna, blonde, dark-eyed and pretty, was the opposite of gawky. From her perch on the honeysuckle-screened balcony outside her bedchamber, Caitlin had observed several young men making a determined attempt to lure the pretty elder daughter of the Earl of Bowland into the shrubbery for a stroll.

Quinn Falconer had the most success and had arrived with Anna under Caitlin's balcony where he had even secured a kiss. Quite a respectful and dull one, she had thought critically, but her sister had blushed like a peony and had scurried back to the safety of the lawn.

I wouldn't have run so fast, she had thought at the time. *He is rather good-looking.*

Caitlin had not quite managed to suppress her giggle and Mr Falconer had looked up and glimpsed her peeping out of the tangle of scented foliage. He had winked at her and grinned, she remembered, then sauntered back to join the rest of the party. That wink had troubled her dreams, just a little, for a while.

And now here he was, a newly minted Duke, and here she was, a widowed shopkeeper with a new name, an utterly different life. Strange how fate took unexpected twists and turns, she mused, looking up from her ledgers to stare with unfocused eyes at the wall in front of her.

They had never encountered each other again, if one could count that fleeting meeting of eyes as an encounter. Two years later Cat had barely made her come-out as a not very noticeable debutante when she had fallen head over heels into love, betrayal and ruin.

And then rescue. Dear William, who had employed her first as an assistant, then as his under-manager until he had tentatively asked her to marry him. He had never known that she had been in flight from her very first Season, that before her ruin she would never have set foot in a provincial draper's shop. Bless him, he had accepted her stilted explanation that she had fled an unhappy family life and the prospect of an unwelcome suitor.

It was a fabrication, of course. Her life had been perfectly happy, and she had been only too eager to fall into the arms of her suitor. After Blaine, William had been blessedly unexciting and reliable. Her eyes swam with tears for a moment as they always did when she thought of how William had left her the shop in his will, dear man.

She closed the ledger with a thump, cleaned her pen nib and donned a bonnet to go next door to her friend Madelaine's shop. Lemon tartlets were not the cure for all evils, but they certainly made life easier to bear, and besides, she should tell her neighbours about the Duke's proposal. Michael Dangerfield and his daughter were visiting his mother in Bishop's Forde, she knew, but Madelaine Arnaud had been doing brisk business all day.

She beamed from behind the counter. '*Bonjour*, Cat. Will you take coffee with me? And a cake, of course.'

The shop had six little tables that could seat two at

each, perfect for ladies refreshing themselves after a shopping expedition—or, more likely, after browsing in Cat's shop while their maid and footman scurried around the butcher, greengrocer and fishmonger or their husband was measured for a new pair of boots. Only one table was occupied now by Mrs Turnbull, an elderly widow with her companion, both of them absorbed in the journals that Madelaine bought for customers.

'Thank you. And a lemon tart if there are any left, please.' Cat took the table furthest from the two readers and waited while Madelaine brought over a tray.

Her friend was, so far as most people knew, the widow of a French royalist. They had fled the Revolution to En-gland, where her son Pierre, now Peter, was born and her husband had then died. The real story, she had confided in Cat, was that Louis had become abusive, taking out his frustration at his new life on her and putting her in fear for herself and the baby.

Madelaine had run away from Louis four years ago, changed her name from Beaufoy to Arnaud, and had set herself up as a confectioner in this obscure town. Mr and Mrs Brown at the bakery had decided to retire to live with their daughter in Aylesbury, and had been trying to sell their shop for several months to no avail. Madelaine had given them as much as she had, and they agreed that she could pay off the balance, month by month.

As she put the skills she had learned almost as a pastime to good effect, the business flourished, she cleared the debt and was able to improve the business. She was still fearful that Louis might find her, but as the years went past she had gradually relaxed and her wide smile was seen more and more often.

'What news?' she asked, settling beside Cat and lifting the coffee-pot.

'Ssh, we must speak quietly. I have had a visit from the new Duke of Harland.'

'Vraiment?'

'Yes, truly. He is full of plans to make Duke's Forde bustling and prosperous again, including building an hotel with an assembly room and a circulating library.'

'But that is wonderful!' Madelaine cocked her head on one side. 'But I sense you do not think so? Why is that?'

'It is all excellent, of course, except that he wants to build his hotel here, right where we have our shops.' Cat had a sudden twinge of anxiety in case Madelaine would be delighted to sell and relaxed when her friend put down her cup with a snap.

'Absolutement, non. This shop is perfect, just in the right place and I have made it exactly what I want. And Peter and I love our home above and our big garden at the back.' She gestured angrily at the marketplace outside. 'He owns all that, does he not? Let

him build his hotel somewhere out there then. *Un Duc? Pah!'*

'That is what I said to him, more or less,' Cat told her, smiling at the Gallic outburst. Madelaine's English was extremely good, the product of her upbringing as a very minor aristocrat, but when she lost her temper, or was surprised, she became very French.

'So, what is he like, this duke?' Madelaine subsided and took a sustaining bite out of a cream puff.

'Tall, dark and handsome,' Cat said, trying for a judicious, not appreciative, tone. 'Thick dark brown hair, very dark eyes, good bones, stubborn jaw.' *Long legs, broad shoulders...* 'Not quite thirty, I would say. Dangerous.'

'How so?'

'He knows he is handsome, rich and powerful and so he expects to get his own way. He tried flirting, very subtly, when I refused him, but he saw immediately that would get him nowhere. I suspect he is intelligent and he seems to be admirably forward-thinking. His ideas for the town are excellent, if he can carry them out, but he is also stubborn. He had decided on the site he wants for this hotel and he does not like being thwarted.'

'Because it was a woman saying no to him?' Madelaine asked.

'Hmm.' Cat gave it some thought. 'No, I don't think

it was that. But he was very aware of me as a woman and of the fact that I probably found him attractive.'

'A pity he is a duke,' her friend mused. 'You are too young to be a widow, and an intelligent, handsome, rich new husband would be ideal. But dukes do not marry shopkeepers like us. They have other connections in their minds.'

'Very true.' And it was true too that Cat sometimes chafed against her status. She had married widower William Brandon three months after he had given her employment and a room of her own, impressed by the way she had dealt so decisively with his accident, and had stayed to nurse him back to health and to look after his two young assistants.

William had been twenty years older than her, with a weak heart, and theirs had been a warm friendship, then a marriage of convenience and, eventually, a true marriage. Cat had found a sheltering roof over her head, a community to belong to, a source of employment and had felt she had been exceedingly fortunate in finding such safety.

Sometimes, at three in the morning, she wondered what would have happened if she had not skirted around that puddle, or the yapping lapdog had not escaped his mistress just then. Where would she be now? *What* would she be? The possibilities made her shudder.

'He did not come to ask me to surrender my shop,' Madelaine remarked, pouring more coffee.

'There was no point if I refused, as I hold the central building. I admit, I am relieved that you do not wish to sell—it did not occur to me that I might be going against your wishes when I said no to him.'

And that refusal had been instinctive, territorial, without rational consideration of the pros and cons. This was her place, her business and her hard work, building on William's legacy. Just because a duke demanded it, she was not going to give it up.

If she was being honest with herself, she realised, her refusal had been stronger because of the flutter of attraction she had felt on setting eyes on Quinn Falconer again. She was an independent woman, a *businesswoman*, and she would not be swayed by feminine weaknesses. Never again.

'So, what do we do now?' Madelaine asked.

'We wait and see what he does and tell Michael Dangerfield about his plans when he returns, although with neither of us willing to sell, Michael's shop will hold no attraction for the Duke. And I will have another lemon tart to recover from the encounter.'

Madelaine chuckled and signalled to her assistant behind the counter. 'I imagine that he is the one who will need to recover. How many independent women do you think he comes across? It will be all, *Yes, Your Grace, no, Your Grace, of course I'll lift my skirts for you, Your Grace, if you will just come into my bedchamber.'*

'Madelaine! *Hush*.' Cat tried to sound reproving and failed. After all, the thought of being alone within reach of a bed with the Duke of Harland produced a very disturbing tingle, right down to her toes.

'His Grace is not a man to hang about,' Michael Dangerfield remarked two weeks later as he and Cat stood outside his shop watching the gang of workmen attacking the Harland Arms. Tilers, bricklayers and carpenters swarmed over the building on the opposite side of the marketplace and waggon after waggon of rubble and rubbish was being carted away.

'No, he isn't. And it will be a very good thing to have it looking smart and attracting travellers to stop for the night, even before his precious hotel is built.'

'He was in my shop yesterday,' Michael said. 'He wanted new boots. I could see his old ones were by Hoby—that put me on my mettle, believe me! I was so bold as to say I was surprised he hadn't sent to London again, and he said he believed in encouraging local trade if the quality was good, which he could see mine was.'

'Papa has quite the swollen head now,' a mischievous voice remarked from the shop doorway.

Cat smiled at Michael's fifteen-year-old daughter. 'He is right to feel proud of his work, Phoebe.'

'Of course. Am I not an example of how superior it is?'

'What you are, Miss, is a pert young thing,' her father said. 'Run along now or you'll be late for Mrs Newnham's class.'

The Vicar's wife and daughter taught the daughters of the tradesmen, merchants and yeoman farmers of the district, instilling literacy, numeracy, deportment and needlecraft along with French, the use of the globes and watercolour painting for some of them with more aptitude, or with parents who could pay the extra.

'Yes, Papa. Good morning, Mrs Brandon.' Phoebe set out across the marketplace for the vicarage behind the church, plaits bobbing below the rim of her sunhat, skirts swinging.

'She'll be putting her hair up soon,' Cat said. 'And my seamstresses will be letting down her hems and the next thing you know, you will have a pretty young lady on your hands.'

Michael shuddered. 'And I will be an anxious father, polishing his shotgun and warily eyeing every young lad who comes within five feet of her.'

'Did the Duke ever say anything to you about buying our properties?' Cat asked, more to distract the anxious father than from any belief that he might have done.

'Not a word, thankfully. I would not have liked to

disoblige such a powerful customer, as I would have if he had asked.'

'That is true. You might have lost trade, whereas neither Madelaine nor I can expect any business from him, unless he has a mistress who wishes to purchase a hat or a dress length, or he likes cake.'

'I'd be surprised if he hasn't—got a mistress, that is,' Michael said frankly. 'As a man I suppose I am no judge, but I would guess he is attractive to the ladies.'

'Oh, yes, indeed he is,' Cat said. 'And he knows it.'

Chapter Three

The next day was a Wednesday, market day, which kept Cat and her two staff busy as the womenfolk from all around came into the town. Madelaine had to set tables out on the pavement to accommodate the demand, and every time the shop door opened, the voices of men standing around outside Michael's shop discussing belts, boots and rifle bags swelled in.

'He's out there again.' Helen came back from polishing the glass in the door and hissed in Cat's ear.

'Who?' Cat wrote a sale in the ledger and made a note to order more silk stockings.

'The Duke!'

'Ssh.' Cat tried to sound reproving, then spoiled the effect by whispering, 'What is he doing?'

'Walking around looking at things and talking to a young fellow who's writing it all down in a notebook and tripping over his feet while he's about it,' Helen said with a giggle. 'The young fellow, I mean. Not the Duke.'

'He is a secretary, I suppose.' Cat congratulated herself on not strolling over to the window to look.

Helen, however, had drifted back. 'Oh! He's coming across, Mrs Brandon. Heading right for us. They both are.' She opened the door and curtseyed before Cat had a chance to collect herself.

'Good day, Mrs Brandon.'

'Good day, Your Grace.' She smiled past him to the young man who followed him in. Lanky, with a pair of spectacles perched on his nose, he clutched his notebook and peered nervously around.

He looks like nothing so much as a curate finding himself in the Hell Fire Club, Cat thought wickedly. *All these frightening feminine frills and furbelows. He might glimpse the hem of a petticoat or an inch of ankle if he isn't careful.*

There were six ladies in the shop and they turned towards the male voice like so many compass needles seeking true North, then had to find things to pretend to look at to disguise their fascination.

'How may I assist you?' Cat enquired.

'With advice, Mrs Brandon, if you can spare me the time. I realise this is a busy day for you.'

'Indeed it is.' She glanced around the shop. This was going to cause gossip and the best way to deal with that was by being as open as possible. 'I confess I feel the need for some refreshment. Shall we see if Madame Arnaud has a table free?'

That has put the cat amongst the pigeons, she thought. Outside, there were more interested glances in their direction as one of Madelaine's assistants hurried to place two extra chairs at the one free table, which, of course, was on the pavement, ensuring maximum visibility on such a busy day.

Well, this is business, and I suppose the more people who see that, the better, she thought as she tucked her skirts in neatly. She had absolutely no desire to feature as the object of the Duke's amorous desires, the local substitute for the mistress he undoubtedly kept in London. And, if he tried flirting, then he was going to receive an "accidental" cup of coffee in his lap for his trouble.

'You said I might be able to advise you, Your Grace,' she said, and saw by their neighbour's reaction that her voice had carried to the nearest table. *Good.* 'A glass of lemonade and a macaron, please, Maria.'

'Coffee for two, nothing to eat,' the Duke ordered without asking his secretary, who folded his notebook open neatly in front of him and sat looking rather like an alert gun dog, awaiting his master's command to retrieve something.

'I have studied the market today. It appears well attended and to have a good range of fresh produce. I am surprised that the sellers do not go into Oxford where there are so many more customers.'

'And where the journey is longer, the fees for stalls

are much higher and the competition is greater,' Cat pointed out. 'This is almost all very local produce. It sells well at good prices because it is fresh, or homemade, and the buyers know the sellers. Your own cook buys provisions here.'

'I see.' He nodded to the secretary, who scribbled busily. 'How is the market organised?'

'Your Mr Yorke could have told you that—he employs a warden to collect fees, resolve any disputes and to organise the cleaning of the marketplace. The parish constable patrols to watch out for pickpockets or confidence tricksters.'

Maria returned with a tray and placed the coffee-pot for Cat to pour, which she did. 'Milk, Your Grace?'

He shook his head.

'Mr–?'

'Turnbull, ma'am. No milk, thank you.'

'Is that all I can help you with?' Cat enquired, nibbling her macaron.

'I was hoping you might tell me which shops are lacking.'

'Hmm.' She gave it some thought, tipping her head to one side, then saw she had caught the Duke's attention.

'Have we met before, Mrs Brandon?'

'Not to my knowledge, Your Grace,' she said composedly, although her heart felt as though it were banging against her ribs. If he recognised her... But how could he? It was ten years ago and she had been above him, almost hidden in the creepers. An exchange of glances was hardly a meeting.

'No, of course not,' he said, then murmured something she could have sworn was, *Honeysuckle.*

The effort to keep her expression bland was almost painful. Scent was one of the most powerful triggers of memory, she once read, and Cat had found it to be true. The smell of fresh linen, dried on the line, took her straight back to the laundry at home where she had been allowed to wash her dolls' clothes and had been strictly forbidden to touch the rollers of the big mangle. Roses brought back Mama's dusting powder, and anyone sucking peppermint drops immediately brought to mind Miss Travis, the meek little governess who had tried so hard to instil information and decorum into Anna and herself.

Now the scent of the flowers twining around her as she hid on the balcony was so strong in her memory that she almost glanced over her shoulder, expecting to see a plant creeping over the doorway behind her.

She pretended to frown in thought, hoping to disguise any reaction. 'Let me see… There are two butchers, a fishmonger, a baker and two greengrocers already, although all would benefit from improvements to their premises. A good general provisions shop would be exceedingly useful and a bookshop—one that perhaps sold stationery and materials for painting and crafts as well. Although you were talking about a circulating library, I think, so that might answer some of those needs.

'We are in sore need of a good ironmonger's shop. You would need to speak to local landowners and farmers to see what they need in the way of feed supplies and equipment. Oh, and there is nothing in the way of a gentleman's outfitter, only one tailor who undertakes repairs and alterations. There, that is all I can think of for the moment.'

She took a much-needed drink of lemonade and managed a bright smile. 'I hope that is some help. Now I have to get back to my customers. We shopkeepers must never neglect them, you know,' she added brightly in an effort to remind him just who she was.

What had triggered that memory in him. Something she had said? But she hadn't spoken on that sunny afternoon, only smiled at him through her screen of creepers.

Then do not smile!

'Thank you for my refreshments.' She stood and was away before the two men were hardly out of their seats. It felt like flight, she could only hope it did not look like it.

The same customers were still in the shop, so she approached the ones at the counter and took over from Ben. 'Goodness me, what excitement,' she remarked generally. 'His Grace is set on improving all our commerce, it seems, so I have done my best to tell him what additional shops might benefit Duke's Forde. What do you ladies think?'

'Have you got all that, James?'

'Yes, sir.' The son of his godfather might look awkward, and he was certainly prone to falling over his feet when deep in thought, but he was an excellent secretary and, thankfully, happy not to stand on ceremony.

Quinn thought sometimes that if anyone else "Your Grace-d" him he would scream. It would be perverse not to be grateful for all the benefits of his inheritance, but at the same time it took freedoms from him he had been unaware of possessing. All these new staff doing work he had performed for his father and then for himself when his father had died: now he had to learn to delegate, to accept being above it all.

'I have received a letter this morning from Abernathy, the architect, and it contains his proposals for moving the site of the hotel towards the corner. He does not sound happy at the need for the changed location but he agrees that your idea of putting the assembly room, the library and the billiards room on the short, narrow end of the marketplace is an excellent use of space, sir.'

'It was not my idea,' Quinn said. 'It was Mrs Brandon's.'

Curse her. He was too honest with himself to deny that it would not be an insurmountable problem to move the hotel, whatever his architect thought, and he did not like the suspicion that his initial fury over Mrs Brandon's refusal to sell had simply been the arrogance of his new title talking. Nobody said "you cannot" or "you may not" to a duke, he had discovered. Except for self-possessed haberdashers, it seemed.

There was a tingling at the base of his spine as he recalled her reaction to his moment of flirtation. She had been angry, but her pupils had widened, one of the signs of attraction…

And he had to stop thinking of her like that. Respectable women, along with servants and innocent young ladies, were out of bounds for a gentleman with any semblance of honour. There were courtesans aplenty, only too happy to attract a member of the nobility as their protector, and any number of dashing widows amongst the *ton* with whom a pleasant dalliance might be arranged for mutual pleasure with no risk of scandal. He had enjoyed such a liaison himself before he had inherited the title, which, he accepted ruefully, was why he hadn't been trying too hard to find a wife.

And that, Quinn realised, was what was confusing his instincts. Mrs Brandon was a widow who had all the confidence, poise and manner of a lady of breeding, and he did not believe those had been assumed.

Something must have happened to cause her to slide down the social scale from, perhaps, a squire's family, or a clergyman's. The death of a father often left widows and unmarried daughters in a precarious position, giving them few options other than to become paid companions or governesses. Or worse.

That still did not explain that nagging feeling that he had encountered her before. Quinn pushed away the thought as he lifted his coffee cup and found the maid at his side.

'Would you like anything to eat now, Your Grace?' the maid asked as she removed Mrs Brandon's cup and plate. 'A fresh batch of pastries has just come out of the kitchen.'

Quinn opened his mouth to refuse, then saw James's expression. Despite being so thin he still managed to absorb quantities of food and always seemed hungry.

'Bring us a selection and fresh coffee, if you please.'

She bobbed a curtsey and hurried off while Quinn resigned himself to being the focus of attention for a while longer. If he was going to bring this sleepy little town back to life, he supposed he had better get used to it. He was aware that many would consider his new wealth the excuse to indulge himself in all the pleasures that money and status could bring. But he had been raised to believe a man worked for a living and for self-respect and that the more you had, the more you owed to those who had less.

'Oh, I say, sir!' James had sighted the approaching basket of pastries and Quinn had to remind himself once again that his secretary was twenty-three, not fourteen.

Although they did look tempting...

'What is he doing now?' Ben demanded.

'He and his secretary are eating pastries,' Helen reported from the shop window where she should have been creating a display of gloves. 'He even manages to do that elegantly, even though I would swear that's his third. The Duke is very good-looking,' she added with a sigh. 'And that secretary is too, in an odd kind of way.'

'Fortunately we have no customers just at this moment to hear your very inappropriate comments, Helen,' Cat said sharply. 'Kindly finish that display quickly. And you, Ben, bring through those new rolls of muslin.'

'Yes, ma'am,' they chorused.

'And then you may go and have your luncheon as all our customers seem to be doing the same thing.' *Or gawp-ing at the Duke.*

At least she might have a quiet half hour to get over her fears, which surely must be irrational. No young man who has just kissed a girl is going to be paying any attention to a naughty chit of a schoolroom girl peeping out at them. And she looked nothing like her sister, which was a blessing.

The thought of being discovered, of word spreading through the community that was now her home, that she was actually Lady Caitlin Montgomery who had eloped with a plausible rake and been besotted enough to lose her virginity to him before she had a ring on her finger, sent cold chills down her spine.

Blaine Wykeham had deceived all the sharp-eyed matrons into believing that the great-nephew of the Bishop of Wessex must be an eligible and respectable gentleman with good prospects. But it seemed that the Bishop and his family had suppressed the information that he was no longer received by any of them, had a mountain of debts and a history of heartless seduction amongst the local girls.

Blaine had charmed her into falling in love, had lied to her that her father had refused his suit when, in fact, he had never asked him for her hand, and had lured her into an elopement that very night. Along with the contents of her jewellery box and almost a full quarter's allowance, which he had taken as he had crept out of the inn that night, leaving her slumbering.

Sometimes, when sleep deserted her in the small hours, Cat marvelled that she had escaped relatively unscathed from that terrible misjudgement. Perhaps her very innocence had protected her, had made her decisive when she should have been terrified. And she wondered too why it had never occurred to her to go home, to confess what had happened. Or even to make up some story about an escapade with friends and hope that she would not find herself with child.

Perhaps it was because she knew what would happen, that her parents would find her some complaisant man to marry her, whether she liked him or not. She was a daughter of the Earl of Bowland and possessed of a generous dowry—those two things alone would attract any number of gentlemen, and she would have been disposed of briskly and without fuss. After all, she had always been the unsatisfactory daughter, the gangly, "difficult" one. The dreamer, nose in a book, head in the clouds.

Well, she wasn't gangly now, she told herself. And her head was firmly attached to her shoulders, and daydreams and novels had given way to ruthlessly practical thinking. She had made a new life for herself and she was proud of that. It was simply fear of losing everything she had built that made her so nervous of the Duke of Harland.

Chapter Four

The next day, Thursday, Cat was sitting at the breakfast table with her two staff, meditatively eating toast and bacon as she mulled over the possibility of adding cor-setry to her stock.

'Goodness, whoever is that at the door at this hour? Go and see, Ben.'

'It's Mr Newnham, ma'am.' Ben returned from the back entrance and ushered in the Vicar.

'Good day, Mr Newnham. May I offer you some coffee? Or tea?'

'Nothing, I thank you, Mrs Brandon. I do apologise for a call at this hour, but there is something that has been worrying me for days, and I simply cannot sleep and I felt I had to speak to you.' He spoke hurriedly, and Cat recognised the signs of the onset of one of his recurrent, almost crippling, attacks of anxiety.

The Vicar was an excellent parish priest, but he found dealing with conflict, raised voices and any form of violence, almost impossible. She suspected there must have been some traumatic incident in his past to account for it, but had never felt able to enquire.

'Come through to my sitting room, Vicar. Ben, go and start making the shop ready, Helen, please clear up in here.' She ushered Mr Newnham, who was wringing his gloves between his hands, into the comfortable parlour and closed the door. 'Do take a seat and tell me how I may help you,' she said, making her voice calm and placid.

'It is the Duke,' he said. 'You are acquainted with him, are you not?'

Cat felt her spine stiffening and her chin came up. If he was here to lecture her on some imagined impropriety…

'I have met him,' she said coolly. 'He has enquired about purchasing these premises, which I refused. He has also asked my opinion on possible improvements to the town. If you call that being acquainted, then yes, we are.'

'Oh, dear, now I have offended you.' The Vicar's gloves were going to be ruined if he continued to torture them like that. 'I have no intention of implying anything…untoward.'

'Not at all. I simply wish to be clear. In my position one cannot be too careful.'

'Yes, of course. I had better explain. It was the late Duke and the almshouses, you see.'

As she did not see, Cat simply waited, unwilling to fluster him further with questions.

'His grandfather paid for them, and the parish council manages them, but he did not endow them with any funds for their maintenance. So when I first came to the parish and saw some dilapidations, I called upon the Duke, who was here on one of his rare visits, to ask for his assistance.'

He was working himself up into an agitated state, so Cat said soothingly, 'That seems a very reasonable course of action. But he was not inclined to help?'

'He became…furious. Red in the face, shouting about ingratitude. His language was terrible. I have never been able… It is a great weakness when I am called upon to defend my flock, but I simply…'

For an awful moment Cat thought the poor man was about to dissolve into tears. 'It must have been quite terrifying, Vicar. And you were in no position to exert any moral authority over him when he clearly had such a disregard for your calling and the needs of the poorest in the community. But do I understand that the need is greater now, and you want to try the new Duke to see if he will be more reasonable than his great-uncle?'

Mr Newnham took a deep shuddering breath. 'That is it exactly. You see, the roofs are beginning to leak and it seems that there is rot in some of the beams. I have had to move Widow Forest from her dwelling into a vacant one on the men's side, which is irregular, especially when we have elderly male parishioners who have a claim on the dwelling.'

Cat thought about the parish council, none of whose members seemed likely to overcome their awe of high rank sufficiently to put a cogent argument to the Duke, especially if there was some reason behind the last Duke's furious refusal, some history that the Vicar knew nothing of.

'He already has workmen swarming all over the Harland Arms,' she said thoughtfully. 'Surely it would not delay the work too much to divert some of them to the almshouses for the roof repairs at least. I will see what I can do, Vicar.'

He was almost incoherent with gratitude as she showed him out.

When was the best time to beard a Duke in his den and ask for money? Cat wondered. Her father always dealt with business in the morning, which seemed a reasonable time for anyone with large estates and a major project on hand. Perhaps if she went to Harland Park now and asked for Mr Yorke, the steward, she could discover how best to approach the subject.

Cat kept a pony and gig at the stables at the Arms, and Treacle, the pony, had not had any exercise for several days, so she had no excuse for delaying, she decided, and went to find a sensible bonnet and a light pelisse.

'I will be out for several hours,' she informed Ben, who was just drawing back the bolts on the shop door. 'You and Helen can manage, I hope?'

'Yes, ma'am. It's always quiet after market day,' he said confidently. 'I thought I'd give everything a good dust and polish and then turn out the ribbon drawers.'

'Excellent. I will be back by luncheon,' she said.

And even earlier if the Duke sends me packing with a flea in my ear for impudence.

Treacle, a sturdy dark brown beast, was always keen to set out on an expedition after being cooped up in his stable. He trotted briskly across the marketplace and down Church Street next to the almshouses as though full of oats.

It would take twenty minutes at that rate to reach the gates of Harland Park, Cat estimated, running various versions of her speech through her mind.

Your Grace, you may be aware that a generous ancestor of yours... You might not know that there was no endowment... Worthy elderly citizens are in need... Unfortunately your great-uncle, not being a resident... And being a bad-tempered, miserly old... No, perhaps not that. *It seems he felt unable to support...*

As she turned in between the lofty wrought iron gates, flanked by a matched pair of lodges, Cat still wasn't quite sure what she was going to say, let alone how to explain why she, and not the Vicar, was making the request for funds.

If it were not for the man she was going to meet, this would have been an enjoyable outing. The parklands drowsed in the gathering warmth of a summer's morning, the deer already clustered under the shade of spreading oak trees. The carriage drive turned and she saw the house for the first time. Large, stone-built and imposing, it did not look very welcoming. She was most certainly not going to present herself at the front door, she decided.

As Treacle trotted closer, Cat saw the bulk of what must be the stable block and turned him into the track leading to it. The yard, reached through a brick arch, was bustling when she drove in, and she soon saw why—the Duke was just dismounting from a raking bay hunter and the grooms had gathered around him to discuss some issue with the animal's left foreleg.

They all looked up as she drew Treacle to a halt under the arch. It was too late to back out now, even if the pony was likely to oblige her—he never liked going backwards.

'Please do not mind me,' she called. 'I can wait. It is not an urgent matter.'

That could have been better put—it sounded as though she expected the Duke to drop everything and attend to her, and it seemed he thought so too, judging by the somewhat wry expression on his face.

And, of course, he came striding over immediately, gesturing to one of the men to take Treacle's reins.

'Mrs Brandon. Was I expecting you?'

No, of course you were not, you provoking man!

'I took the chance on finding you at home and able to receive me,' she replied sweetly. 'Or possibly Mr Yorke. I have come on an errand from the Vicar.' That at least was a most respectable excuse, if there was such a thing for a lady visiting a bachelor in his own home, unaccompanied by a chaperone.

'Mr Newnham? Will you not come inside and take tea while you carry out your mission?'

'Thank you, Your Grace.' Cat climbed down from the gig, placed her hand on the Duke's outstretched arm and attempted to look ladylike.

'We will go in through the back door, if you have no objection, and collect a maid on the way,' he said as they set out across the yard.

'Thank you, Your Grace,' she said again. Either he was being thoughtful by providing her with a chaperone or he was protecting himself against being compromised. Probably both—he was not a stupid man.

'Harland,' he said abruptly. 'Or Falconer. I am weary of every communication being wrapped around with *Your Graces.*'

'Very well, Harland,' she said. 'I imagine that the formality can become somewhat trying when one has not actually been raised in a ducal household.'

Falconer was far too close to how she had known him before, and instinct told her that the less she thought about that, the less risk there was that she might betray herself.

'Exactly, although I am having trouble with the staff. My uncle was a stickler for correct form and none of them are comfortable yet with calling me simply *sir*.'

'Yes, I can understand that might make them wary of overstepping.' And as he clearly understood that, it might make him more sympathetic to Mr Newnham's nerves.

None of this was helping her own qualms. He was too close, too male and, if his memory ever retrieved that elusive glimpse through the honeysuckle, he would be her ruin.

The Duke—*Harland*, she reminded herself—ushered Cat across a yard, through the back door and into the kitchen passage, then opened the kitchen door— behaviour eccentric enough to make any cook faint away in the average aristocratic household.

There was a faint squawk from inside, and he said, 'Tea for two to the Chinese drawing room, if you please, Mrs Simpkins, and one of the parlourmaids to look after my guest. Ah, thank you, Tilly.'

A rather flustered girl emerged, smoothing down her apron. She bobbed a curtsey in Cat's direction, then followed them as Harland led the way up the back stairs, through the baize door studded with brass dome-headed nails that reminded staff, even in the dark, they were entering the world of "Upstairs", and across the hallway into a charming small drawing room decorated with painted wallpaper.

'You can sit over there, Tilly,' Harland said, waving at a chair in the furthest corner. Then, when the maid had retreated, he offered Cat a seat near the window where, if they kept their voices down, they would not be overheard.

'Let us wait for our tea before discussing the Vicar's business. You drive a neat little pony, Mrs Brandon.'

'Treacle? I would describe him as shaggy, rather than neat. He gets as fat as a butterball if I do not exercise him enough, and he has a rooted objection to backing up, but yes, he is a willing fellow and very gentle. I do hope your hunter is not lame.'

'A bruised hoof, I believe. Nothing serious, my head groom assures me.'

Idle chat about horses bridged the gap until the arrival of the tea-tray and, by the time she had lifted the teapot, Cat saw that the little maid was quietly dozing in her corner.

Even so, she kept her voice down as she said, 'You are aware of the almshouses in the marketplace?'

'Certainly.'

'They were paid for by an ancestor of yours, I understand. Your grandfather, possibly? Or perhaps his father. They are managed by the parish council and the Vicar. However, no endowment was made for their maintenance and, in recent years, they have become dilapidated beyond the resources of the parish to repair.'

'A curious oversight on the founder's part. The Vicar is hoping that I might deal with the matter now, I imagine.'

'Er, yes.' Now he was going to ask…

'But why can the Vicar not approach me directly?'

'I should tell you that Mr Newnham suffers terribly from his nerves,' Cat began, with a hasty glance to make certain that Tilly was still enjoying the unexpected treat of a soft chair in the middle of the morning. 'He is an excellent parish priest, but is quite prostrated by violence, anger and bluster. I suspect some distressing incident in his past is the cause of that but, naturally, I have never felt able to enquire.'

'And he fears my anger?' Harland's eyebrows rose and he looked, for a moment, exceedingly forbidding. That look alone would probably cause poor Mr Newnham to faint dead away.

'He does not know you. But he did venture to make the same request to your late great-uncle, with most unfortunate results.'

'Ah.' The eyebrows descended and something close to a rueful grin twisted his lips. 'My Great-Uncle Dominic took a very robust view of poor relief. Essentially, I do not think he believed in such a thing as a deserving pauper. Then a case in one of the villages on his Norfolk estates, where the poor fund was embezzled by the vicar, did nothing to soften his view.'

'Oh, dear. Well, the result was that Mr Newnham is almost prostrate with anxiety about approaching you, but feels he must, because the roof is giving way and one dwelling is now uninhabitable and there are people in need of the accommodation.'

'How many does it house now?'

'It should hold six men and six women.'

'Clearly, in a place the size of Duke's Forde it needs extending as well as repairing. Is there scope to build out at the back?'

'I…believe so,' Cat said, flustered by not having to put forward any of her half-organised arguments. 'I have to say, this feels as though I was putting my shoulder against a heavy door, expecting resistance, and it has simply swung open.'

'I may be new to this, but I hope I know my responsibility to my tenants and the parishes on my estates,' Harland said. 'But why are you the one to bring this request to me? If the Vicar is prostrate with nerves, surely a delegation of the parish council would be an alternative?'

'Mr Newnham feels they would not be able to withstand you if your reaction mirrored the late Duke's, and as he is aware that we are acquainted…'

'I see.' Now Harland was looking very grim indeed. 'It would appear that in seeking you out to ask your opinions I have exposed you to gossip. I apologise and I will do what I can to make that right.'

'There is no need,' Cat said hastily. 'There is no gossip, and it was clear from the way he spoke to me that Mr Newnham had, in no way, misinterpreted the situation.'

There was a silence while they both studied their teacups. Cat contemplated "the situation". Goodness knows what Harland was contemplating.

Now what is he going to say?

Chapter Five

It seemed the Vicar was not only of a nervous disposition, but somewhat naive, Quinn reflected. If there had been anything improper in his relations with Mrs Brandon, then it was tactless in the extreme to have sent her on this errand and, as Mr Newnham clearly knew her to be the respectable lady that she was, he should have realised that she might find it very embarrassing to be asked to call on a single gentleman.

But as she *was* here…

'Can you spare me an hour more of your time to discuss this in more detail, Mrs Brandon?'

'Certainly, if that would be of help.'

'Tilly!'

The maid jumped so much that her cap slipped rakishly over one eye.

'Yes, Your Grace. I mean, sir… Sorry, sir.' She jammed the cap back with one hand.

'There is no need to apologise. I startled you. Would you ring the bell, please.'

'Yes, sir.'

One of the footmen appeared. Augustus, Quinn thought. His uncle called all the footmen *James* and all the maids *Maria*, which saved him the effort of remembering anyone's name.

'Ah, Augustus, isn't it?'

'Yes, Your, er sir.'

'Please will you find Mr Yorke, give him my compliments and enquire whether he is free to join me here with, if he has them, the plans of the almshouses in the town.'

'Yes, sir.'

'And, Tilly, ring for more tea and another cup, please.'

The tea arrived before his steward and came with a plate of scones.

Quinn was just spooning raspberry jam onto his second one when Yorke came in, his arms full of battered rolls of paper and with a cobweb in his hair.

'I am sorry, sir, I hadn't realised the almshouses were ours. These were buried deep in one of the cupboards.' He dropped the rolls on the table, saw that Quinn had a visitor and took a hasty swipe at his dusty clothes. 'Good morning, Mrs Brandon.'

'Good morning, Mr Yorke. May I pour you some tea?'

Quinn, watching the exchange from under hooded lids, was even more certain now that Mrs Brandon had received a genteel upbringing. She was dispensing tea like a natural hostess and setting Yorke at ease as she did so.

'The almshouses are not estate property, I believe,' he said. 'They were given by one of my forebears, although without adequate endowment for their upkeep. I understand there are repairs urgently required and a pressing need to enlarge the accommodation. Mrs Brandon is aware of what the most urgent priorities are.'

'Roof repairs,' she said briskly, passing the jam to the slightly bemused steward. 'Although there are undoubtedly other problems.'

In the end, when the tea was cold and the scones merely a memory of crumbs, the decision was reached that Yorke, accompanied by the master builder working on the Harland Arms, would inspect the almshouses and immediately undertake whatever was required to make them all habitable. Meanwhile the architect responsible for the plans of the hotel would be directed to inspect the site and draw up a scheme to extend the building.

'We should be able to double it in size,' Yorke said, peering closely at the old plans.

'The Vicar will be delighted to hear this,' Mrs Brandon said as she got to her feet. 'I am sure you will be receiving a call from him soon, Your Grace.'

He noted that, instinctively, she was addressing him by his title in front of his staff.

'I will walk you back to the stables, Mrs Brandon. This time we will take the front door, I think.'

She stopped beside him for a moment on the top step and gazed out over the parkland, bathed in sunshine. 'How very lovely this is.'

There was a wistfulness there that surprised him. Mrs Brandon had always seemed so practical, so down to earth.

'It is, isn't it?' he agreed, realising it fully for the first time. Up until that moment it had simply been part of his inheritance, a source of work and worry, something to be enjoyed later, when he had the time. If he ever did.

Now, seeing it through her eyes, he felt a sense of beauty and of peace. This was England and this piece of it was the home of his ancestors. They might be a somewhat dubious collection—a few heroes, a number of very ordinary types and an embarrassing handful of colourful rogues, but they were his, as was this now.

'You made me see it, Catherine,' Quinn said without thinking. Then he heard her sharp intake of breath beside him. 'I apologise, I had no right to presume.'

'That isn't... My friends call me Cat,' she said. Then, 'And that was presumptuous of me, to make an assumption.'

'Not at all. A cat may look at a king, so the saying goes, so I am sure a Cat may be friends with a duke.'

That startled a breathy laugh from her, a sound that seemed to go straight to the base of his spine and send decidedly inconvenient signals elsewhere.

Quinn gave himself a brisk mental shake. He was not going to be attracted to Cat Brandon, he told himself firmly. That was unwise, unsuitable and any number of other *uns*. On the other hand, it was rather late in the day to come to that conclusion, because he was already finding her attractive, both physically and mentally. She was unfashionably tall, unfashionably intelligent and undoubtedly independent—more *uns*, he thought—and one did not matter and the others added to the attraction.

He cleared his throat and offered his arm to descend the short flight of steps to the carriage drive. Dukes did not fall for shopkeepers. Dukes did not get involved with shopkeepers. Not if they had any sense, which he clearly did not.

'What would be best for our nervous Vicar?' he asked, the cleric being the least erotic thing he could call to mind. 'For me to write to him, or for you to tell him what we have discussed and say I will be calling on him later?'

'I will speak to him today and tell him what we have discussed,' she said decisively. 'Thank you for being so understanding.'

'Not at all. It would be most unfortunate to find myself at odds with the Vicar.'

She smiled and he wondered if she was relaxed enough with his company to allow him to ask a few personal questions.

The mystery of just how this young lady—because she was both—had come to be married, and then widowed after what must have been quite a short marriage, in some obscure Oxfordshire town was niggling at him, as it had been almost since he had first encountered her.

'Have you lived in Duke's—'

'Oh! Oh, just look at Treacle. Thank you!' She almost ran from his side to where Tompkins, one of the grooms, was just straightening up from oiling the pony's hooves. He had been groomed until he shone, his mane and tail were neatly trimmed and he was looking as smug as a pony might, after all that attention.

'Not at all, ma'am,' Tompkins said, hastily moving the jar of oil away from her skirts. 'He's been in livery at the Arms, I daresay. Adequate, no doubt, but not up to *our* standards. It was quiet, so I had the lads give him a bit of attention. He's not so very large, except around the middle,' he added with a grin.

'Oh, and look at the gig—all swept out and washed. Thank you very much.' She beamed at him. Quinn, caught at the edge of the smile, blinked. Tompkins looked besotted.

* * *

'My goodness, Treacle, we *are* moving in exalted circles,' Cat said as they trotted away down the winding drive. 'And just look at you, smart as a London carriage horse. They'll not recognise you at the Harland Arms.'

Treacle flicked one ear back to listen but, correctly interpreting this as having nothing to do with speed or direction, trotted stolidly on.

Mr Newnham would be both relieved and delighted, she knew, and she was excited to tell him the good news, but the church clock struck one, then gave its ugly *clunk*, as she drove into the yard at the Harland Arms. She must go to the shop first and have her luncheon. Mrs Newnham would not be delighted to have her own meal interrupted, even with such tidings.

Treacle was received with some surprise by the stable lads at the inn, but Cat did not enlighten them about where he had received his elegant grooming. That would most certainly start the rumour mill into action.

Cat was halfway across the marketplace when she saw Madelaine come out of her shop, hatless and still wearing her apron. She ran to Cat, who saw with a stab of anxiety that her face was white and there were traces of dried tears on her cheeks.

'Whatever is wrong?' She caught her friend's hands, turning her so they were walking side by side, hoping she was shielding her from any curious eyes. 'It isn't Peter, is it? Or—not Beaufoy, surely?'

'No,' Madelaine managed. 'Peter is well and my... Beaufoy has not found us. It was that horrible architect of the Duke's. He wants my shop.'

'He what? But— We cannot talk out here. Come with me. Have you eaten? Has Peter?'

'He has, I could not...' She gave a little hiccupping gulp as though swallowing fresh tears.

'You will be better for something. Come along, and when you feel calmer you can tell me about it.'

Fortunately the three customers in the shop were gathered around Helen, who was showing them the newest gloves, so Cat whisked Madelaine though to the back before any curious eyes noticed her distress.

Ben was just finishing his meal and jumped to his feet to clear the table. 'Good day, Madame. May I get your luncheon, Mrs Brandon?'

'No, that's all right. I would like to speak to Madame Arnaud about a private matter if you would not mind...'

'I'll take a turn round the marketplace,' he said cheerfully. 'I could do with a breath of air, it's very warm.'

'Sit down.' Cat pressed Madelaine into a chair, then began to assemble food on the table: some ham, sweet pickles, fresh bread and butter and a bowl of fruit. It was probably all her friend could manage. She poured cider for both of them from the stone crock keeping cool in the pantry, then sat down and began to cut bread.

'Drink. I am certainly going to.' The cider was crisp and fresh and it seemed to revive Madelaine a little.

'Now, what is all this about an architect?'

'It is the man who has been doing the drawings for the hotel. He seems very cross that he cannot build the one he first designed, which would have meant knocking all three shops down.'

'The Duke seemed happy enough with the new plans, I thought,' Cat said, puzzled. 'He said the architect agreed that the assembly room and so forth could go at the short end.'

'Now he says that he has revised the plans and it is obvious that the façade will be cramped and not impressive enough. If he has my shop to demolish, then it will be vastly better.'

'Well, that is just too bad.' Cat attacked the ham with a sharp knife. 'If he comes back, you tell him… No, if he pesters you, you say you will complain to the Duke. I most certainly will. I saw him this morning and he said nothing at all about wanting your shop.'

'Vraiment?'

'Truly. This architect just has his nose out of joint, or he misunderstood the Duke's intentions. Now, have something to eat and you will feel much better. Besides, neither the architect nor the Duke has any power to make you sell, have they?'

Madelaine took a healthy gulp of cider. 'No, they don't, do they?' She smiled ruefully. 'I was just so frightened…'

'Because you finally feel safe and settled here, and you and Peter are doing so well, then anything that seems to threaten that is alarming. That's perfectly understandable. Now, eat and I will tell you why I was talking to the Duke this morning and about some good news. But you must promise to keep it a secret for the moment.'

A minor crisis with an order and a polite wrangle with Miss Twite, who was making an attempt to return a pair of gloves which had clearly been worn and had a stain on them, delayed Cat longer than she had planned and it was past three o'clock when she broke the news at the vicarage.

'The Duke has agreed to pay for the repairs? And for new almshouses? *Twelve* new ones?' Mr Newnham gaped at her. 'And he was not annoyed?'

'Certainly not. The Duke said he felt it was his duty and responsibility. He wishes to call on you, along with the master builder who is working on the Harland Arms, so the repairs can be put in hand urgently. Then he will have his architect draw up plans to extend. It looks as though there is space for twelve, but of course it will have to be measured out to be certain.'

Cat braced herself, because the Vicar looked ready to faint with delight onto the polished boards of the vicarage drawing room. Fortunately Mrs Newnham was made of stouter stuff.

'That is excellent news, Henry,' she said briskly. 'Now, we must bestir ourselves so we are fully prepared to explain what is needed, ready for when they arrive.'

'Um… It is too late for that. Here they are.'

Chapter Six

Cat, facing the window, could see the five men who were advancing to the front gate. There was the Duke, his secretary, a sturdy man with a low-crowned hat who Cat had seen directing the builders at the Arms and a willowy fellow in a highly fashionable coat and a hat of exaggerated design. That, surely, had to be the architect. He had his assistant at his heels, burdened with rolls of paper and a large portfolio.

She would not mind having a word with that fashion plate about bullying women.

'Henry dear, take a deep breath and compose yourself,' Mrs Newnham said as the sound of the doorknocker reached them. 'His Grace is clearly on the side of the angels in this.'

There was an initial flurry of introductions—Mr Flowers the master builder, Mr Abernathy the architect and Potter, his assistant—then the ritual of tea being offered and politely refused, then the Newnhams took Mr Flowers off to inspect the repairs needed, leaving Cat to entertain the Duke, Mr Turnbull and the architect and his assistant.

No time like the present, she thought, her anger at the memory of the tear tracks on her friend's face still fresh in her mind.

'I had understood that you had abandoned the idea of placing your new hotel on top of our shops, Your Grace,' she said with a tight smile that even the most dense man could not have misinterpreted as one of pleasure.

'I have,' he said, warily.

'Then apparently this has not been adequately communicated to your architect as he was harassing Madame Arnaud this morning. She was most distressed.'

'What is this, Abernathy?' Harland demanded, swinging round to stare at the man.

'Yes, I spoke to the woman, Your Grace. It was hardly harassment. We had agreed, had we not, that the best of the designs would appear pinched without the space occupied by that coffee shop?'

'And I requested that you modify the design because that space is not available,' Harland said tightly.

'And, naturally, I have done so,' the man said with an airy wave of his hand towards his assistant, sitting on a sofa some way back, peering over the top of the armful of plans and clearly wishing himself elsewhere. 'But I felt it worthwhile to have another word with the woman. The ladies so often change their minds, do they not?' he remarked with a smirk. 'Perhaps she had not quite comprehended the advantages of your very generous offer.'

'*Ladies* may change their minds, as may anyone,' Cat said before Harland could speak. 'But intelligent businesswomen with successful enterprises take careful consideration before making up their minds in the first place and are not to be bullied into the wrong decision by some puffed up London architect with too much pride to listen to their patron's instructions.'

'Madam!' He jumped to his feet. 'I am not to be spoken to in such a way!'

'But I have just done so,' Cat replied calmly and gave him a "and what are you going to do about it?" look.

'If I might get a word in edgeways,' Harland said, his tone chill. 'Abernathy, you acted entirely without my authority. You will write an apology to Madame Arnaud—I cannot imagine she will wish to receive you in person—and if that is not satisfactory I am sure Mrs Brandon will inform me of it. I suggest you and Potter now take yourselves off to survey the almshouses and draw up a proposal for their extension before you cause Mrs Brandon further aggravation.'

'Your Grace.' Abernathy drew himself up, snapped his fingers at the unfortunate Potter, who was probably going to feel the backlash from this humiliation, and inclined his head towards Cat. 'Madam.' He then swept out.

'Goodness, I could almost hear his train swishing,' Cat said, more lightly than she felt as her anger subsided. It left her feeling slightly nauseous.

'I apologise for that performance. You wonder why I tolerate him, I imagine.'

'It is not my place to wonder at your actions, Harland.'

'Yet I have made it your place, have I not?' he asked, looking at her thoughtfully. 'I have asked your advice about the town, engaged with your concerns about the almshouses. It appears that you are now my official advisor on Duke's Forde.'

'Very well, if that is the case,' she said, ignoring the slight feeling of dizziness, as though she peered over the edge of a chasm. 'Why *do* you tolerate him?'

'Because he is a very good architect, which anyone seeing the cut of his coat and his deplorable taste in hats would be perfectly justified for disbelieving. I would not allow him anywhere near the interior decoration of so much as a shepherd's hut but, as for the buildings themselves, he has every right to be proud of his work.'

'Yes. I see. And you want the best for the town.'

'I do.' Harland smiled a trifle ruefully. 'I will admit that, at first, I saw merely a shocking waste of rental revenue here and, I suppose, I felt a distaste for seeing a place allowed to deteriorate that way. Then I began to enjoy the process, the challenge. I like the way that the grooms at the inn's stables have begun to smarten the place up, without being told to. I felt satisfaction when some of the shop tenants approached Yorke to discuss improvements. I suspect I will feel some pride when the almshouses are enlarged.'

Cat nodded her understanding while, inside, she felt a decidedly sinking feeling. *I like the man. I like him far too much for safety. He said we could be friends. Perhaps we are...but I want more than that. And I cannot have more because of who I am now. And because of who I was.*

The thought of being exposed as the ruined Lady Caitlin was appalling. Her parents would descend on her, shocked and lecturing, it would all leak out and Society would be full of whispers and speculation. That she could ignore, but this was her home now, her friends were here, her whole world—what would the people of Duke's Ford make of her pretence? What would Harland think of her?

Dukes don't ma— Her thoughts skidded away from the word. *Dukes do not become* involved *with shopkeepers. Dukes do not become involved with the disgraced daughters of earls either.*

Not for the first time Cat wondered just what her parents had told the world to explain her disappearance. It must have been convincing, whatever it was, because she had seen nothing in the newssheets, even those most given to scandalous gossip and tittle-tattle. She had hardly been "out" and, she suspected, she had made very little impression on polite Society in those early weeks of the Season, so it was hardly as though an accredited beauty had vanished from the scene.

She decided that what she would have done in their position was to put it about that she had suffered a nervous collapse, being unable to cope with the excitement and punishing round of social engagements, and had retired to the country to live quietly with an elderly relative. Uncle Alexander in his remote Scottish retreat would be perfect.

She had left them a note explaining what she was doing, so it was hardly as though they would worry that she had been kidnapped—even if that was not far from the truth—or had met with an accident. There had been no need to call out the Bow Street Runners and risk a scandal.

Had Papa set out after her to try and bring her back, she wondered? Or had they decided that the less satisfactory of their two daughters had made her bed and could lie on it? Anna had snared her viscount, heir to an earl, and had been expecting her second child. Her oldest brother, Giles, was expected to seek out and court an heiress. Yes, they would probably have washed their hands of her and prayed earnestly that she vanished into decent obscurity.

Which I have, by some miracle.

'A penny for your thoughts, Cat.'

'Oh. I beg your pardon, Harland. Had I fallen into a brown study?'

'Somewhat. Will you share it or is it personal?'

'I suppose it is. I was thinking about my arrival in Duke's Forde.'

Harland had settled back comfortably into his armchair, his fingers steepled, one long leg crossed over the other, the picture of a relaxed man having a conversation that interested him. 'I have to confess, I have wondered about that. May I be so intrusive as to say that I do not believe you were born into a family of shopkeepers?'

'No, I was not,' she confessed and realised this was the perfect opportunity to throw up a smokescreen to hide her past, to deal with any lingering wisps of memory about their one past encounter.

'My parents— Papa owned some land.' *Just a few thousand acres.*

'A squire?'

'Yes,' Cat agreed. After all, that was what the landed aristocrats were to their tenants, simply squires on a very, very large scale. 'But then when they…' She let her voice trail away, despising herself for how easy it was to allow just a touch of grief to colour her words. She gave herself a little shake, pretending she was pushing away the unpleasant memory of her bereavement. Had that worked? It was the most dangerous part of her story, the part that wasn't true and the part that left a day and a night unmentioned.

'I found myself with very few resources, far less than I had ever imagined. Life had seemed very secure and safe before that. There was an uncle in Scotland, but he was always a trifle peculiar, so they said. Besides, he was a very long way away and we had never met.

'So I decided that I must seek employment. I did not have any talents to be a governess, so a companion seemed the most genteel option. Oxford must have many elderly ladies and several employment bureaux, I thought, so I set out for there. I stopped in Duke's Forde to break my journey.'

Because I had almost run out of money and could travel no further...

'I went to the baker's shop that Madame Arnaud now owns. On the way I passed the haberdashers, just as the owner tripped over someone's lapdog, hit his head and was laid out on the floor, bleeding terribly. Nobody seemed to know what to do, so I went in and, I suppose, took control.'

'And the rest is history,' Harland said with a nod. She had been aware of his close attention, and he had shown no sign of finding any part of her tale so far unconvincing.

'I suppose it is. William was older than me and his

heart was weak, so on his doctor's orders he was laid up in bed for some time to recover. I simply moved in and helped nurse him and look after the shop. Ben and Helen were there then, but much younger, of course, so we managed. When William recovered he offered me employment as a sort of assistant manager, I suppose. I found I enjoyed the work, was good at it. Then, after a while, we married, more for companionship and, well, to preserve appearances.'

'But you were happy?'

'Yes,' she agreed. 'I was. Content. I had found a place to belong, an occupation I enjoyed. I made friends here. And then William died of the heart condition he had been suffering from for so long, and left the business to me.'

They were people I trusted, people who would not betray me, even if they ever discovered the truth about me, people who cared about more than status and wealth.

'And you are still content?'

His dark, intelligent eyes were fixed on her face, she realised, and his gaze made her shiver, inwardly. What did he see there? Guilt? Lies?

'Yes. Yes, of course I am. My business is successful and nothing has changed, except that your plans should make Duke's Forde more prosperous, a more interesting place to live.'

It was certainly that now, although she had heard

that the Chinese believed that living in interesting times was a curse, not a blessing. Quinn Falconer had brought danger with him, although, worryingly, it often felt more like excitement than peril.

Stop being seduced by a pair of fine eyes and an even finer pair of shoulders, she scolded herself. *If he recalls who I am, this...this friendship will be over and my standing in local society will be ruined. Respectable Mrs Brandon actually the ruined daughter of an earl? Deceiving us all this time?*

'I confess that, of all the things that I expected this town to be, *interesting* was not one of them,' he said.

Cat shrugged. 'Why should you find it so? You must be used to London Society, to the Season, to country house parties, summers by the sea, perhaps. Shooting parties in the autumn. A depressed little town and its problems could hardly be called *interesting*. Except, I suppose, as a sharp contrast. That could be enlivening, like finding a slice of lemon in an oversweet posset.'

Harland laughed. Not polite amusement at her simile, but a full-throated, vastly amused shout of laughter.

It was hopelessly contagious and Cat found herself laughing too, although she had no idea why, only that he was so attractive with all of the sophistication stripped away, all the ducal gloss lost.

'Why are we laughing?' she asked, a full minute

later as she scrabbled in her reticule to find a handkerchief to mop her streaming eyes.

'I have no idea,' he confessed, emerging from behind his own large square of white linen.

Another way that men have an advantage, she thought, locating her own little scrap of lace-edged nonsense, scarcely adequate to absorb one tear.

'Here.' He dug into a pocket and produced another, immaculate handkerchief, sharply folded. 'My valet sends me out with two, just like Nanny used to.'

That set her off again, even as she reached for the cloth and their fingertips brushed. Cat retreated behind what would have done duty for size as a tray cloth until she thought she had her expression under control. Nothing could be done, of course, about her eyes and her nose would, of course, be red. *Delightful.*

She had to think of something safe to talk about. Something serious and dull. Drinking troughs? No, drains, that would do it.

'Harland—'

'Call me Quinn,' he said abruptly. 'I call you Cat, after all.'

'It would be most improper,' she said, attempting to sound shocked instead of alarmed. *Do not think of him as Quinn Falconer. Do not think of honeysuckle and balconies...*

'What do you call this?' He gestured at the space

around them. 'We are alone and unchaperoned, the door is fully closed. Now, this *is* improper.'

'But in a vicarage…' she protested feebly.

'Where anyone might call at any time. They might take a quick peek through that wide window as they come up the path, just to see who is at home.'

'That is not amusing. Go and join your beastly architect at once, Quinn, and I will go and find Mrs Newnham. She will be mortified if she realises that she has left me alone with you.'

'To be the victim of my wicked wiles?' he said, clearly expecting her to protest that she suspected him of no such thing.

'Exactly.' Cat stood up. 'I shall leave by the back door. You go out of the front.'

Quinn started to rise politely as she did, and Cat put out a hand to wave him back in his chair, but he was too fast, and she was too near, and instead of empty air her palm hit his chest.

She staggered a little and he caught her by the forearms to steady her. 'Cat.'

They were very close. Close enough for her to smell the faint, discreet hint of lemon verbena and warm male skin beneath the scent of freshly laundered linen. Close enough for her to hear that his breathing had hitched on one breath as he caught her.

She should thank him and step back. Now, before

this became...something. A thing. A situation. She did not move.

'Cat,' Quinn said again, and she felt the slight pull, no more perhaps than his hands tightening on her arms.

If she stepped forward, their bodies would touch. If she stepped forward and looked up, he would kiss her.

She had wondered for years what his kiss would be like.

And then, before she could react, decide—lean in or step back—he released her and moved away. 'Do you feel steady now?'

Cat looked him in the eye and let anger replace all those other emotions fighting in her head. 'No, not particularly. But I am not going to fall...over. Not now, Quinn.'

He did not move as she walked steadily out of the room, closing the door behind her. He did not speak.

Chapter Seven

Quinn bit back the words, the curses at his own stupidity. What had he been thinking—other than that he wanted his hands on Cat's body, his mouth on hers?

And in the vicarage drawing room, in front of a window, of all places, to add stupidity to completely reckless behaviour.

He was fortunate that Cat had not slapped his face and had the restraint to simply cut him with words. No, she was not going to *fall*, respectable, decent woman that she was. Sensible woman too. She had her eyes wide open and she knew better than to be dazzled by the prospect of a dalliance with a duke. It could never end well for her, and she had everything to lose if the slightest whisper of gossip got out. It would all be gone—her good name, her business, her place in this community, her world.

Quinn knew he wanted her and he knew too that he could not always have what he wanted. Certainly not this woman.

He cracked open the door and listened, heard Cat's voice coming from the back of the house.

'Mrs Newnham is still at the almshouses? She must have been delayed by something urgent. I will not wait, but perhaps I might go around and see if I can find her. May I use your kitchen door, Mrs Gordon? Thank you.'

Best to stay where he was until she had been gone some minutes. He settled back into the armchair, an undeservedly comfortable place from which to consider his own folly.

Instead he found himself thinking about Cat and her story. It must have been a terrifying experience, finding herself alone and having to discover some way to make a respectable living. Despite her best efforts, he had sensed the fear that lay under her calm recounting of the situation she had found herself in.

Quinn frowned. Something had not rung quite true, now he ran through her words, her tone, her expression, again. The story of how she had found herself working for, then married to, William Brandon, had felt right, but there had been something...

It was the lack of relatives, he realised. What had she said? *There was an uncle in Scotland, but he was always a trifle peculiar, so they said, and he was a very long way away.*

Who had said that? Could one uncle really be her sole relative? No godparents living, even? And surely, even a peculiar relative in the wilds of North Britain would be better than risking life alone in a world that was terrifyingly dangerous for an unprotected woman?

There had been the memory of natural fear there, of course, he realised. But more than that—there had been anger.

Cat was a young woman who had learned to hide her emotions behind the face of a successful shopkeeper. She was firm with staff, and no doubt with suppliers and creditors; always pleasant, whatever she was feeling, with customers. But he was coming to know her now, and he had played enough hands of cards in clubs and hells to be able to recognise the subtle "tells" in an opponent.

Not that Cat was an opponent, but she was certainly hiding things from him. It was her business, of course, and he should not pry. And yet...

What if she had been forced to leave her secure home after the death of her parents? What if one of those non-existent relatives—and he found it hard to believe there were none—had done something to make flight the only option? A predatory uncle by marriage, or a male cousin, perhaps, wanting something in return for a roof over her head? Was that uncle in Scotland not just "strange", but dangerous?

He was a duke now, he reminded himself. Someone with resources, powers and influence far beyond those of the well-born, well-off gentleman he had been. If he could discover Cat's history—all of it—might he find something that would restore her to the position in the gentry he was sure she had been born to? And if one of those non-existent relatives had tried to harm her—then he would deal with them as they deserved.

She would not like it if she knew what he was intending, and that gave him a qualm. On the other hand, he would be totally discreet, with only her best interests in mind. If there was nothing to be found, or nothing to be done, then he would forget everything he learned about her.

There was one obvious place to start: the parish registers of Duke's Forde that would contain her marriage record, unless she and Brandon had gone into Oxford. But why would they have done that? It was not as though they had anything to hide and they were to return here after the wedding.

Quinn got up and let himself out of the front door, then, ignoring the group standing in front of the almshouses, walked around to the south door of the church. If he could find what he was looking for without having to ask, all the better. As he entered, the clock struck five, ending with its distressing *clunk*. He supposed it was his duty to have the clock repaired as well, he thought ruefully, then decided that Yorke could deal with that.

Registers were usually kept in the vestry, so he

made his way to the chancel and tried the low door in its north wall. It opened onto a small room with two cassocks hanging on the wall, a cope chest for the vestments, a cupboard sporting a large lock—containing the church plate, presumably—and a bookcase holding a number of large volumes in varying states of repair.

He took down the nearest one and opened it on the table. It was very new—only a year's worth of baptisms, marriages and burials. He took the one before it and began to page back through the marriages. The Vicar had handwriting that was clear enough, but even so, the entries were crammed together with small groups of weddings set between baptisms and burials. Then he found it in September eighteen hundred and twelve.

William Brandon, bachelor of this parish, of full age and Catherine Ransome, spinster of this parish, of full age, were married by banns. So, there had been no attempt at discretion by having a licence and thus avoiding banns being called from the altar steps on the preceding three Sundays. These were two people with nothing to hide, at least, within their community. And, of course, unless they chose to place notices of the marriage in the national newssheets, then there would be no reason for the wedding of two shopkeepers in a small town to attract any interest beyond the parish.

But he had Cat's maiden name now, and an approximate age—if Cat was more than twenty-five or twenty-six, then he needed spectacles or she was a witch—and that would be enough to set a skilled investigator on her trail.

He had inherited one of these, most conveniently. His new man of law, also acquired along with the title, had mentioned that he employed just such a man.

'One never knows when one might require discreet investigations to be carried out, Your Grace,' Mr Grainger had said. 'People are inclined to believe they can take advantage of those of high status.' He had smiled a smile that put Quinn in mind of an illustration he had once seen of a Nile crocodile. 'We do not tolerate that.'

Very well, he would summon this man to Harland Park to discuss the matter—he was not going to risk putting anything on paper—and see what he could do.

Quinn put the registers back in place and let himself out of the church. Time to see if a plan for the repairs had been put in place and whether Abernathy had recovered from his tantrum. He was good, but it was time to remind him that there were other architects, equally talented, out there.

When she saw him emerge from the church porch and take the path across the graveyard to the gate into the almshouse yard Cat wondered what the Duke had been doing there. She hadn't seen him go in, but he couldn't have been there long. Just time for a quick prayer to give him patience in dealing with his architect, perhaps?

Or a brief tour of family memorials, although all those Harlands who had died since the middle of the last century had been interred in the mausoleum in the park of the big house. There were some handsome table tombs with knights and their ladies reclining on top, the men with lions at their feet, their wives with lapdogs, except in one case where a particular smug-looking cat had been immortalised, a mouse under its paw. When the sermon was failing to hold her attention, she had sometimes wondered if that was a clue as to the couple's relationship.

She was glad to see him, despite her nerves over the way they had parted. There was no need to worry, she realised as he joined their group, politely doffing his hat to her and to Mrs Newnham. Not by a flicker of an eyelash did his expression betray either any special awareness of her or any feeling of awkwardness.

'A timely arrival, Duke,' she said. 'Mrs Newnham and I are having difficulty in impressing upon Mr Abernathy that the residents are more interested in space, convenience, warmth and the proximity of adequate earth closets and a wash-house than they are in colonnades, finials and architectural decoration, which I believe will make several apartments depressingly dark.'

She managed to maintain her smile, which she had

feared had been about to turn into a snarl at the architect.

'Your Grace.' Abernathy's own smile was almost a grimace. 'I have been attempting to explain to the ladies that the almshouses should reflect the prestige and the generosity of their donor and be an ornament to the town.'

'I have not the slightest interest in any of that,' Quinn said. 'These dwellings are to provide for the elderly inhabitants of this place in a fitting and dignified manner. I require you to produce plans to double the number of apartments in a manner and style that reflects what is already there and including all those elements and features which the Vicar, Mrs Newnham and Mrs Brandon desire. If you find yourself unable to do that, then I am sure that there are others who would be only too pleased to undertake the work.'

Quinn thought the architect would have turned on his heel and flounced away if he had been dealing with anyone other than a duke. As it was, he made an abrupt bow. 'I shall produce an outline for approval as you direct, Your Grace.'

He stalked off, his assistant at his heels, and Quinn said, 'I apologise. It seems to me that, if he does what he is told, this is the fastest way to get the new apartments ready, but if he causes you any further problems—Vicar, ladies—I will replace him.'

Mr Newnham, who had looked ready to take flight

if an argument had ensued, mopped his brow. 'We are much obliged, Your Grace. And the excellent Mr Flowers has undertaken to send workmen over first thing tomorrow, to remain with us until all the repairs have been completed, which he considers will take a week. Thank you for giving us your valuable time.'

Cat watched as Quinn made little of his assistance, thanked the Vicar for drawing the matter to his notice—which made Mr Newnham blush and shake his head—and then turned to make his way back to the marketplace.

'I must congratulate you, Cat, on not felling Abernathy with a set square and throttling him with his own measuring chains,' he said as he caught up with her and opened the gate.

'It was tempting, I have to admit,' she said.

'Especially as you have had to deal with enough male idiocy for one day,' he added.

Was that an apology? She supposed it must be. And now she had to decide how to react to it.

She could snub him, she could pretend not to know what he was referring to or she could make some gesture of acceptance, which was what every instinct was telling her was the right thing to do.

Dangerous, of course, but honesty had always been important to her. And he had not pressed his advantage when, she was certain, he had sensed how close she had been to leaning in for that kiss. He shouldn't have put them in that position in the first place, she thought severely, but penitence was attractive…

'Men can be thoughtless creatures,' she observed, looking up at him. 'Creatures of impulse and instinct. A woman must learn to rely on her own instincts to know where she can trust.'

Those dark eyes were rueful, and there was something like admiration in his expression. 'And your instincts tell you what, Cat?'

'That Abernathy will one day be found buried in the foundations of his latest masterpiece. He gives me a headache. Otherwise, my day has been…satisfactory.'

Had she gone too far? Would he take that as encouragement or the mild teasing she had intended.

'Thank you, Cat,' he said with a smile that made something inside her give a little flip. 'I have learned a number of useful things today.' He raised his hat and turned away to cross to the Harland Arms, leaving her wondering just what he meant by that.

He had learned about the almshouses, certainly. He had learned about the Vicar's delicate nerves and, she supposed, he had learned exactly where flirting with her got him. He had learned about her arrival at Duke's Forde as well. Had she said too much about that?

No, Cat thought as she opened her shop door, she had said just enough and in exactly the right tone. Her secrets were quite safe.

Chapter Eight

In the two weeks that followed it seemed to Cat that she had somehow become the Duke's representative in the town. Mr Flowers, the master builder, came and asked her opinion of exterior paintwork colours, brandishing a handful of wood chip samples. Mrs Newnham and the Vicar dropped by daily with progress reports on the repairs and to show her the first draft plans and drawings from Abernathy.

'They seem very fine,' Mr Newnham said anxiously one day. 'But my wife wonders about the position of the, er, earth closets and the size of the laundry. But I am sure Mr Abernathy knows best, so...'

'No, he doesn't. He only cares how it looks,' Cat had said, firmly wresting the plans from the Vicar's grasp. She circled the inadequate washhouse and wrote, "Bigger!" across it, then pencilled in an additional set of earth closets in the new rear yard.

'There.' She handed it back. 'Or shall I tackle him?'

'No, thank you,' Mr Newnham said, squaring his shoulders. 'I am resolved to deal with this myself.'

Madelaine teased her gently about it when she took advantage of a quiet afternoon towards the end of the month to indulge in a cup of chocolate.

Her friend brought her drink to the table and joined her with her own cup. 'Now, let us see how long we can sit here before someone comes and asks you something about the Duke's works.'

'Nonsense, there is nothing that I can tell anyone.' Cat dropped a quite unnecessary piece of sugar into her chocolate and stirred it energetically.

'Not even the Duke?'

'How did you—? Oh, I walked right into that one, did I not? Well, it doesn't seem right to tell people what to do, or to listen to suggestions or criticism and not pass it on. So, yes, I do send him the occasional note.'

She was not blushing, she was almost certain. Not that there was anything to blush about, not with notes that were simply reports, signed "Yr. obedt. servant, C. Brandon."

She saw no reason to confide that the answering notes thanking her began, "Dear C" and were signed, "Yours, Q."

He is not yours, she would remind herself sharply whenever she received one and locked it away in her desk. They were strictly practical communications and to the point with no attempt at flirtation—except that greeting and signature.

Dear Cat, she thought, and sighed.

'Oh, good afternoon, Mrs Brandon,' a voice said beside her, making her start.

'Mrs Allsop.' Cat smiled at the Squire's wife. 'What a lovely day, is it not?'

'It is indeed. I was wondering if you could tell me about the assembly room.'

'The assembly room? Why, I believe the Duke is planning to include one with his new hotel, but it is most unlikely to be ready for this winter, don't you think?'

She gestured to where the team of labourers was demolishing the row of shabby shops and houses at the end of the marketplace facing up towards the church. The work had only just begun there because of having to find new premises and accommodation for the displaced tenants.

'Quite. So considerate of his Grace to rehouse everybody, don't you think? Or perhaps it was your good offices?'

'It was nothing to do with me,' Cat said firmly. 'The Duke is clearly a very conscientious landlord.'

'That is good to know. I had wondered…' The older woman cleared her throat. 'It was the old assembly room, the one in the inn, I meant. You recall? It had to be closed up because part of the ceiling came down.'

'That was before I came to Duke's Forde,' Cat said. 'I hadn't realised that there had been one.'

'Oh, yes. And many an assembly was held there. Excellent dances—the floor was very good, you know—and there was a nice little balcony for the musicians. Such a pity we have not the use of it any longer.'

Mrs Allsop had three daughters, one already out and two on the verge of it. No wonder she was anxious to have dances in the town once again as soon as possible, Cat thought.

'Why do you not ask the Duke himself about it? I can see him approaching now,' Madelaine said brightly, nodding towards the window.

'My goodness! I suppose...we have met, after all. He was good enough to call, you know, but I hardly like...'

'Why not take my chair, Mrs Allsop? Your Grace.' Madelaine got to her feet as the shop door opened. 'May I serve you coffee? Mrs Allsop was telling us about a question she has for you.'

'Thank you, Madame, a coffee would be delightful. May I, Mrs Brandon? Mrs Allsop, do tell me how I can be of help.'

The Squire's wife looked ready to faint as she grappled with the problem of a casual conversation with a duke—*a duke*—in a tearoom. Madelaine seemed delighted to have him patronising her establishment again, and Cat could almost feel the pressure of eyes on her, almost hear the speculation.

Quinn waited patiently while Mrs Allsop gathered herself to answer. He did not enjoy the fact that his title so often made a barrier to normal social interaction, reducing perfectly sensible people to stumbling formality. Goodness knows what it must be like to be a minor royal.

'Well, Your Grace, it is the assembly room, you see—the old one, I mean, in the Harland Arms. Only it has been closed up for years, owing to the ceiling—so fortunate that the bass viol player was not more seriously injured, although Miss Fortesque had strong hysterics afterwards—but as the inn is being put into such good order and the new assembly room in the hotel will be some time yet...' She lost herself and sent Cat an imploring glace.

'We were hoping that the room at the inn would be fit to be used again for this winter Season,' Cat said, smoothly picking up the thread. 'Although perhaps you feel it would be a waste if there is to be the new one, Your Grace.'

'It is being taken care of. I believe the Coroner is anxious to have the use of it again for inquests, and there are various societies that have been enquiring about it,' Quinn said, smiling his thanks to Madelaine as she brought him his coffee. 'The Glee Club and the Horticultural Society to name two, and then I believe that some of the ladies want it for charitable sales of work.

'The ceiling has been repaired and the walls are to be painted and so forth. I believe that there was some issue about the correct treatment of the floor if it is to be used for dancing, but I know nothing about that.'

'Now that I do know about,' Mrs Allsop said. 'I was on the committee of ladies when it was in regular use.'

'Then perhaps you would consider forming such a group again, ma'am? It would be a considerable benefit to the town, I am sure. If it would not be an imposition,' Quinn added when she hesitated.

'Oh, no. Not at all. It would be a pleasure, Your Grace. With whom should we communicate our thoughts on the programme and use?'

'I will tell Longford, the innkeeper, and James Turnbull, my secretary. Between them and you and your ladies, I am certain there will soon be full use of the room. I will ask Turnbull to contact you. Please let him know of any supplies your committee might need—writing paper and so forth.'

He smiled politely at her enthusiastic thanks and drank his coffee. He had wanted to speak to Cat, not for any specific reason, but because he was beginning to fear she was avoiding him. Her polite notes were always entirely businesslike—and why should they be anything else? he asked himself irritably—

and he found he was missing her practical common sense, her lack of deference and those sudden flashes of tart humour.

Now he found himself having to make polite conversation with Mrs Allsop under the interested gazes of a dozen interested ladies.

'You said that you had a suggestion for me concerning the provision of a waiting room for ladies using the stage or Mail coaches, Mrs Brandon,' he said as inspiration stuck him. 'I can see the benefits of that. Perhaps you would not mind indicating exactly where you had thought suitable?'

He mentally crossed his fingers that Cat would not simply stare at him and deny all knowledge of that spontaneous invention, but she took a final sip from her cup and stood up.

'Of course. I am delighted that you approve the idea. Travel by public stage is something of an ordeal for an unaccompanied female and the jostling one endures at inns can be intolerable. Would you excuse me, Mrs Allsop, if I leave you and show His Grace what I had in mind?'

'What on earth are you talking about, Quinn?' she demanded as soon as they were out of earshot. 'I made no such suggestion. Not that it isn't a good one.'

'It just came to me. I am glad that you think it useful. Do mind that puddle, Cat.' He offered his arm but she skipped lightly over the wet patch without his aid.

It seemed that the accidental almost-kiss in the Rectory was not forgotten.

'I think it an admirable idea,' she said as they continued across the square. 'But where are you going to put it? It needs to be on the ground floor and close enough for travellers to see and hear what is going on so they do not have to keep emerging to find out when their coach arrives.'

The Oxford Mail coach was just leaving with a musical display on its horn by the red-coated guard. As the yard cleared of passengers Quinn strode across to a boarded-up lean-to shed. 'This looks big enough.' He prised open the door and looked in.

'Cleared out, the walls properly lined to keep it warm and with its own earth closet, it would be perfect,' Cat said. 'Such a good idea.'

'I will give orders for it to be done. Shall we look at this assembly room? What do you think of it?'

'I have never seen it.' She came with him willingly enough as he made his way into the main body of the inn and took the main stairs to the first floor.

'It's along here, I think. I only glanced at it before.' He paused by a set of double doors, very aware of her close by his side, of the fresh scent of her hair, the swish of her skirts on the bare boards.

He should go to London, spend some time...relaxing. For quite a while he had enjoyed a very pleasant liaison with Lady Ansley, a charming widow who saw no reason to remarry and lose her independence, and no reason either not to continue to enjoy the pleasures of the marriage bed. They appreciated each other's company and respected each other's independence.

It occurred to Quinn that they had not been together for months. Perhaps all he needed was a little… diversion.

'Dingy,' a brisk voice beside him said. 'It needs more light.' Cat took off her bonnet and laid it on a chair. 'That's a little better. With these latest hats one might as well be wearing blinkers.' She stared around her critically. 'But all it needs is a good clean, a coat or two of whitewash and new curtains. The seats and benches need recovering, but the floor is good, I think.'

Cat took four running steps into the room, then twirled around, skirts belling out around her. Coils of her hair, confined now by neither cap nor bonnet, fell to her shoulders. 'My goodness, how long is it since I last danced!'

She was laughing and irresistible, and Quinn walked to her and held out his hand. 'Do you waltz?'

'I know the theory but I have never been ap— I mean, I have never had the nerve to try it.'

Now what is wrong? Cat was flustered, but not by his presence, he was sure. What had she just been about to say?

'Then let us try it now.' He swept her into a hold

and started to hum the last tune he had waltzed to. '*One*, two three, *one* two three…'

And they were dancing, Cat was laughing. She fell over her own feet once and then found her rhythm, following him as they covered the dusty floor. He tried a fancy turn and she stayed close, her cheeks flushed, her eyes the soft hazel brown that he had come to understand showed she was happy. The dangerous green glint was what he had to beware of, he thought, smiling down at her.

Cat smiled back and began to hum along with him, now that she had caught the tune.

Should he stop? There was no orchestra to draw this reckless dance to a close, only his own instincts. And they were saying, *Stop. Enough. There is peril here!*

His arms were full of laughing, warm, delicious woman. Dangerous woman.

Quinn stopped humming, stopped dancing—which would have been ideal if the suddenness had not made Cat trip, over his feet this time, and he caught her awkwardly, falling to his knees as he cradled her clear of the floor.

Her arms went around his neck. Instinct, what remained of his functioning brain told him. Instinct, nothing more. His nostrils were full of the scent of her, of warm woman, of herbs and flowers. His body could feel the impress of her curves against him. Under his fingers her pulse beat hard.

They stared into each other's eyes for a long, silent, moment, then Cat's lips parted and her arms tightened. Quinn bent his head and was lost in the kiss.

It was not gentle, but hungry, as though both were famished. She was not an innocent, that glimmer of thought reminded him. She had been married. But this was not right. Not there, not now. Not ever.

That was his conscience, shouting at him against the thrum of his blood, the aching need and desire for her, the answering desire Cat's body was signalling. Her mouth was open under his, the heat, the dart of her tongue and the nip of her teeth acting like a shot of brandy in his blood.

They were as one in passion and, it seemed, in tune in more ways than that, because, in a split second it was over. She drew back, even as he lowered her carefully to the floor and straightened, stepped away.

'That was a very bad idea,' Quinn said, controlling his voice with an effort. 'I apologise.'

'That realisation appeared to strike us both at the same time. No apology is needed.' Cat sounded equally breathless, but she held out her hand and he took it to pull her to her feet.

She moved away a little, but not, he thought with relief, out of wariness, but to brush the dust from her skirts.

'We agreed that a cat may be friends with a duke, did we not? But friendship is as far as it can go.' Her clothes apparently ordered to her satisfaction, she looked up and met his gaze squarely. 'I am not in the market for a *carte blanche*, Quinn. And no other offer is conceivable, is it?'

'Dukes have married actresses,' he said, surprising himself as the words left his lips. Was that what he wanted? Marriage? *Marriage?*

'But not shopkeepers.' Cat picked up her bonnet, scooped up her tumbled hair and efficiently trapped it inside. Her hands were shaking a little, he saw, as she tied the ribbons.

He wanted to tie them for her, but he was afraid his hands were shaking too. And if he touched her again...

If she could behave with dignity in the face of this situation, then so could he. 'No, not shopkeepers. Society has a strong aversion to trade, I fear.'

'So irrational, as without it we would all be naked and starving.'

She was angry now, he could hear it in her voice. He suspected it was mutual, although quite who he was angry with he was not sure. Cat had wanted that kiss as much as he had. Not that it gave him any excuse for taking it.

'Quite.' Quinn opened the doors and looked out. 'The corridor is empty. I suggest you leave first.'

Cat swept out past him, then stopped a few feet along the corridor and looked back. 'Thank you for my first waltz.' Then she was gone, and he stood there as the sound of her heels on the uncarpeted boards faded away.

My first waltz. And what was it she said? *I have never been ap*—

Young ladies making their come-out in London had to be approved by the Patronesses of Almack's before they could accept invitations to waltz, or risk condemnation for being fast. Did some kind of approval exist in other social circles? Or were his vague suspicions about her origins correct?

If Mrs Brandon had encountered the Patronesses, then her come-out had not been the one a country squire's daughter or a vicar's child would have experienced. Tickets of admission to Almack's were devilishly hard to come by for all but the loftiest of the *ton*, and not even for them if the Patronesses took a dislike or scented scandal.

Just who was Cat Brandon *née* Ransome? If Mr Grainger had set his man Foster on her trail by now, he might not have long to wait to find out.

In the meantime he had every intention of riding back to Harland Park and taking a swim in its lake, the coldest thing he could think of, given that the ice house had been neglected and stood empty, home to spiders, snails and gardeners' tools.

He had to get this growing obsession with Cat under

control, because he was learning that being a duke—at least, one with any concern about his duties and obligations—needed all the concentration he could give it.

Chapter Nine

Cat was halfway across the marketplace when it occurred to her that this was the second time she had walked from the inn towards the haberdashery after fleeing from the embraces of a man.

Only this one took responsibility for his actions, she reminded herself, slowing her near-run to a more ladylike stroll. To compare Quinn Falconer with Blaine Wykeham was to insult one and flatter the other.

That kiss had been as much her fault as Quinn's, she knew perfectly well. She had wanted it, dreamt about it and had thoroughly enjoyed it—for the moments it had lasted. Unfortunately there was a price to pay for pleasure and that was physical in the bodily yearnings she felt and, much more long-lasting, in the social awkwardness of living with what had happened. How was she going to face him again? And then there were the emotions to deal with.

It did not help that it had been so good. Losing her virginity to Wykeham had been unpleasant, and William's polite and considerate attentions had only gone to show just how selfish and uncaring Wykeham had been. But she had always felt there must be something more than "polite and considerate" and now she knew that she had been right.

How very fortunate that Quinn was not just a duke, but also a gentleman, or matters might have become considerably more complicated than they already were—she didn't trust her own willpower one inch.

The shop was busy when she entered, so Cat went through to the back, gave her skirts a thorough brushing, redid her coiffure and fixed on her cap. There was nothing like a cap for making a woman feel respectable, she thought, rather shakily.

The shop door bell tinkled. More customers. She could not afford to spend her time brooding over what had just happened. Or thinking of Quinn Falconer at all. She was an independent woman with a living to earn.

The smile felt fixed, but nobody appeared to notice anything amiss as she emerged into the shop and greeted customers and her staff. The new arrival was, to her surprise, male.

Men came to the shop, of course, accompanying their wives, or as servants attending on the lady of the house. But this one seemed to be neither.

A superior kind of clerk, Cat decided. He was thin and middle-aged and neatly dressed without any fashionable details, and he was clearly feeling out of place amidst bonnets, laces and ribbons.

'May I help you?' Cat asked when he ventured up to the counter.

'Er, handkerchiefs, if you please.'

'I'm afraid we do not stock gentlemen's handkerchiefs,' Cat apologised.

'But you do sell linen? You see, I suffer from summer sneezing,' he said, leaning a little across the counter and lowering his voice. 'Well, it starts in the spring. Some say it is the dust and others the pollen and another school of thought is that it is the sun itself that causes it. But it is a miserable affliction.'

'It must be,' Cat agreed. She had seen sufferers with streaming eyes and sore noses retreating inside on the brightest, most pleasant of summer days.

'And I use so many handkerchiefs and they really are expensive to buy in quantity, especially good quality ones. So my landlady suggested that I buy the linen and she would hem them for me. Only there are no shops selling good enough linen in my little town and sending off is too much of a risk. But I am travelling to Oxford and stopped at the inn across the way and overheard a lady remarking on the quality of your fabrics.' He came to a halt and regarded her hopefully.

'I see. You would need something very soft, but strong enough for constant laundering, I imagine.'

'Exactly that, ma'am.'

'Do take a seat, sir, and I will see what we have that might suit.'

She sent Ben to bring four rolls of plain white linen and set them on the counter in front of the man, now perched on one of the bent-wood chairs, and went through their various qualities with him. 'This one washes very well, but never becomes soft. I would recommend it for aprons. This one is very soft, but not hard wearing. Of these two, this is the more economical, but slightly less soft. Three yards of any of them would give you eighteen squares.'

He pondered and finally decided on the more economical choice.

'We could cut it for you, ready for hemming, at no extra cost,' Cat offered, rather liking the earnest little man and the respectful way he stroked the fabric. She approved of people who took an interest in quality.

'That would be most kind, ma'am.' He settled into the chair more comfortably as Ben took the roll to the cutting table and began to measure out squares. 'I hope it is not impertinent to enquire, but it clearly takes much knowledge to manage a store of this quality. Does it involve an apprenticeship?'

'Well, Ben and Helen were both apprentices, but I married into it, as it were.' She was not telling him anything that local gossip would not. 'I had no background in shopkeeping, only in shopping! It took me a while to learn all there is to know, of course. I have to admit to already possessing a liking for fine fabrics and for laces and ribbons, although what young lady does not? It would have been much harder to have found myself in an ironmongery or a grocery.'

'I can quite see that. I do find it interesting to study anyone who has a skill or a trade, whether it is a farrier or a painter.'

'Surely you have your own skills,' Cat said lightly.

'Oh, I suppose so. I am a lawyer's clerk, so one does need to acquire knowledge in that field.' He gave a little chuckle. 'But it is dusty, serious work and it would be a pleasure to be surrounded by such colours and softness. But I suppose there is a full measure of work at a desk with pen and ink and ledgers as well and young ladies are rarely taught accountancy, I imagine.'

'There are household budgets to learn to balance, although, I have to admit as a girl, I was always bored with that and imagined that with a competent housekeeper I wouldn't need to know such dull stuff. I had to learn rapidly.'

She calculated the cost and wrote him a receipt when he paid her and watched with a smile as he left the shop full of thanks and clutching Ben's neatly tied parcel.

'A nice little man,' she murmured to Ben as he came to gather up the rolls of linen. 'I do hope he has a good landlady. But as she is offering to sew his handkerchiefs, I imagine she is pleasant enough.'

Helen came over, her brow creased by a frown. 'Mrs Brandon, Miss Appleby says there is a new fabrics warehouse in Oxford, a large one. But she says it is expensive—London prices. Do you think they will take business away from us, though?'

'It might. I had better go and see and discover what they have and what they are charging. Do you know where it is?'

'Broad Street.'

'Hmm. Quite high rents, I imagine, if it is a large place. Yes, we must visit, Helen. Tomorrow is Tuesday, it is always quieter before market day. Can you manage alone, do you think, Ben?'

'Yes, ma'am. We're not expecting any deliveries,' he said confidently.

'Then best bonnets, Helen. We will pretend to be ladies on a shopping expedition and see what we can discover.'

And Oxford was a nice safe distance from the Duke of Harland. Wherever else she might encounter him, it wasn't going to be in a haberdashery emporium in the middle of a university city.

A plan to take her away from Duke's Forde for a day was soothing, but even so, Cat kept catching herself going over and over those few passionate moments at the inn, with consequent tingles in places she found it easier not to think about.

Thank goodness they had both realised what a mistake it was, and thank goodness she had not misjudged Quinn's character, and he had not proved to be the kind of man who would have refused to stop after her first reckless response.

One of the reasons she, and her neighbours, had so stubbornly resisted any move from their premises was the space at the back. There they each had a large garden, divided by walls about six feet high and opening through doors at the end onto a lane. That meant Billy Upwell who scythed their grass and pruned their shrubs had easy access.

Michael Dangerfield grew vegetables and Phoebe enjoyed her little flower patch. Madelaine left hers to grass and shrubs so Peter could run and chase his ball and make dens to his heart's content. Cat had a small paved terrace, a lot of grass and beds where she grew bulbs, herbs and anything that caught her fancy and which didn't need too much time spent on it. A garden was for relaxing in, not somewhere to make more work, in her opinion.

Now she sank down on the bench on the terrace and tried to clear her mind of everything except the distant sounds of the town settling down for the evening. Ben had gone to join some of his friends at the skittle alley in the alehouse in Church Street, and Helen had taken scraps from their fabrics to the sewing group that made patchwork quilts and infants' clothes for charitable distribution.

Was it possible to make one's mind a blank and think about nothing at all? She tried, then was distracted by the sound of hinges creaking. Someone had opened and closed Michael Dangerfield's back gate. Then the sound of another gate—Madelaine's. She heard her friend's voice raised in greeting, and guessed that she too was relaxing in her garden.

Their voices were audible but, unless she strained her ears—which she was careful not to do—she could not make out what they were talking about.

None of my business...

'You are *not* a widow?' Michael's voice carried clearly.

There was the sound of Madelaine's, lower, but with her accent much more pronounced as it always was when she was excited or upset.

Cat stood up. She should go inside.

'Where is the swine?'

'I do not know. There is nothing to be done.' Madelaine was very clear now.

Then there was the sound of her gate closing and, a few moments later, the squeak of hinges and a bang as Michael's was shut with some force.

Oh, lord, he has asked her to marry him and now she has had to tell him the truth. Why did I not see that might happen?

Michael was always helpful to both of them, always the perfect gentleman, and Cat had never had any inkling that he thought of the Frenchwoman as anything but a friend and neighbour. And had Madelaine feelings for him? How upset was she now?

Cat sat down again. She could hardly go around and admit to inadvertent eavesdropping. If Madelaine needed her support, she would ask for it. Now that was all three of them in turmoil over their personal lives. Being in company was no consolation at all.

With so much on her mind, Cat had not expected to sleep that night but, strangely, she woke refreshed at six the next morning without even the memory of dreams to disturb her.

The journey to Oxford with two passengers was not fair to Treacle, so she would hire a horse and gig from the Harland Arms for her expeditions into the city.

The idea of anyone she had known in her past life arriving in Duke's Forde never worried her, but Oxford held more potential dangers so she always wore a veil.

Duke's Forde might be perilous too when all of Quinn's plans came to fruition, she realised with a pang of anxiety. Then she told herself she was being foolish. Who would recognise the shy debutante of eight years ago in the mature widowed shopkeeper she was now?

Helen, smart in her Sunday best, took her place beside Cat in the gig and, out of the corner of her eye,

Cat could see her smiling as they left the yard. An entire day away from the shop was a treat for both of them.

'Oh, look,' Helen said as Cat was focused on turning the bay gelding out onto the road. She had never driven him before and she was wary of taking his obedience for granted.

'What?'

'It's His Grace and that secretary of his, the gangly one. They've been over at the almshouses, I think. That is a very smart curricle he is driving.'

The bay broke into a trot and Cat reined it in, cursing under her breath. When she had it walking sedately again, she looked across and bowed slightly.

Quinn raised his whip in salute and then, to her horror, sent his pair of chestnuts across the marketplace towards them.

'Good morning, Mrs Brandon, Miss Helen.'

'Your Grace, Mr Turnbull.'

'Have you abandoned poor Treacle for this rakish fellow?'

'We are going to Oxford, which is rather far for Treacle,' Cat said. At least her blushes were hidden behind her veil.

'But that is our destination also, we can travel together.'

'How delightful,' Cat said between gritted teeth and was aware of the sharp look that he sent her.

'May I ride with you, Mrs Brandon?' he went on. 'Turnbull will be delighted to drive my chestnuts, and Miss Helen might enjoy joining him. I am sure she is adequate chaperonage, given that we are all in open vehicles.'

She could hardly refuse, not without seeming churlish, or as though she did not trust him, and he knew it.

Quinn gave the reins to his secretary, who was having difficulty controlling his broad grin, then came and helped Helen down and onto the seat beside Turnbull in the curricle before taking her place in the gig.

'I suppose you would prefer to take the reins,' Cat said. She had never yet encountered a man prepared to be driven by a female, unless he was teaching her.

'Not at all. I am glad to relax and to allow Turnbull his treat. Besides,' he added as Cat sent the bay into a trot, 'this gives me the opportunity to speak with you alone in perfect propriety.'

There were better moments to be dealing with remarks such as that, especially when one was driving an unfamiliar horse. They were approaching the tricky left-hand bend as the road left the marketplace and swooped down to the even sharper right-hand turn to the bridge.

Cat breathed in hard and concentrated on her driving, keeping the pace to a controlled trot. Even the Mail coach drivers, famously flamboyant, took this section of road with caution.

'Indeed?' she queried once safely on the opposite bank and negotiating Duke's Forde's straggling outskirts.

'Indeed. Do not pretend you have no idea what I am talking about, Cat. The incident is firmly impressed on my memory and, although I should not say so, I would be surprised if you had no recollection of it.'

'We kissed, that is all.'

Quinn made a sound suspiciously like a snort.

'Passionately,' she admitted. 'Also foolishly, reprehensively and, very fortunately—briefly. We are two adults with the usual desires and instincts, which propriety and self-preservation require us to keep under control. For a moment we did not. Then we regained our senses. Fortunately the…incident…was unobserved. The matter is now closed.' Cat was quite pleased with her crisp, unemotional tone.

Quinn, apparently, was not. 'Cat, I am a gentleman. And when a gentleman–'

'You are a duke. I am a shopkeeper. Different rules apply.'

The bay picked up the agitation she was not allowing to show in her voice and broke into an extended trot. As they had reached the edge of the town and were clear of small boys chasing chickens, coal carters unloading and maids twirling feather dusters out of windows, she could only hope Quinn assumed she had intended the change of pace.

'It certainly means that I do not take advantage of my position.'

'I can only assume you mean your position in Society. I am not in your employ and I own my own freehold. In no way am I in a situation where you have any power over me, *Your Grace*. We are back to a situation between a man and a woman who have discovered a mutual attraction which they know it is unwise to pursue. Fortunately we both realise that.'

'Has anyone ever told you that you are a most infuriating female, Cat?'

'No. And I can only assume you find me infuriating because I can produce a reasoned argument without bursting into tears, fainting away or pretending to less intelligence than I actually possess.'

The bay broke into a canter and Cat made no attempt to rein him in. With any luck Quinn might fall out, she thought savagely and realised she had lost her temper.

To her further annoyance Quinn laughed. 'Ouch, a palpable hit. Please, allow me to apologise, and do rein in that beast or James will assume we intend to race.'

Confound the man. Laughter was very disarming. The bay obediently dropped back to a fast trot at the pressure of her hands on the reins.

'Apologise for what, exactly?' Cat enquired.

'For calling you infuriating for all the reasons you named. May we begin again, Cat?'

'As what?' she asked cautiously.

'Friends? Friends who have the sense not to be too alone together? If you still trust me.'

If I trust myself...

'Very well.' That sounded grudging. 'Yes, I would like that and I do trust you.'

'Excellent. Then I will presume on our friendship to ask why you are setting out for Oxford, both of you looking, if I may say so, Bond Street smart.'

'You may.' She felt her shoulders relax as though she had been on a slippery slope and had regained safe footing. 'We are on an espionage expedition, setting out to spy on a new potential rival to view their quality and prices and, if possible, gain a clue as to their suppliers.'

'Intriguing. May I join you? Or no, that might give rise to speculation. We must enter quite separately. Do they sell upholstery fabrics, do you know? James and I can browse for those. Or we could be looking for ribbons or lace as a gift.'

'Can you do so incognito? I would hate for them to be able to announce that they are patronised by the Duke of Harland.'

'I do not have a false beard with me, but I will pretend to be James's secretary and he can show his card should the occasion arise.'

That made her laugh. 'Then he pays you too much if you can afford that hat and the pin in your neck cloth.'

'I can see I would have been useless as an intelligence officer against the French.'

Chapter Ten

They passed the journey pleasantly, talking—rather carefully, Cat thought—of neutral subjects. The passing scene, progress on the almshouses, whether the dust and noise from the demolition in the marketplace was causing a nuisance for her and her neighbours.

'There were a few days when Madame Arnaud could not set her tables outside, but she is conscious that the works will eventually be to all our benefit, so she was not at all annoyed.'

'Even so, I should have thought of it. I must speak to her about compensation. There are the outskirts of Oxford ahead. I had better resume my own vehicle. What is the address of this place?'

Cat drove off the moment Helen was settled beside her again. 'The Duke is going to investigate this warehouse as well,' she explained as they passed St Clement's church and crossed the River Cherwell by the long Magdalen Bridge and began to pick their way along the High Street.

'This is exciting,' Helen said, staring around her at the ancient colleges and the pavements bustling with pedestrians, many of them in academic cap and gown. 'A secret mission with the Duke—and I had a marvellous drive with Mr Turnbull. I could see he was a little nervous at being entrusted with that pair, but he drives ever so well.'

'I am glad you are enjoying yourself,' Cat said, most of her attention on negotiating the right turn into the Corn Market. 'We need to look out on the right for Ship Street—this place must be somewhere between that and Broad Street. Look for an inn with stabling.'

'There!' Helen pointed and Cat just had time to turn in to the inn yard's narrow entrance.

With negotiations for a few hours' stabling complete, they strolled out and began to explore, demurely ignoring the smart curricle with two gentlemen that was slowly making its way past.

'There it is. *Walton's Warehouse of Fine Fabrics and Haberdashery.* They have certainly spent enough money on sign writers.'

'And it is large—a double front and it seems to go back a long way. Oh, and there's a big staircase,' Helen reported, peering in the window. 'There must be two floors.'

'I think that I am a very fussy banker's wife and you are my dutiful unmarried sister,' Cat decided as they approached. 'Mrs... Doubleday.'

A doorman doffed his hat and opened the door for them.

'I can't see Ben doing that,' Helen whispered.

'No.' Cat was beginning to feel apprehensive. If this place held a very good stock and made its customers feel pampered and important, might she begin to lose trade?

'May I be of assistance, ladies?' A smartly suited floor-walker approached.

'Velvets. In blue,' Cat said.

'Certainly, ma'am. This way, if you please.'

They were installed on chairs in front of a counter.

'No female staff,' Helen murmured.

'No, that's a mistake. I know they think male staff are superior, but ladies like to talk to another woman.'

The assistant began to produce rolls of fabric. Cat fingered each in turn and, out of the corner of her eye she could see Helen looking surreptitiously at the labels on the end of the rolls. She asked the price of the best quality fabric and where it came from. The price made her raise her eyebrows behind her veil but the assistant was vague on the origins.

'Nothing is quite right,' she said with a sigh. 'Where are the silks?'

The floor-walker came and escorted them to another area and they were just seated when Quinn and James came in.

'Oh, look, Miranda,' Helen said brightly. 'Gentlemen. Aren't they smart? Whatever can they be doing in here?'

Their escort left them abruptly and a buzz began to circulate as word of their new arrivals spread amongst the assistants.

'Blue silk for an evening gown,' Cat said crisply, making the man on the other side of the counter start and drop his shears.

'Certainly, ma'am.'

They went from there to browse the cottons and muslins, then to look at ribbons and lace.

Meanwhile the men had attracted a little train of attendants as they strolled through. 'Like a comet with its tail,' Cat murmured.

After half an hour and the purchase of a yard of ribbon, they left.

'Oh, quick, Mrs Brandon, I must write everything down before I forget it.'

Cat spotted a tiny green area in front of a church and they sat down on a bench while Helen scribbled in her notebook. 'There.' She passed it to Cat. 'Not all the rolls and bales had suppliers marked, but I've got all I could.'

'Well done,' Cat said. 'I thought the stock is of an equal, or less good quality than ours, but more expensive. Except for the silks. Those were very fine. I wonder where they found those.' She stood up and brushed down her skirts. 'Overall, I am encouraged.

We can let our customers know that they will find the same quality but at a better price with us. Except for those silks…'

'There's the Duke and James… I mean, Mr Turnbull.'

The two pairs met, apparently by chance, as Cat and Helen were about to cross to the inn. 'There is an inn, the Globe, a mile outside the town,' Quinn said without looking at them. 'I will take a private parlour there and we can have luncheon and compare notes.'

'But your business in Oxford?'

'Is swiftly accomplished, a matter of some properties I need to look at briefly. If I hurry and you dawdle— Allow me to assist you across the road, ma'am.' Quinn tipped his hat as though he had just seen her, and offered his arm.

Once on the other side the men strode off.

'Shall we *dawdle*?' Cat said to Helen with a laugh. 'That shoe shop looks very tempting.' She was feeling very light-hearted, almost frivolous, she realised. Not at all the kind of emotion a sensible businesswoman should be feeling after sizing up a rival.

An hour, and a pair of shoes, later, Cat drove into the yard of the Globe where a groom was leading Quinn's curricle away. The landlady met them at the door. 'Your brother and his friend are already here, ma'am. The parlour is just through here.'

'My brother?' Cat said by way of greeting when the door was closed.

'It seemed best. I have ordered the chicken pie with a fruit compote to follow, but if that does not suit, I can ring and change it.'

It suited very well, so Cat swallowed her instinctive reaction to order something else entirely, on the principle that men ordering for ladies without asking was irritating. She took off her bonnet, gloves and pelisse and sat down.

James poured lemonade. 'We thought their silks were excellent.'

'I agree,' Cat said. 'Unfortunately we could see no labels to identify the suppliers.'

'Oh, I asked,' James said. 'I remarked that I only bought the best for my wife and wanted to know which mercers were they using. It is all Spitalsfield silk, apparently, and I have a list of the suppliers.'

'None from Coventry?' Helen said alertly.

'Ribbons only, apparently.'

They stopped talking as the maid brought in the food and another jug of ale for the men and there was an appreciative silence while they tried the pie. Then Quinn said, 'I will ask my man of business in London to approach these suppliers and establish costs, for whatever you want. James will buy it, and you then sell it, undercutting the Oxford warehouse prices.'

'I could not possibly involve you in trade!'

'Absolutely not,' he said with a grin that made her want to grin back, it was so infectious. And made her tingle all the way down to her toes. 'I am shocked you should think I might do such a thing. It is James here who will take on a new role as a silk merchant.'

'And we will split the profit,' she said, eyeing him warily.

Quinn inclined his head in assent.

'In that case it is a quite brilliant suggestion.'

'Thank you, Mrs Brandon. I have to agree.'

The laughter from that exchange stayed with Cat like a warm hug as she drove back to Duke's Forde. Quinn peeled off before they reached the town, taking a cross-country route home and leaving her to drive into town with no risk of tongues wagging at the sight of them together.

The meal had been delightful, she thought. Convivial, friendly—and potentially profitable, which was the important thing, of course. Somehow all of the tension that had been between them like an overtightened violin string ever since that kiss had relaxed.

It hadn't quite vanished, there was still a thrum of awareness, of...*excitement*, she realised. But it was under control, she assured herself, almost something to be enjoyed, which was decidedly peculiar, given how dangerous the entire situation could be.

It is almost like falling in love for the first time, Cat

realised, recalling that secret, bubbling feeling. *And remember how well that turned out.*

Now, of course, she was older, more experienced and recognised it for what it was—physical attraction and something surprisingly close to friendship. Nothing that a mature, sensible woman could not deal with perfectly well. Nothing that would not soon settle down into a simple business relationship.

As they drove, she and Helen worked out what they would say to their customers who already knew about the Oxford warehouse. 'We will be shocked at the amount they charge compared to our wares at the same quality, and will say so,' she decided. 'I know we cannot match them for choice, though, that is my only concern.'

'Once they see our beautiful new silks they won't care,' Helen said stoutly. 'Wasn't it wonderful of His Grace to offer to buy for us? Mr Turnbull, I mean.' She blushed.

'Helen, has Mr Turnbull been flirting with you?'

'Oh, no.' All wide-eyed innocence.

'Or have you been flirting with him?'

'I might have been.' Her smile slipped away. 'But he's the son of one of His Grace's godparents, so flirting is all it ever can be, of course.'

'I suppose so.'

James Turnbull was probably hoping, with Quinn's patronage, for a career in politics, or in a government department, and he would need a well-connected wife to help with that.

'I don't understand why the gentry are so down on trade,' Helen said. 'I mean, they've got so much money—where has that all come from?'

'Land mainly, or that is what is acknowledged. Lineage is everything. How long have your ancestors been in England? How old is your title? Your estates are the proof of that long bloodline, I suppose. But they all have links to trade, only at arm's length—just as the Duke is doing with us. And younger sons often end up as merchants in the East India Company, for example. But you mustn't be seen actually *working* for your money, being employed, that is the important thing.'

'That's, what's the word? Hypo-something.'

'Hypocritical. I agree. But appearances are everything in polite Society. Unless, of course, the head of the household has gambled all the wealth away and the heir has to make the huge sacrifice of marrying for money,' she added tartly. 'And then he is pitied and the heiress is sniggered about behind her back because her father bought her a title.'

'Well, I think it is foolish,' Helen said. 'Anyone would call *you* a lady, even if you do own a shop.'

'Owning it might not be quite so bad, but *serving* in it? After that it doesn't matter how pure my vowels are,' Cat said with a laugh that, she realised with surprise, was quite genuine. She really didn't care.

Early the next morning Quinn left James writing to various London silk mercers with requests for samples and price lists, while he went outside to meet with a thin, precise little man in the summer house out on the south lawn, where he could be certain of not being overheard.

'Your Grace.' Foster stood up as he entered. 'Good morning, sir.' At first glance he looked to be exactly what he purported to be, a lawyer's clerk, but he shed the precise, slightly anxious air as he straightened up and met Quinn's gaze with a look of sharp intelligence. This was their second meeting

'Good day to you, Foster.' Quinn waved him to a seat and took one where he could keep an eye on the lawn for wandering gardeners. 'What have you to report?'

'That the lady is, indeed, a lady, and not simply a member of the squirearchy or lesser gentry. I have made a study of accents and I have had the opportunity to observe members of many aristocratic families and their manner closely. If Mrs Brandon was not raised in such a household I would be very surprised indeed.'

'Could she be a baseborn child taken into the family?' Quinn wondered aloud. 'It is not unknown.'

'Indeed, sir, and that is one possibility. However, I would expect such a daughter to be married respectably and not to a tradesman, however high-class.'

'True. What of her maiden name?'

'The name she used when she married.' There was a faint suggestion of a correction in Foster's tone, and Quinn nodded in acknowledgment. It did not do to take anything at its face value.

'Ransome. Catherine Ransome. Now, I have started from the assumption that the lady had either been dispossessed of her position and her home, or that she had fled it, presumably to escape something. It might have been something inflicted upon her—ill-treatment, an unwelcome marriage, for example—or she might have been running from scandal of some kind. A compromising relationship, perhaps. If she had been dispossessed, then again we are back to a scandal and her family disowning her, or perhaps a change of circumstances with the death of her father without a son and therefore the title and estates going to a distant, unsympathetic relative.'

'I agree, but that does not get us much further forward.' Quinn shifted impatiently on the hard bench.

Foster was unruffled by his impatience. 'We know the date Mrs Brandon arrived at Duke's Forde. I imagine that is not something she would deceive you about, as it is common knowledge in the town. I have set my assistant, who knows nothing of the circumstances, to scouring the scandal sheets, the Court news and so forth to see if there is any clue there—a death and an inheritance by a distant cousin, tittle-tattle about a young lady and so forth. So far, he has found nothing likely.

'However, I have been searching *The Peerage* and *The Landed Gentry* myself for the name Ransome. There is the Honourable Alexander McTavish Ransome living on some island in the far reaches of North Britain. He is a widower and childless—'

'She said something about an uncle in Scotland and that he was…eccentric, was it? No, peculiar and a long way away.'

'That would fit, sir. He is certainly about as far as it is possible to get without taking to the sea and landing in Norway,' Foster said dourly. 'There are any number of Ransomes, with and without an "e" in *The Landed Gentry*, but none I could find with a daughter born in the years around 1790, which seems about the right date of birth for the lady. Or, rather, none who could not be accounted for by marriage.'

'What about *The Peerage*?' Quinn asked. This was like groping around a strange room in the dark, hoping to stumble across the door. 'If the Ransome in Scotland is a younger son of an earl–'

'Which he is, sir. The Earl of Havering.'

'Never heard of him,' Quinn confessed.

'Neither had I, sir. It seems he was not active in

politics or Society, but lived rather secluded in Wiltshire. He died several years ago and his son shows similar tendencies to a retired life. However, there is a daughter, Lady Annabelle Ransome.'

'Too old, surely?'

'Indeed, sir. But she married the Earl of Bowland and they have a daughter born in the year 1792. Lady Caitlin Montgomery.'

'Bowland?' And there it was, the memory of the honeysuckle swamping the lingering scent from the cheek of the girl he had just kissed so very respectfully. And looking down at him from the balcony above, laughing at him, the face of another girl just visible through the tangle of stems. She had been younger, still a schoolroom miss, but her eyes had been alight with intelligence and amusement.

'I knew her older sister. Ann, is it?'

'Anna, sir. She is married to the Viscount Dorrington, Lord Castlebrook's heir.'

'And Lady Caitlin?'

'Named for an Irish cousin, I believe, but that is all I have discovered so far. She appears to have vanished from the record. Certainly there is nothing about a marriage or her death.'

'Lady Anna was blonde and petite, as I recall. Mrs Brandon is a tall brunette.' He searched his memory for the parents. 'Lady Bowland, I recall, is fair and small. Bowland himself is brown-haired and tall, as is the son.'

'Giles, sir. Viscount Wintercombe. He is, I understand from the gossip, on the point of offering for Miss Langley, the daughter, and only child, of Sir Hardwicke Langley. A very wealthy gentleman,' Foster added with a faint smile. 'He, and his parents, are staying with the Langleys at West Marsh Hall, just outside Aylesbury. An announcement is expected daily.'

'I went to school with Felix Langley,' Quinn said slowly. 'And Aylesbury is not so far from here, twenty miles or less, cross-country. Do you know, I might find myself just happening to drop in on my old friend as I pass by.'

They hadn't been particularly close, but he and Felix had always got on well enough for it to be a reasonable thing to do if he was in the district.

'The weather is fine, I foresee a day on horseback in my near future. Meanwhile, see what you can pick up about Lady Caitlin.'

'Sir.' Foster stood, picked up hat and notebook and bowed himself out. A minute later, when Quinn scanned the gardens, he could see no sign of the man.

Chapter Eleven

Quinn strolled back to the house, puzzled. If Catherine Brandon really was Lady Caitlin Montgomery, how on earth had she ended up in Duke's Forde married to a shopkeeper? It clearly had not been a love match; the late William Brandon was not the reason she had left home.

Noble families did not throw out erring daughters to fend for themselves and cause further scandal. No, they packed them off to remote country estates, or to be companions to elderly widows in Bath, or, in extreme cases, had them locked up in private asylums.

So young Lady Caitlin had been escaping from home, right at the start of her first Season. She'd hardly had time to cause a scandal, surely?

Somewhere a clock struck nine. Quinn strode off across the lawn to the stables. 'I need to ride about twenty miles today,' he told Simpson, his head groom. 'I want a mount that will be comfortable with that and also one from which I can plausibly remove a shoe at the end of it.'

'I'd have said Monty,' the man said. Either he was too discreet, or too used to the eccentricities of the aristocracy, to show any surprise at the request. 'But he was shod yesterday. Lady Dove would do you, Your Grace,' he said, jerking his head to where a big Roman-nosed grey watched them from her loose box. 'Go for miles, she will, and a favourite of the late Duke. And she's due for shoeing in about a week, I'd say.'

'Lady Dove it is. I'll be back for her in half an hour, Simpson.' All he needed was to consult a map to have a possible destination somewhere beyond West Marsh Hall, have Cook pack something in his saddlebags so he did not have to stop for refreshment on the way, change and be on his way with a sturdy hoof-pick in his pocket capable of removing a horseshoe.

Cat had hoped to spend the day busy with shop work and reviewing her stock of silks so she was ready to order from the London mercers that Mr Turnbull made contact with.

That plan lasted until just past ten when she was discussing the Oxford warehouse with the ladies who had first brought news of it.

'I visited yesterday,' she told them. 'A large selection of course, but the prices certainly reflect the rent they must be paying.'

'And the fact that they will reckon their customers believe that a keen price is a mark of low quality,' Miss Appleby said disapprovingly.

'I did approve their silks, however,' Cat said, doing her best to sound even-handed. 'I have news of a supplier in London who should be able to secure some as good for me, so we will have them in stock in plenty of time for the coming Season.'

Miss Appleby and her friends were at the centre of the area's network of gossip, and that news, Cat was confident, would soon spread.

She turned back to the counter when the sound of the doorbell made her look back to see Madelaine. Something was wrong, and she could guess what, she thought as her friend forced a smile and a cheerful greeting for the ladies in the shop.

'Come through to the back,' Cat said, taking her arm and guiding her. 'You are upset,' she said as she closed the door and Madelaine sank into the nearest chair. 'You don't look as though you have been sleeping.'

'That is because I haven't been,' Madelaine said grimly. 'Not last night, anyway. Cat, Michael asked me to marry him, and I had to tell him why I could not.' Her lips quivered and Cat saw her set her jaw.

'You couldn't just refuse him, I suppose?'

'No. I want to marry him, I have done for oh, months, now. Peter likes him. He is a wonderful father to Phoebe. I couldn't just say "no" as though I had no feelings for him.'

'He will be totally discreet,' Cat said. Not that that was the problem, of course.

'I know he will! But I cannot marry him. I converted to your church when I left Louis, but it would still be a sin.'

'It would be against the law, which is rather more of an immediate problem,' Cat pointed out. They had to be practical about this. She had no idea what the penalties for bigamy were, but they were bound to be severe. 'I cannot imagine that, if Louis ever did find you, he would politely pretend he had not and go away. He would delight in having the law on you.'

'I don't even know if he is still alive. He was such a quarrelsome, violent person that someone may have killed him by now,' Madelaine said.

'If he is still living, I must point out that the penalties for murder are worse than whatever they would be for bigamy,' Cat said, hoping to herself that she was only joking and that the warning was not needed.

'Oh, yes. Never fear that I will do something foolish. Nothing could be worse for Peter than if they took me from him.'

'Perhaps an enquiry agent might be able to discover whether Louis is still alive,' Cat mused. 'But how to find one who one could rely upon to search thoroughly—and one who would not try and double his fee by taking a bribe from Louis if he found him?'

She regretted speaking as soon as she saw her friend's face whiten. 'No! I could never risk that.'

'I suppose an irregular arrangement would be out of the question? You and Michael could go away for a month or so, and return "married". It would not be against the law unless, I suppose, you signed legal documents as a married woman.'

'It would still be a sin,' Madelaine said dismally. 'And a scandal if Louis ever finds me. And that would reflect on Phoebe, as well as on Peter and me.'

'True.' Cat got up and began to make tea. There was nothing she could do, unless—

There was one person she knew who would have access to lawyers and their enquiry agents, men who would carry out orders with scrupulous discretion. And that was Quinn.

Should she suggest it to Madelaine? She was certain the other woman would refuse from a mixture of shame, pride and fear. But if she did not tell her first… Either nothing could be discovered, in which case Madelaine never need know. Or proof could be found of Louis's death, in which case Madelaine would probably forgive her. If he was found, still alive, then perhaps Quinn's lawyers would be able to advise whether a Roman Catholic marriage in France was legally binding in England.

Cat had no qualms in asking favours for Madelaine, although she would not have dreamt of it for herself. The only reason she had accepted Quinn's offer to buy silk was because she could pay him back, with a profit. Accepting favours put one in someone's power, as this would, but the needs of Madelaine and Peter—and Michael—overrode that.

She would have to ask him, face to face. This was not something she could risk writing about.

Madelaine finished her tea, put a bright, determined smile on her face and stood up. 'Enough of feeling sorry for myself. Nothing has changed, not really. I must get back to work. Thank you, my dear.' She kissed Cat's cheek and let herself out.

Last week she would have called me chèrie, Cat thought anxiously. *She is trying to make herself as English as possible.*

The shop, when she emerged, was busy. From listening to her customers it was clear that the word had spread about the prices in the Oxford warehouse. Although she was sure most of the ladies would rarely go into the city for their shopping, the fact that they had good value on their doorstep seemed to have encouraged them to come and browse—and buy.

'It must be the lure of a bargain,' she murmured to Helen.

'But we haven't lowered our prices,' Helen whispered back.

'I know, but I am not complaining!'

She saw Mr Yorke drive past and cross the marketplace to the Arms. 'I won't be more than a few moments, but I have just recalled something I need to tell Mr Yorke,' she said, snatching up her bonnet from under the counter and hurrying out.

She met him as he left the inn yard.

'Good day, ma'am. May I be of assistance?'

'There was something I needed to discuss with His Grace. Is he likely to be coming into town, do you know?'

'Not for a few days, Mrs Brandon. I am expecting him to be away for three or four days. Perhaps I could help?'

'Thank you, Mr Yorke, but, no. It is not urgent.'

They exchanged polite bows and she walked back to the shop, not certain which was more concerning— that she could not talk to Quinn, or the fact that she felt so adrift discovering that he was not near.

Definitely the latter, she decided as she removed her bonnet and prepared to engage in an earnest discussion of hat ribbons with two of the Allsop girls who were close to squabbling over which would have blue, and which green, for her new hat.

This was the reality of her life, she told herself firmly. Not intimate little chats with good-looking, intelligent dukes. She was playing with fire becoming as close as she was to him, and she was putting her heart at hazard. If only she could find something to dislike about him, life would be so much easier.

Quinn had no difficulty in finding West Marsh Hall, although it was six o'clock by the time he led the mare up the carriage drive. Her near fore shoe was in a ditch a quarter of a mile back and he took his time, making certain she was walking on soft turf at the side of the drive.

They were received efficiently in the stable yard and one of the men ran to find Felix Langley.

Once his old school friend arrived, the rest had proved very easy. Of course Harland must stay the night, there was no question of Quinn going on his way at this hour, although of course the village smith would be summoned.

'We've a small party here already, and always delighted to add another bachelor to the mix.' Felix nudged Quinn conspiratorially. 'Wintercombe is here doing the pretty with my sister Adelaide. We're expecting him to talk to Papa tomorrow, but I'm looking forward to seeing his face when an unmarried duke turns up and Addie bats her eyelashes at you, which she will, the minx. Now, I see you've no baggage, so let's see what my valet can fit you out with for the evening. We're much of a size.'

* * *

Giles Montgomery did, indeed, poker up when they were introduced by a beaming Sir Hardwicke Langley, who clearly felt a duke under his roof added a certain cachet to the party.

Quinn shook hands and smiled amiably at the suitor. 'We have met, Wintercombe, but it's an age ago. I tried, and failed, to attract the interest of your sister Anna, clearly a wise lady.' He lowered his voice. 'I believe I should wish you luck with Miss Langley—you are a lucky man.'

'Thank you. You haven't been around Town, Harland,' Giles said. Judging by his stiff manner, he was clearly not certain if Quinn had turned up at the last moment to try and cut him out with the heiress and was quite prepared to defend his territory.

Quinn had no intention of explaining about lost horseshoes and chance arrivals to set the other man's mind at rest. If he was so uncertain of the lady, then he deserved to be teased a little.

'No, the Season never held much charm for me, and my father's health was poor, so I spent several years managing the estate. Then I inherited.' He shrugged. 'And that, as you may imagine, has been somewhat time-consuming. Now I am feeling the need to settle down.' He didn't have to add, *And take a wife*, to unsettle the other man.

The reaction of Miss Langley, who did, indeed, flutter her eyelashes as predicted by her brother, had Lord Wintercombe glowering. Quinn thought he had gone far enough and did nothing to charm the young lady beyond common politeness. Instead he turned to Wintercombe's mother.

Yes, there was the resemblance to Cat that he had expected. Lady Bowland had the same blonde hair as her older daughter, but Cat had the same hazel eyes and straight nose. She was also a full head shorter than Cat, but her husband more than made up for that, and there was no mistaking the likeness between Cat and Giles, who had the same colouring and his father's height.

So now he was certain that Mrs Brandon was Lady Caitlin Montgomery. The puzzle remained—why? What had happened to her?

'I recall a delightful garden party during the Season when your very charming daughter came out,' he said. 'Lady Anna is the Viscountess Dorrington now, is she not?'

Lady Bowland beamed at him, clearly still pleased with the match. 'Indeed, yes. Such a devoted couple. Dorrington quite dotes upon her.'

'I am not surprised. And you have another daughter, have you not? I am so long out of London Society that I cannot recall her name.'

The smile became fixed. 'Caitlin? Ah, yes. Sadly the dear girl has never been robust and the strains of her first Season quite overcame her. She retired to the country after a few weeks and has a very simple routine now which suits her very well.'

Methinks the lady doth protest too much...

'That is Society's loss, I am sure, but if her happiness and health depends upon seclusion, than that is a wise course for her to take. I imagine she finds Bowland Court most soothing,' Quinn said, naming the family's Leicestershire seat.

He could almost hear Lady Bowland's teeth gritting, but her smile did not fade. 'Dear Caitlin spends most of her time as companion to an elderly relative. The usual round—Bath, a quiet seaside villa with Cousin Dorothy and then back to a little house in the Norfolk countryside.'

Quinn was prepared to wager a large sum that Cousin Dorothy did not exist and an even larger one on her family not having the slightest idea where Cat was now.

He made a non-committal reply and turned the subject before his curiosity became too obvious. Beside him, Lady Bowland relaxed, but Quinn was conscious of an unsettling sensation in the pit of his stomach.

What was the matter with him? He made himself concentrate and answered a comment about the King's health, allowed himself to be drawn away by his hostess and managed all the right apologies for the intrusion and thanks for her hospitality, then took in Lady Langley when dinner was announced.

It was easy enough to maintain the façade of enjoying the evening, but below the surface of polite chit-chat Quinn had less than half his mind on what he was saying. The rest of his brain was wrestling with why he was feeling so unsettled when he had answered the question of Cat's identity.

She appeared to be a well-born lady because she was one. That was plain enough. What had caused her to leave Society was still a puzzle, but that was not what was so disturbing—it was his motive for wanting to know, he realised.

He was attracted to Cat and, he now realised, there was no reason why he should not marry her. As the daughter of an earl she was an eminently eligible bride for someone in his position. The fact that she had been running a drapery shop could easily be fudged over—after all, the family had been maintaining for years that she was living retired in the country, apparently without discovery. All she needed to do was stage a complete recovery and emerge into Society.

But *marriage*? He had found several eligible young women attractive before and never felt the slightest urge to wed them.

And what would you have done if it had turned out that she was not *Lady Caitlin?* his conscience demanded. *Would the word marriage even occur to you?*

It doesn't arise, so you don't have to think about it, Quinn told himself, but he felt uncomfortable nonetheless. He pushed the uneasy question to the back of his mind.

Cat has been done wrong by in some way, so the next thing is to discover what happened and put it right.

But how? Cat trusted him, he was sure. He could simply ask her outright. She might be grateful that she need no longer hide. A wrong would be righted, everything would be perfect.

So why was his gut telling him that he was treading on dangerous ground? What if she put the same question he had asked himself: *And if I was not Lady Caitlin? Would you care then?*

Chapter Twelve

Three days after Cat's conversation with Madelaine, Quinn called at the shop, soon after she and her assistants had finished breakfast.

'Oh, good, I need to talk to you.' She realised that she was clutching at his arm in her urgency and made herself let go and step back.

Strangely, Quinn did not appear annoyed that she had crushed his sleeve—his coat really was rather splendid, she thought—or that she was behaving like a hoyden. In fact he seemed pleased.

'I was hoping to talk to you too. It is a fine morning, perhaps a short drive would be pleasant?'

As she needed to talk in the utmost confidence, that suited Cat perfectly. 'I will get my bonnet. I won't be long,' she told Helen. It shouldn't require much explanation to make Madelaine's plight clear to Quinn. And of course, that was the only reason she was feeling so…so deliciously unsettled.

There was a phaeton standing outside with one of

the local lads proudly holding the horse. A phaeton and not his usual curricle, and no tiger up behind, she puzzled. And Quinn was looking very smart. Perhaps he was going on to another appointment after their conversation.

He handed her up to the high seat, tossed a coin to the boy who snatched it out of the air with a huge, gap-toothed grin on his face, and climbed up beside her.

'Where are we going?'

'Oh, just along the riverbank, I thought.'

Quinn seemed rather tense, but perhaps that was a new horse, or a new carriage—she hadn't seen either before—and there was the nasty bend down to the bridge to negotiate, which certainly needed concentration.

The narrow track that followed the course of the river on the other bank was a popular spot for walkers, fishermen and picnics, but at that hour it was deserted. Quinn drove along to one of the places popular for *al fresco* meals, a flat area shielded by weeping willow trees, and reined in.

'Oh, good, nobody is going to overhear us here,' Cat said as a coot flapped away across the water in a panic.

'That is what I thought,' Quinn began and took a deep breath.

'I need your help,' Cat said. She was in no mood for

a lengthy discussion. 'But you have to promise me to keep this absolutely confidential.'

He blinked at her like a man who has turned over two pages of a book at once and has lost the thread. 'Yes. Of course.'

'Only it is not my secret.'

'It isn't?' Quinn seemed surprised, which was strange.

'No, it is Madelaine's. She is not a widow, you see—her husband is still alive. He was violent, a horrible man who took out his frustration about being an exile on her. And then he became rough and impatient with little Pierre—Peter—so Madelaine knew she had to run away from him before he began to hurt the child as well. She changed her name and came here and she is only just beginning to feel safe.' The words were tumbling out of her and she stopped, took a deep breath and tried to slow down. It was important that Quinn was clear about what was happening, what she was asking of him.

'But now someone wants to marry her. A good man whom she loves. But she has no idea whether Louis Beaufoy is alive or dead. It would not surprise her if he had been killed in a fight or a quarrel, but she has no way of finding out. I wondered whether you knew of a really good enquiry agent, one who would be utterly discreet.'

After that initial look of confusion Quinn appeared

to be keeping up with her torrent of words. 'As it happens, I do. My lawyers employ an excellent one who has just completed a task for me.'

'Would he help with this? I would pay his fee and expenses, naturally. Madelaine is my friend and I want to help her.'

Quinn made an abrupt, dismissive gesture with his hand. 'There is no need for that. She is a lady of my acquaintance who is in distress. I will deal with it.'

'You will?' Cat would not have taken his charity for herself, but she had no idea what it might cost and she had been anxious about that. Quinn's response was doubly a relief.

'Of course. Now, I will need all the information she can give me about the man.'

'Oh, no, we can't tell her about this. She hates speaking of it and she only told Mich—the man who wished to marry her, because she could not deceive him, let him believe she did not care for him.

'Louis Beaufoy is a *comte* from Aquitaine. From what she has told me over time, I know that he is tall, with very dark hair and brown eyes. He is an excellent swordsman and he might well be teaching swordsmanship now. He has a scar on his right cheek from a knife fight, apparently, an ugly one. It runs from here to here, and he hated it because he is very vain about his looks.'

She reached out and touched the outer corner of

his right eye and trailed it down almost to the corner of his mouth.

Quinn went very still and she snatched her hand back again. *Friends,* she reminded herself. *Do not provoke anything more.* She had been in such a hurry that she had not put on gloves and his skin was warm under her fingertip, with hardly any sensation of stubble. He must have had a very close shave that morning.

The reaction to her own foolishness made her voice harsh when she said, 'What did Madelaine do to deserve being tied to that man? Marriage is such a risk for a woman. You give up everything—your name, your money, your free will, your children—to someone who may be a saint or a monster.'

'Most of us attempt to be something in between,' Quinn said mildly, although he did not smile. 'Your husband was a good man, was he not?'

'He was a very good man and I was exceptionally fortunate. In the end,' she added, almost under her breath.

'You have never been tempted to repeat the experiment?'

'No. Never,' Cat said with a shiver. Blaine Wykeham, her seducer, had been entirely convincing. She had not simply liked him, she had fallen in love with him, thrown her hat over the windmill for him, as the expression went.

Her judgement of men was clearly flawed, and it

had only been the experience of living so closely to William that had reassured her that she fully knew his character and could take the risk. Under normal circumstances a lady could hardly ask to live with a man for months so she could assess him thoroughly before committing herself.

'I see.' Quinn was sounding very dry now, and she supposed it was most ungrateful of her to ask a favour of him, to accept his offer to pay for the enquiries, and then to give vent to her feeling about men and marriage as though he was the sort of man Beaufoy was.

'I apologise for expressing myself so forcibly to you,' she said carefully. 'You are my very good friend, never think I do not know that and appreciate it.' Then she remembered how they came to be there. 'But I have been talking for an age. What was it that you wished to speak to me about?'

'I forget. Whatever it was, it is nothing as important as Madame Arnaud's situation.' There was a slight pause, then he said, 'Would you take the reins while I note down what you have told me about this man Beaufoy?'

'Yes, of course.' The horse stood steadily as they made the transfer and Cat watched as Quinn took a small notebook and pencil from his breast pocket.

'Louis Beaufoy,' he said as he wrote. 'Comte, Aquitaine. Tall, dark brown and brown, severe scar right cheek. Swordsman. Quarrelsome. Is there anything else? How old is he?'

'Older than Madelaine I am sure. Thirty?'

Quinn wrote that down and returned the notebook to his pocket. 'Ah, I have recalled what I wished to tell you. Turnbull says he has the silk samples and prices and will call on you this afternoon if that is convenient.'

'Yes, thank you, it would be perfectly suitable. Please tell him to come whenever he wishes.' But that had not been what Quinn had driven to the riverbank to say to her, she was quite convinced. He could have given her his secretary's message in her office at the shop.

Puzzled, she glanced at his profile as he turned the phaeton, but his expression was unreadable.

'You must tell me if I am being inquisitive, but did you have pleasant travels over the last few days?'

'You *are* being inquisitive,' he said in what Cat recognised as a return to his usual, amiable tone. 'And, yes, they were interesting and profitable. I was seeking information and found exactly what I wanted.'

Something to do with the improvements in the town, no doubt. 'I am glad of that. London?'

'No, Miss Curiosity. A country house near Aylesbury. Now, tell me honestly, are you finding the works troublesome?'

'Not very. Now the demolition for the hotel site is

over, the dust and noise are much reduced, and Madelaine says the screens that have been erected next to her café have proved very successful. Although apparently some of the ladies have rather missed being able to sit and admire the workmen's muscles while drinking their hot chocolate, I'm sorry to say.'

Quinn gave a sort of amusement. 'Disgraceful. I am deeply shocked.'

'So was Mrs Allsop when she discovered what was behind her daughters' sudden passion for cream buns.'

The horse began to walk back towards the bridge, the phaeton lurching a little on the rough track. Cat fought the temptation to hold on to Quinn's arm. Their thighs were very close and if she leaned towards him, just a little, they would be touching all the way down their bodies. It was hard to suppress the shiver that thought provoked.

She sought desperately for some neutral topic. 'The new almshouses are coming along very well,' she said, recalling what the Vicar had told her the previous day. 'They are drawing up lists of those eligible to occupy them now. There will be toasts raised to your name when the fortunate old people move in.'

'It is no more than they deserve after a lifetime of hard work, I am sure. It is gratifying to be able to do something for them. I have no doubt that Mrs Newnham will have a list of other projects she would like me to undertake.'

'Oh, yes, and I can tell you most of them. A school, for a start. And a reading room. I don't mean a subscription library, but a free one for working men where they can have the newspapers and some journals and might be a focus for the donation of books. There is a small informal group that meets in members' houses, but a dedicated room would be wonderful. And—'

'Very well, I shall leave you and Mrs Newnham to draw up a schedule of works.' He appeared to have recovered from whatever it had been making him appear so stiff.

'Well, you will soon be bored when the hotel is built and the inn renovated and all the new shops are trading,' she said in a rallying tone.

'Then I will have all the business of the estates and my tenants and deciding where my loyalties lie when I take my seat in the House of Lords,' he countered.

'Whig or Tory?'

'I can find faults and virtues with each. I shall probably sit cross-bench and vote with my conscience,' Quinn said, rather absently.

Yes, he certainly had something in his mind.

It was only as he was handing her down in front of the shop that a thought struck Cat. What if he was off somewhere to propose marriage to a lady? The elegant clothes on a weekday morning, the smart phaeton, his air of seriousness... Had he been going to tell her of his plans?

As a friend might, she thought, swallowing a sudden lump in her throat. Because that was what they were. All they ever could be. Just friends.

Whatever he had been intending to say, something had made him change his mind.

That could have gone better, Quinn thought as he flicked a coin to the lad who had run out again to hold his horse steady as he had helped Cat descend. *Much better.*

So much for your first attempt at a proposal. You didn't even get one word out, and now you are committed to sorting out someone else's marriage.

He'd had it all worked out in his head. First he would have declared his affection and respect, then made the proposal. Cat would have protested that dukes could not marry shopkeepers, and he would have pointed out that she was no merchant, but an eligible lady. He would then have announced his intention to right whatever wrongs she had suffered that had caused her to flee her home, and she would have accepted him.

Possibly. Probably, he told himself. Cat was not a woman for foolish flutterings and pretences at modest shyness. A kiss would have sealed it, because nobody could deny the passion that had flared between them. That moment when she had touched his cheek had felt as intimate, as erotic, as if her hand had caressed his bare chest.

He forced his mind away from the demands of his body and back to his plan. Once Cat accepted him, arrangements would have to be made to hand over the running of the shop to her two young assistants with guidance from a distance by Cat. Meanwhile they would develop a story about her recovery from her weakness and her family would have to be brought into line, which they surely would be without much trouble. No one with any sense turned down the advantages a duke in the family would bring them.

That was where he had got to, and by now they should have been at the stage of passionate kissing and making plans. Should have been. Instead he had been shown very clearly that Cat was wary of marriage and had no very high opinion of his sex in general.

Quinn tooled the phaeton out of town with a rueful smile on his lips. What was it that Robert Burns had written? Ah yes, he had it.

The best laid schemes o' Mice an' Men
 Gang aft agley,
An' lea'e us nought but grief an' pain,
For promis'd joy!

Well, he was certainly not experiencing any joy, or promises of it, at the moment, but perhaps his lady would be in a more receptive mood if he could put her mind at rest about her friend.

When he returned to Harland Park he went directly to his study to write to Foster. He had no need to mention Madame Arnaud's name, or Duke's Forde, so he could risk putting what he had in writing.

Take care for your own safety. I am told that this man is violent, quarrelsome, with a nasty temper and a short fuse. He is skilled with a blade. A definite sighting of him alive, or proof that he is dead—in which case with details that would allow his widow to remarry—are what is required and should not require you to come into actual contact with the man. It is possible that he has returned to France, in which case it will be necessary to have enquiries made there, but if that is the case, report back to me before taking any action.

He found James Turnbull in the stable-yard, about to ride into town to deliver the silk samples and quotes to Cat.

'I have put the latest report and figures for the Harland Arms on your desk, sir,' he said from the saddle of the raking grey he favoured. 'I would say it is finished, save for a few furnishings.'

'Excellent, thank you, James.'

Quinn handed the phaeton over to the grooms and strolled back to the house in a pensive mood. So much for driving out in his newest, shiniest vehicle, all dressed up as though to make morning calls in Mayfair. Cat couldn't have been less interested.

But she was loyal, he thought. Loyal and fierce and sensible. He had seen the hesitation, then the calculation in her eyes when he had said he would pay for the investigation into Beaufoy. Pride almost had her refusing, he realised, then she had accepted his argument and decided that, after all, he could well afford it, whilst she could not, although she would have gone short herself to help her friend if that is what it took. Her sense of duty was strong, but she was also pragmatic and, he acknowledged with amusement the fact that she had no scruples about employing his wealth and influence in a worthy cause.

And that felt good, he realised. The almshouses pleased him a great deal and even his architect had stopped sulking, although that had taken a while.

He rang for coffee and settled himself behind his desk, where stacks of carefully docketed and labelled files and a pile of letters awaited his attention. It was tempting to sit back, savour the fragrant brew and brood on tactics for winning Cat, but duty called.

He was halfway through the report of the Harland Arms when the idea struck him. He would hold an assembly, free to all the inhabitants of Duke's Forde, to celebrate the first completed project and to thank them for enduring the disruption of the works.

Quinn took a clean sheet of paper and began to jot down notes. Food, drink, a band, fireworks. Yes, fireworks on the opposite bank of the river to be viewed from the grounds at the back of the Arms. Which meant those had to be tidied up considerably. He added, *Gardeners. Terraces?*

And that would be the perfect time and place to propose to Cat. An evening of music and dancing and fireworks. Everyone happy. And he would lead her out into the garden—no, whatever they did to improve the area, it was no place for an intimate conversation, not in the middle of a party. A boat, that was it. He would row her out into midstream and propose. How romantic.

Brilliant. What could possibly go wrong?

Chapter Thirteen

Cat was deep in discussions with six of her best customers when Quinn strolled into the shop the next morning. The silk samples that Mr Turnbull had brought her were spread out and the ladies were excitedly discussing which they thought would be most popular and which they already wished to place orders for.

She had spent hours the previous day with the figures, working out what she would have to charge by the yard to cover the mercers' price, transport, her own profit and a reasonable return for Quinn. She had been worried that it would make it all too expensive, but the ladies were enthusiastic.

'Oh, just look at those lovely pastel shades,' Mrs Allsop was saying as Quinn entered. 'I can see my girls in those—the primrose for Clementina, Jane in the pale rose and Bella in the blue. The shimmer! And the drape! How much did you say, dear? Why, that is very fair indeed for such quality. Not dagger cheap, but one must pay for quality, I always say. Let me order a dress length of each of those now. And that wonderful plum shade for myself—'

She became aware of him and broke off with a little gasp. 'Your Grace!'

'Mrs Allsop, Mrs Brandon, ladies.' Quinn bowed and they curtsied, all of a flutter. 'How very providential—I was hoping for guidance, and I find assembled the ideal advisors. The work on the Harland Arms is complete, save for the grounds, and I thought to hold a grand assembly for all the inhabitants of the town to celebrate. What is your opinion?'

'A delightful prospect. By ticket?' Mrs Baggott enquired.

'No, freely available to all.'

'It sounds most generous and very exciting,' Mrs Allsop ventured. 'But might there be a difficulty for the, um, humbler inhabitants who perhaps would not feel comfortable mixing with their employers and the gentry?'

'Then the stable-yard and the barn could be used,' Cat said. 'Like a Harvest Supper. There would be room for dancing and a fiddle band out there and food and drink could be provided. Then I imagine all the guests could find where they would be most comfortable themselves without any guidance.'

'I knew you would solve all my difficulties, Mrs Brandon. And ladies.'

'We could form a committee,' Cat said. 'Mrs Longford, the innkeeper's wife, would be just the person to organise the outside party.'

The others all started talking at once, and Cat saw a look of mild alarm cross Quinn's face. 'There is no need for panic,' she told him quietly. 'I will sort it out. Have you other business in the town today?'

'Quite a bit.' He was edging towards the door away from the animated discussion, like a man who has nudged a stone and discovered he has started a landslide.

Behind her, Cat could hear ideas being tossed around. What *had* he started?

Two bands...buffets...cider and ale in the yard... Fancy dress? Too complicated... Should there be a pig on a spit? Two? An ox?

'Go and take coffee at Madelaine's when you have finished your business and send me word. I will come and report,' she murmured, close to his ear. 'And the silk is wonderful. Thank you.'

The look he gave her brought the colour warm into her cheeks. It seemed that she had been wrong, thinking that he was intending to ask someone for their hand the other day. Unless he was a complete rake and had no trouble courting one lady with a view to marriage while entertaining decidedly improper intentions about another.

A duke had any number of reasons to dress elegantly, even in the depths of the country, she told herself. The suspicion that he had been on his way to propose to someone said more about her inner thoughts and yearnings than it did about Quinn's intentions, she told herself firmly.

The maid from Madelaine's shop came along after an hour, and Cat followed her back to find Quinn seated at a corner table with a plate of cakes and a coffee jug in front of him, along with two plates and cups and saucers.

'A committee has been formed, or rather, the ladies are over at the Arms enlisting the help of Mrs Longford on how to make sure everyone feels comfortable. They assure me they will report back with an agenda for the first meeting,' Cat said as she took her seat.

'Now, do not look like that,' she teased. 'I know perfectly well that you called at the shop in the hope that something like this would happen, or that I would suggest it. Shall we liaise with Mr Turnbull?'

'If you would. He can place orders or deal with any payments that have to be made in advance.' Quinn poured coffee for both of them, then nudged the plate of sweet temptation towards her. 'Please, take the lemon tart, I know that is your favourite, not that one could not guess.'

'Why on earth would you think that?' she asked, laughing at him. They were the only customers, she realised. It was that dead spot in the morning when there was food shopping still to be done while everything was fresh and no excuse yet for a relaxing interlude for refreshment.

'It is attractive, delicious and somewhat tart under the sweetness. Or perhaps, rather, it is sweet under the tartness.'

Quinn's comment had her freeze, her fingers hovering just above the tart.

'Oh.' Goodness, she was blushing. She didn't blush like a green girl any more, for goodness sake. A little warmth in the cheeks sometimes, of course, but now she was certain her colour must resemble the strawberry crowning the other little tart in the selection.

'Either you are teasing me, Your Grace, or you are flirting. One is unkind, the other dangerous.'

'You tease me,' he countered, lifting the strawberry from the top of the tart and biting it in half. 'Friends tease each other, provided it is kindly, and I spoke no more than the truth. And as for flirting…surely that is safe enough between two persons of impeccable morals such as ourselves?'

That startled a laugh from her. 'I know nothing of your morals, Quinn, whereas you are quite correct about mine. There is nothing like life in a small provincial town to ensure that one can have no secret vices, so I live a blameless life.'

'No secrets at all?' He finished the strawberry in a flash of white teeth and licked his lips.

Oh, goodness, those lips...

'None,' Cat said flatly. All her secrets were in the past and there they could stay. She covered her unease by lifting the lemon tart from the serving plate to hers and carefully cutting it into segments. She ate a piece, glad of the sharp bite of citrus that seemed to clear mind as well as palate.

Change the subject, pretend you pay no heed to talk of flirtation.

'And when will this grand assembly be?'

'Your hard-working committee of ladies will need to know that,' she added, praying the colour in her cheeks had ebbed.

'The third week in August?' Quinn said, sounding like a man who had just plucked a date out of thin air.

'That gives us just over seven weeks,' she said in alarm and took a reviving gulp of coffee.

'Not long enough? I am hoping my gardeners will turn the riverbank grounds of the inn into something more civ-ilised by then, and that is all we need to wait for, so far as the building is concerned.'

'Men never have the slightest idea how long these things take.' It had always seemed to involve weeks of planning whenever Mama had planned a major entertainment and that was with a full household of staff to carry out her orders. Cat had a strong suspicion that she would be involved in a great deal of running around, seeing to details.

'And you do?'

It seemed an idle remark, just a reaction to her statement, but Cat bit her lip. What would a shopkeeper know about organising a ball, which, in effect, this was?

'I observe and I have imagination. But enough of that, there will be a long list of queries before very long, I am sure, but in the meantime, I must thank you for the arrangements over the silks. I believe they will do very well for us.'

Quinn shrugged. 'Thank Turnbull.'

'I have. I have also worked out costings—what I should charge and therefore the return you should expect. I will give those to him.'

'No need. I have every confidence in your calculations, Cat.' He selected a delicate Florentine biscuit. 'Now, I have put in hand that other matter we were discussing. I will let you know when I have news.'

'Thank you.' Cat started guiltily as Madelaine emerged from the rear of the shop in answer to the tinkle of the bell suspended above the door. 'I hate to see her so unhappy,' she said quietly as her friend greeted the two ladies who had just entered.

'She looks her usual self.' Quinn glanced across.

'She is putting on a brave face. For one thing, she does not want Peter to sense her mood and, for another, when you have to earn your own living you learn to never show your real feelings.' She shrugged. 'Nobody wants to employ someone who looks miserable, or to buy from someone whose mood lowers your own.'

She had learned that very early. Look confident, seem positive, and no one will wonder what is wrong and you do not look like a victim, someone to be preyed on.

'Shopkeeper's wisdom,' Quinn said lightly, but she thought he gave her a quizzical look.

'Anyway, I must get back to work. Thank you for the refreshments.' She stood up, waved to Madelaine and walked out before Quinn had the chance to open the door for her.

Dukes do not open doors for shopkeepers, only for ladies.

Chapter Fourteen

August arrived with fine, hot weather and Cat did a brisk trade in muslins and fine cottons. In what spare time she had, she did her best to keep the Grand Assembly Committee, as they called themselves, from turning a dance and party for the community into something more fitting for coronation celebrations. Then she dispatched the results to James Turnbull.

Madelaine began to recover her spirits, the work on the new hotel continued apace and the new almshouses were finally ready for their new occupants.

On the fourth of the month, much excitement was caused by the delivery of the first consignment of the new silks from London. Cat put one roll of leaf-green with a fine gold thread running through it aside for herself, scrupulously entering in the ledger the amount that would have been due to Quinn had she sold it. Miss Tomlinson, the dressmaker that Cat often used on behalf of her customers, bore it away wrapped in calico, along with a plate from the latest edition of *La*

Belle Assemblée, promising that Cat's evening dress would take precedence over all other orders.

Cat rewarded Helen and Ben for all their hard work with a dress length, gloves, slippers and silk stockings for Helen, and the cost of a new evening suit, waistcoat and shoes for Ben.

'Christmas has come early,' she told them when they stammered their thanks.

She saw little of Quinn, except for glimpses on his almost daily appearances in town. He would go into the hotel, ducking under wooden scaffolding and around ladders, then emerge to stride across to the Harland Arms, presumably to talk to the gardeners. As the new shops opened beside the Arms for the tenants displaced by the hotel—a grocer and a hardware shop and a new arrival, a men's tailor—he made a point of calling in on those as well.

The Vicar held a tea party to welcome the new residents in the almshouses and both Quinn and Cat were invited to that, so she did have the opportunity to ask, under cover of polite chit-chat over tea cups, if there was any news from his enquiry agent.

'The man's alive,' Quinn said, his voice low. 'And in some trouble with the law. He killed a man—'

'*Some* trouble?' Cat almost choked on a biscuit in the effort to keep her voice down. 'You are saying that he's a murderer now? What happened?'

'I'll tell you later, but the Vicar wants me to go and

say a few words and cut the ribbon on the new washhouse door or something.'

Cat was left almost twitching with nerves while Quinn made a short and gracious speech, welcoming the new arrivals to their homes and thanking the old inhabitants for their patience and helpful contributions during the planning and building.

When he finally extricated himself from a crowd of gratified elderly men and women and regained her side she hissed, 'Tell me at once! Is Beaufoy in prison?'

'When we are alone,' he murmured. 'May I escort you home, Mrs Brandon?' Quinn offered his arm as he bowed to Mrs Newnham on their way to the front gate. 'A delightful interlude, ma'am.'

'It was a brawl in a gaming hell off St James's Street,' Quinn said without preamble once they regained the marketplace. 'A gentleman called Hampden accused Beaufoy of cheating. Beaufoy knocked him down and stormed out, but Hampden got to his feet and pursued him into the street, demanding satisfaction, followed by several fellow gamblers who, fortunately, were not too drunk to be good witnesses.

'They just reached the doorway in time to see Beaufoy draw a blade and stab Hampden in the belly, pull out the knife, wipe it on his victim's coat and stroll away, clearly imagining that he was unobserved.'

Cat gasped and clutched his sleeve.

'I'm sorry, I should not have described it in such detail.' He put his hand over hers. The reassuring weight felt so good and, under her hand, the long muscles in his forearm felt disturbingly good too.

'Nonsense. I want to know. Have they imprisoned him? When is the trial?'

'He was still on the run when Foster wrote to me. The witnesses shouted, Arnaud took to his heels and they lost him in a maze of alleyways behind Almack's assembly rooms. Hampden's friends called out the watch and went to Bow Street to offer a reward, so now Beaufoy has a price on his head.'

'Oh, good heavens,' Cat said. 'That means little Peter has a murderer for a father.'

'And not for the first time, I imagine. His reputation is, so Foster writes, shocking, and none of the more reputable gaming houses would let him in their doors any longer. If they catch him, there is no doubt he will hang.'

'Poor Madelaine. She must have loved him once. For him to come to such an end...'

'I know. She will be free, but I cannot imagine she would want it to happen in such a way. Will you tell her?'

'Not yet, I think. It will give her nightmares thinking about it, wondering where he is. Perhaps when they have caught and tried him and it...it is all over, then I imagine it will be in the newspapers, won't it?

That way she need not know that I have been interfering.'

'But you have done no such thing.' Quinn stopped and swung around. 'You have simply tried to help her by discovering whether her husband is still alive.'

'I suppose so,' Cat said uneasily. 'But I told you about her secret.'

'You meant it for the best,' Quinn said.

'One of the most damning comments possible,' she said bitterly, wondering why he winced. 'I should have suggested an enquiry agent to her and offered to help with the cost if she chose to go ahead.'

'And she would probably have refused out of sheer pride, if nothing else. Sometimes we have to do what we can to help our friends, even against their wishes.'

That was said with some meaning, she thought. Had Quinn once interfered for a friend and received little thanks for it? But surely the law would catch up with Arnaud, and then Madelaine could read about it and know she was free, even if it was by such horrible means.

'You have a very tender conscience, Cat.' Quinn's hand tightened over hers.

'Perhaps.'

I have secrets of my own and know how I would feel if a well-meaning friend probed into them for my own good. Time to change the subject.

They had slowed almost to a standstill as they discussed Beaufoy, reluctant, perhaps, to draw any closer to Madelaine's shop. Cat went to an ancient mounting block that stood at the edge of the pavement and perched on the edge of it, surveying the marketplace. Behind her she heard a scuff of boots on stone, then silence, as though Quinn had thought to join her, then chosen not to. Her hand felt cold now the warm weight of his had gone.

There were changes in the familiar scene before her, but it was still recognisably the place where she had taken those first, fearful, steps into her new life. The Harland Arms was like a familiar friend dressed in new clothes, their hair freshly styled, their expression optimistic. The far end, where the hotel, as yet unnamed, was rising within its armour of scaffolding, was very new of course and so were the smart shopfronts adjoining the Arms. But it was the atmosphere of the place that had changed, she realised.

She had grown to love Duke's Forde because it had taken her in, accepted her, provided her with sanctuary, a living and, in time, with a small army of friends and acquaintances. But it had been weary, scuffed around the edges, accepting of its own place in the world as nothing more than a big village, with the market the only remnant of its once vigorous life. Local gentry still shopped there, and the three shops with Cat's in the centre had helped keep them loyal, but how much longer could it have continued with no new blood coming in to provide employment, pay the parish rate, fill the collection plate in church on Sundays?

'Your grand assembly will mark the end of your rejuvenation of Duke's Forde, even though the hotel is still to be completed,' she observed without looking back at the man behind her. He was close, she could feel him as though he was touching her.

'Yes.'

'You must feel very proud of what you have achieved.'

'Proud?' Quinn sounded puzzled. 'It is gratifying, of course. We are seeing results already—I understand that there have been applications for more market stalls and Longford reports that they are getting more passing trade at the Arms now. Travellers are stopping to eat and to rest their horses, and he has plans to buy animals to hire out. Turnbull is placing advertisements in newspapers to promote the refurbished bedchambers and the new dining room. Soon we will have travellers choosing to stay there overnight and not forced to by a lame horse or a sudden indisposition.'

'But you are not proud of that? You should be. You had the insight and the imagination to see that might be done and then the decisiveness to carry it through and be a driving force. You did not simply wave your ducal hand and loftily instruct some minion to improve the place.'

Quinn's snort was derisive. 'Lofty ducal hand? I was not raised to make gestures of that kind. My father's estate was a working one, with decisions constantly to be made to improve the land, the stock, the properties. He raised me to always be looking ahead—what was happening that might change the market for what our farms produced? What would make life better for our tenants and the community? How does one plan ahead for things we can predict and those we cannot. We never expected that my uncle would die with no heir.'

'Rash to allow an only son, heir to a great title, to become a soldier. I had wondered about that.'

'There had been twin boys younger than Jordan, and he was army-mad and would not be denied, arguing that there were two healthy, intelligent boys in reserve. They died in a boating accident in 1813, healthy, intelligent and sixteen years old. Jordan sold out. But when Bonaparte escaped from Elba and it all started again he argued that Wellington needed all the experienced officers he could muster. I believe the old man truly thought that Bonaparte would be cowed by the Allies gathered against him and it would never come to a pitched battle. If he had, I suspect he would have drugged Jordan and locked him in the cellar until it was all over.'

'Poor old man, to lose three sons, it must have broken his heart.'

'He never showed it until Jordan's funeral, then I think he simply gave up. He told me I would have to do the best I could, although, as he thought my late father, his brother, a dangerous radical, no doubt it would all go to hell in a hand cart. Then he simply… died.'

'So, was your father a dangerous radical?'

This time Quinn's snort was pure amusement. 'No. He was progressive, interested in the natural sciences, in agricultural improvement, in extending the franchise and in abolishing the slave trade—that all made him incomprehensible to the old man.'

'You have learned from your father and are applying those lessons to a far greater estate than he ever imagined you would have to. I still say that is a matter for pride, not simply gratification.'

He moved then and came to sit on the other end of the worn old stone block, careless of his elegant clothes as he flipped back his coat-tails. 'Very well, I will admit to some pride, if only in the way in which I have bent one very self-opinionated architect to my will.

'You must feel pride in your business, Cat,' he added.

'Of course I do. I was completely ignorant of shop-keeping in general and the drapery trade in detail. But I learned well from William, and from Ben and Helen, and I applied my lessons and some imagination and a lot of hard work to get where we are today. There is no sin in pride, provided one keeps a sharp eye out for faults and acknowledges the help one has had along the way, as you do of your father's guidance.'

'You knew how to manage staff and a household,' Quinn remarked conversationally.

'Well, yes, but—' Cat closed her mouth with a snap. She had almost fallen straight into that. Like any young lady she was reared to control a household, in her case, with the expectation that it would be a large one. 'Knowing how to manage a live-in domestic and a small household budget is some help I suppose.'

Quinn said nothing. She glanced at him out of the corner of her eye, but he was gazing out over the marketplace with a faint smile on his lips.

The sudden urge to lean over and brush her own mouth against his was so strong that Cat found herself gripping the rough stone until her fingers hurt.

After perhaps a minute, he looked across at her. 'You have a way of making me see what is in front of my nose, Cat.'

So long as what you see is not a foolish creature becoming far too fond of you. It is desire and liking, that is all it is. Not love. You must not *fall in love with this man.*

'So, what are your plans now, Quinn?' she heard herself say, rather too brightly.

He shifted around to look at her directly. 'To visit

all my estates personally—I shall plan a grand tour of them to follow my assembly.'

'And then it will be almost winter, and in the new year there will be the Season to look forward to.'

'You think I should regard that as something of a pleasure in store, do you?'

'Do you not? I understood that you had not been much in London because of your ailing father's need for your presence, and this year there was the death of your uncle and mourning and the need to come to terms with your new position. But now—why, you will be the centre of attention, the most eligible man in town.'

She said it lightly and saw him wince.

'You think that is something to be desired?'

'Well, *you* certainly will be!'

'Desired for my rank and position, for my estates and my wealth. Forgive me if I would prefer to be desired for myself as a person.'

'Then be thankful you are not a lady of rank and connections, because then you would be wanted for exactly those things, but would also have to pass the test of being acceptably pretty and having a spotless reputation.'

'That was said with some bitterness,' he remarked, quirking an eyebrow.

Cat shrugged. 'Observation.'

'Why did you leave home, Cat?' Quinn asked softly.

'I told you: a desire to find a congenial position in which to earn an honest living.' She stood up and brushed her skirts, craning to try and see over her shoulder. 'Have I covered myself in grime?'

Quinn walked round behind her. 'No. Spotless.'

For some reason that got beneath her careful mask and she found herself blushing hotly. *Spotless?* Most certainly not. Any Society matron would label her as spoiled goods.

'I do wish you would trust me, Cat,' Quinn said softly.

'But I do,' she protested. 'I feel completely safe with you, surely you know that?'

'I was not talking about the control of my baser instincts, Mrs Brandon,' Quinn said. He turned abruptly and strode off towards the hotel building site, leaving her gaping inelegantly after him.

She almost called after him, then remembered where she was and composed herself. Goodness knows what they had looked like to any observer. She walked across the cobbles towards the grocery shop in the hope that it would look as though they had parted because they were going in opposite directions, not because they had—what? Quarrelled?

By the time she had bought a jar of preserved cherries that she did not in the least need, Cat decided that Quinn suspected that she was concealing something about her life before she came to Duke's Forde and that she had been considerably better-born than she pretended.

It would not be a difficult conclusion to reach, she supposed. She had never tried to modify her accent for one thing. But it did not matter what he suspected, he could not know who she was. Something about her when they first met had been familiar from that glimpse amongst the honeysuckle tangle, but he had not referred to that again.

The trouble was, Quinn was intelligent and curious and a gentleman. If he suspected something was wrong, then he would try and put it right. Which meant that he was probably going to keep niggling away at it until he found something.

But there was nothing to find, she reassured herself as she paid for the cherries and refused the offer to have "the boy" deliver them.

Quinn's enquiry agent had been given a name, a description and information about Beaufoy's character and had found him, but she had simply vanished and her family had done nothing, had no information with which to trace her after that first day and night.

No, she was quite safe, she reassured herself as she picked her way back across the marketplace.

But if she wasn't, if Quinn discovered who she was? Cat stopped dead, right by the base of the worn old cross. He wouldn't betray her, surely? He was her friend. But he would probably do what he thought best for her, she worried, and she couldn't think of a single nobleman who would consider an earl's daughter running a draper's shop to be for the best for anyone.

She reached the shop feeling so anxious that it was an effort to put a smile on her face and enthuse over the news that Jemima Barlow, daughter of local baronet Sir Percival, was betrothed to the oldest son of a most distinguished Yorkshire family.

Lady Barlow was in the shop with a long list and a pile of fashion journals, all with paper slips sticking out of them. 'So much to be ordered for the dear child's trousseau,' she was declaring as Cat walked in. 'Oh, Mrs Brandon, just the person I need. Now, dress lengths. I need your advice on the best choice for all these gowns. Madame de Freyne in Oxford will be making them up, of course, but I rely upon you for quality.'

Which was all very gratifying, and profitable. Lady Barlow, the daughter of a Bristol merchant, had a sharp eye for value, and Cat need not fear competition from the Oxford warehouse for this valuable order.

She was soon so engrossed with the list and the knotty questions of which cloth was best for a riding habit, whether an almost transparent muslin was too daring for underwear and how many day dresses were an absolute minimum, that she was barely aware of the lad who came in, sidled nervously up to the counter, handed Helen a note and scurried out again.

'For you, ma'am,' Helen said when they finally sank down onto the high stools and drew breath. 'It was that lad from the hotel site.'

Cat took the note, folded into a tight square and sealed with a wafer. The strong black writing read simply, "Mrs Brandon".

The message inside was even briefer. "Sorry. Q."

Cat stared at it.

What am I going to do with the man if he keeps making me like him more?

'Not bad news is it, ma'am?' Helen asked anxiously.

'What? Oh, no. Just the Duke clarifying something that arose today.'

Or muddying the waters even more.

Chapter Fifteen

The days until the Grand Assembly, as it had become immovably known, seemed to run faster as the date approached.

The roofers finished on the hotel, so the scaffolding came down and the sounds of hammering, shouts and curses from inside were mercifully muffled. The gardeners wrought a minor miracle with the Harland Arm's riverbank, creating gravelled walks and a series of small terraces and everywhere in Duke's Forde nothing seemed to be spoken of but the Great Day.

Business in the shop flourished as ladies kept finding a need for alterations and more ribbons, lace and floss trimming. Cat and Helen each had fittings for their evening gowns and were delighted. Ben was struck dumb by his own magnificence in his first properly fitted evening suit after having always made do with one from a second hand dealer.

And the Duke of Harland was frequently seen, but

never called. Nor had he replied to Cat's answering note that read, "There is nothing to apologise for. C."

When the evening finally arrived, Madelaine and young Phoebe, who was thrilled to be allowed to attend her first "grown-up" event, joined Cat and Helen in Cat's bedchamber to change into their finery. Young Peter was spending the evening at the almshouses, where a special supper and music had been laid on for the frailer inhabitants and where several experienced grandmothers—and one great-grandmother—were delighted to have a child to fuss over.

'Oh, we do look fine,' Phoebe said with a happy sigh as she surveyed herself in the looking glass in her very first long dress.

'You look exceedingly grown-up,' Madelaine said. 'So be sure that the young men do not forget your age. Remember what we talked about.'

'Yes, ma'am,' Phoebe said obediently.

It seemed she trusted Madelaine like the stepmother she so longed to be, Cat thought. They would both be keeping an eye on the girl and she would whisper to Helen too. There were no predatory rakes likely to make an appearance at this party, where everyone knew each other by sight, if nothing else, but young men would be young men once drink had been taken and pretty girls were fluttering around them.

Their escorts across the marketplace were waiting

for them below, Ben glowing with pride in his smart suit of clothes, Michael Dangerfield smartly correct and beaming with pride as he looked at his daughter.

He avoided staring at Madelaine beyond a first look and a bow, Cat noticed, hating to see her friends made unhappy. She had no desire to see anyone at the end of a rope, but if a bolt of lightning struck Madelaine's wretch of a husband, she would rejoice.

Even the marketplace had been swept, with not a trace of a cabbage stalk between the cobbles, she noticed as they made their way cautiously in their thin dancing shoes.

Quinn was waiting at the carriage arch into the Arms to welcome his guests. He had made no effort to outshine them, but wore an elegant suit of clothes with just a single onyx stickpin in his neckcloth and the gold of a watch chain with a single fob. He was shaking hands with everyone too, from the Squire to one-armed Jemmy Little who made a living running errands, thanking them for their support and their patience while he turned their town upside down.

He made Phoebe blush by addressing her as Miss Dangerfield and requesting the honour of a dance. She almost stumbled away, overcome by having a duke's name on her very first dance card. Madelaine received warm thanks for her tolerance of the works right next door and the fact that Quinn's nerves had been sustained throughout by her cream cakes and coffee. She too passed into the inn with his name on her card.

Cat dropped a curtsey as her hand was taken and kept a polite social smile on her lips, which turned into a gasp as he murmured, 'You take my breath, Cat. A waltz, if you please.'

She fumbled with the card, then whispered urgently, '*Not* the first set,' as his pencil hovered. 'Ask Lady Barlow.'

He nodded, accepting that she would be a far less conspicuous choice, and initialled the last waltz and a quadrille before moving on to shake hands with Helen, a stiffly formal Ben and Michael Dangerfield.

'My goodness,' Madelaine said, fanning herself as they strolled across the inn yard, admiring the arrangements. 'That man is altogether too charming for his own good. Or perhaps I should say, for the good of any female with eyes in their head. Phoebe is going to imagine herself in love now.'

'A very safe first attack of calf-love,' Cat said. 'She is far too sensible to know that the daughters of superior shopkeepers do not marry dukes, however many novels she reads.'

'Yes, we are all too level-headed for that, are we not,' her friend said, with so little inflexion in her tone that Cat glanced at her sharply.

Had that been a pointed hint that Cat was cherishing similarly foolish daydreams?

'Look what a good dance floor they have laid out here,' she said, pretending not to notice and nodding towards the barn, where the sounds of fiddles tuning up floated out, along with the weird rumble of the church band's serpent horn. 'And three hogs roasting! My goodness, the smell is delicious. It would turn a hermit to sin. Let us go upstairs before my mouth begins to water too obviously.'

She had expected to feel a pang of something—Guilt? Arousal?—when she entered the old assembly room again, but the transformation was so complete that she could hardly believe that this was where she and Quinn had been locked in that desperate, passionate embrace.

The wooden floor gleamed, the stained and cobwebbed walls had been whitewashed and were hung with garlands and all was lit by three candelabra hung from the ceiling and sconces all along the walls. A string band occupied a dais at one end, and chairs and benches had been arranged around the walls. Cat had suggested to the committee that to make it too elegant might deter the humbler guests, and she thought they had done an excellent job of making it smart enough for the gentry, yet not intimidating for anyone nervously venturing upstairs.

Michael requested the first waltz, and Ben shyly asked for a country dance, and soon Cat's card was filling up with initials until she thought Quinn's were comfortably submerged.

The dancing upstairs opened with a cotillion, which she danced with Mr Allsop, trying not to watch Quinn's dark head as he and Lady Barlow wove their way through the intricate measures.

Next she and Ben romped their way through a set of country dances with great enjoyment and numerous mistakes, then went downstairs to see how things were progressing and for Ben to find a mug of ale.

Quinn had come down too, she saw, watching him whirl the landlady, Mrs Longford, dressed in her best crimson satin, through a vigorous turn in a riotous crowd attempting to Strip the Willow.

'Time I was upstairs again,' she said to Ben and fled before Quinn saw her watching.

Michael guided her very correctly through the first waltz, and she thought it a pity that both of them were wishing they were in the arms of someone else entirely, because he was a good dancer and she, able to keep her mind on her steps and not on the body so close to hers, welcomed the opportunity to polish her performance a little.

For Quinn, a little voice murmured.

For me, so I do not make an exhibition of myself, she corrected her thoughts sharply.

The music stopped and, amidst the loud applause,

she went down, found Helen and took her hand. 'Come upstairs.'

'Oh, no, ma'am, I don't belong with the gentry.'

'You are dressed as finely as any lady present and your manners are as good. If His Grace can dance down here, you can dance up there.'

They had hardly reached the head of the stairs when they encountered Mr Turnbull, who promptly asked Helen for the next dance. He led her off blushing, and Cat allowed herself the indulgence of a few romantic thoughts in that direction before following them into the assembly room and encountering the Vicar, who promptly requested she partner him in the set just forming.

After that she lost track of time and simply enjoyed herself.

'My dance, I believe?'

Cat looked up from her seat on the bench that ran around the room and found Quinn in front of her. His immaculate shirt points looked a little wilted and the hair that his valet had brushed into elegance was beginning to curl at the ends. Cat thought he looked better for it.

'Oh, goodness. What is it?' she asked, furling her fan and opening her dance card.

'The quadrille.'

'Which means I have to think,' she said standing

up, taking his hand and letting him lead her out onto the floor to join another three couples to make up their square.

The quadrille was still a very new dance, introduced from Paris by Lady Jersey, one of the patronesses of Almack's. It involved each couple in the group dancing in the centre and then the others copying them. She had tried it a few times at local parties and usually it ended with everyone colliding and collapsing in giggles.

'It would help if the different sections didn't have such ridiculous names and weren't all in different times,' she murmured, glad to have something to take her mind off the fact that her hand was clasped in Quinn's. They both wore gloves of course, but even so, the warmth and strength of his hand was distracting.

'I find it helps to think of them in English—the more ridiculous, the more they stay in the memory.'

They bowed to the other couples, all looking as apprehensive as Cat felt, and she could see that none of the groupings around the room seemed very confident.

The band struck up and Quinn said, 'And off we go with the Trousers.'

That had the unfortunate effect of giving Miss Alison Allsop opposite him the giggles, and her partner, one of the Squire's sons, had to push and pull her quite ruthlessly to keep in step.

By the time they had all stumbled, pranced and,

occasionally, danced their way through *La Pantalon, La Poule, Le Trénis, La Pastourelle* and were about to embark on *La Finale*, they were all half-helpless with laughter.

Across the dance floor at least three couples had fallen and gales of mirth almost drowned the music.

'I can see that there will have to be a number of quadrille parties held before this goes on the programme at any more assemblies,' Quinn said, still grinning as he led Cat off to a chair by the wall. 'May I fetch you some lemonade?'

'You may. And a fresh pair of lungs and new feet, please.' Cat unfurled her fan and used it vigorously.

Quinn wove his way towards the table serving refreshments, and Cat watched him. He really was too attractive to be fair, she thought, almost resentfully. Attractive to look at, attractive in character. He made her laugh and he made her think and both were welcome. He also made her lust and that was far less comfortable.

Attraction, liking, lust—all of those things could be suppressed, given enough self-control. But what could not be ignored, or suppressed, was the fact that she was in love with the man. Which meant that she had to learn to live with it, suffer it, hope it would eventually wither into a dull ache of longing.

What a miserable prospect.

'You seem pensive.' Quinn's voice so close beside her made her jump.

'I am trying to calm myself after all that hard work. Thank you.' She took the glass from his hand and sipped, glad of the excuse not to look at him.

'What do you think of it?' From the corner of her eye she saw Quinn make a sweeping gesture to encompass the assembly.

'I think it a resounding success,' she said warmly. 'And people are mingling, upstairs and down, in great amity. It will be spoken of for years.'

'I am glad it is being enjoyed. I feel genuinely grateful for the way the townsfolk have responded to what I have been trying to do. I must admit, I started this thinking only of improving the rental income, but now, thanks to you, I can look beyond the ledgers and into a community. You make me *see*, Cat. You make me think.'

'Me? But I have done nothing except help where I can with my local knowledge.'

'You have done far more than that.' He sat down beside her and put out a hand to steady her glass which was tilting at a dangerous angle, she realised. 'You are important to me, Cat.'

When she simply looked at him, taken aback, he laughed and stood again. 'I shall go and claim a dance from your Miss Helen before my secretary makes her the subject of talk by asking her to stand up with him for a third time.'

'Oh.' She tried to collect her thoughts. 'Yes, I can see that you would want to discourage that association. A girl from a shop and your secretary. He is the son of one of your godparents, is he not?'

'He is, and why that should make him an unsuitable match for a young woman of intelligence and charm and good character, I have no idea.'

He vanished into the press of bodies, cutting across the dance floor and leaving Cat to stare after him. He couldn't seriously be thinking that Helen would be acceptable to James Turnbull's relatives, surely?

Helen Pardoe had been born into a very respectable farming family, but they could hardly even have been called yeomen, let alone minor gentry. Orphaned at a young age, she had been apprenticed to William Brandon, where she had proved a quick learner. Her Oxfordshire accent and her country manners were soon lost as she copied the customers, but even so… James would have ambitions and for those he would need money and connections.

No, Quinn was teasing her.

The last set of the evening, upstairs and down, was to be country dances and before that, upstairs at least, a waltz. The one she would dance with Quinn.

Cat congratulated herself on regaining her calm and

her poise by the time the preceding set was almost done. She had sat that one out to steady her nerves, horrified to find she was so tense that she had no appetite for the delicious spread of food laid out in the supper room.

The memory of the waltz in this very room, the way it had ended in that kiss, grew more and more vivid as the evening had progressed, and now she wondered if she would have the control to dance in Quinn's arms again now. Surely she would simply melt into a puddle or flee?

'Shall we?' He was at her side while she was still tangled in her thoughts.

Cat found herself standing up, putting her hand in his and saying, with perfect composure, 'Of course.'

Where had that calm come from? The recognition that her reputation depended on behaving as though this were nothing out of the way, she supposed.

'The band is very good, is it not?' she observed as the dance floor began to fill up. Around the edge the less dashing ladies and the younger girls sat watching.

'Excellent. The fiddlers and the church band downstairs are doing a grand job too.' Quinn seemed distracted. 'Cat, are you committed for the last set?'

'No, I thought I would probably be too weary to dance by then,' she admitted.

'In that case, will you join me outside so we can

find a good spot to watch the fireworks?' he asked as the first notes set them dancing.

'Oh, I had forgotten those. Madelaine said she would go and collect Peter from the almshouses and let him watch—the bangs would wake him anyway. Yes, I would like to have a good view, thank you.'

That had carried them over the first awkwardness if, indeed, Quinn felt any. Perhaps he had already forgotten that silent waltz, that kiss. The room did look so very different now, of course. And probably it had not mattered so very much to him.

'It is better with music, isn't it?' he asked, shattering that faint hope.

'Yes. Much better.' She made herself speak calmly, as though she was not so close that she could feel the heat of his body, smell the crisp notes of citrus and, after an evening of vigorous activity, the scent of warm male flesh. That was ridiculously arousing and her hand tightened on his shoulder.

He pulled her a little closer.

'With music and a little practice I am not falling over my feet any more,' Cat said, attempting a light laugh.

See? I am not affected at all by this.

Quinn murmured something close to her hair. Something like... *Falling?*

Then suddenly she found she did not care any longer about where they were, who might be watching, what had happened before. She was in the arms of the man she loved, probably for the last time. The music was glorious and her feet, her body, knew exactly what to do.

Cat closed her eyes, surrendered to her heart and let herself be swept into the dream.

Chapter Sixteen

'The music has stopped.' Quinn's voice was low and gently amused. 'Have you gone to sleep?'

'Oh, goodness, so it has. No, of course I have not gone to sleep,' Cat said crossly as she stepped away and walked briskly to the edge of the ballroom. 'I was simply continuing the tune in my head,' she added as he caught up with her.

'Ah, I see. Shall we go and secure our place for the fireworks? I suggest fetching your cloak, it will be cool at the river.'

It seemed unnecessary to Cat—the summer evening still held the heat of the day and she was thoroughly warm from dancing, and the glow of dreaming in Quinn's arms, but she submitted to having her light cloak draped over her shoulders before being led outside.

'The gardeners have done a wonderful job,' she said, viewing the three tiers of narrow terraces they had managed to create on the long riverbank frontage and the smooth paved area at the top. It would probably be a squeeze, but all the guests ought to have a good view of the display without risk of falling into the water.

On the opposite bank she could see figures moving about, lit by closed lanterns for security so close to all that black powder.

They strolled up and down the top terrace for a while in silence. Quinn made no move to secure a particular spot, which puzzled her vaguely, but she was too happy just to be out in the fresh air, on his arm, alone with him, to give it much thought.

'The music has stopped,' he said after a while and moved to the steps, handing her down to the next level.

Behind them the sound of excited voices grew loud as the guests began to filter out into the night. The stimulus of dancing, alcohol and a party made them boisterous, but the sound was happy and, by some miracle, nobody seemed to have had too much to drink and no quarrels or fights had broken out.

'How far down are we going?'

'Right to the bottom.'

Wouldn't the view be better at the top? Then she saw what was moored at the foot of the steps. 'A boat?'

It was quite a large rowing boat, Cat saw, with rugs and cushions heaped in it and a wickerwork hamper stowed in the bow.

'A boat,' Quinn agreed, as he climbed down into

it and held out his hand. 'Come aboard. I thought we might slip downstream clear of the inn and enjoy a glass of wine alone while we watched the display.'

Cat glanced back. The upper terrace was well-lit, but the lower one only had a few well-placed lanterns to make sure nobody fell over the edge or down the steps. She didn't think they had been seen yet.

Should she? Of course not, it was a shocking thing to contemplate, going off alone into the darkness with a man like this. Not, she thought with an inner smile, that any man could achieve much in the way of seduction in a rowing boat. Not without risking both parties ending up in the water. Her virtue, such as it was, was safe.

A pity, she thought.

She put her hand in Quinn's and stepped down. The boat rocked and he hastily lowered her onto one of the seats, then turned to untie the rope tethering them to the bank.

The scream penetrated the sound of the river, the babble of excited voices above them. It was a woman, her voice piercing, full of horror.

Cat sprang to her feet again, rocking the boat. She clutched at Quinn and he stepped ashore, almost lifting her after him onto solid ground.

The scream came again, and with it a pistol shot.

'That was from the marketplace. Stay here, Cat.'

Quinn took the steps two at a time and vanished into the milling crowd on the top terrace.

'What is it? What's happening? Who screamed? Was that a gunshot?' The questions in a babble of voices were unanswerable.

Cat pushed her way through the crowd. She had an awful feeling that she knew that voice, even though she had never heard Madelaine scream before.

Peter? Had something happened to the little boy? But who was shooting?

People were jammed into the yard, with the crowd in the high arched carriage entrance acting like a cork in a bottle as everyone, reluctant to go outside, stopped dead. Cat kicked ankles, used her elbows ruthlessly, and finally forced her way out onto the cobbles of the marketplace.

It was vividly lit, as most of the businesses around the long rectangle had hung out lanterns for the celebration. To her right, in front of the building site of the hotel, stood a curricle, a light racing model, with two horses. They shifted uneasily, their reins trailing loose.

Next to them stood a man holding a horse. There was something familiar about him, then he moved a little and Cat saw he was the nice clerk who had bought linen for handkerchiefs from her. He looked frightened as he watched the scene in front of him.

And that, when she took it in, stole Cat's breath.

Madelaine stood between the clerk and her shop, confronting a man who had his back to Cat. He held pistols in both hands, down by his sides. One of them, she guessed, he had just fired.

Behind him Michael Dangerfield was slumped against the base of the market cross, a hand to his shoulder. As Cat looked, horrified, he shifted a little, as though to get up, then fell back.

Still alive, she thought. *Thank God.* But where was Quinn?

She began to walk across to Michael, treading slowly so the armed man would not glimpse the movement from the corner of his eye.

The stranger was ranting at Madelaine in French, she realised as she came close enough to hear.

'You sent that little rat to spy on me!' Cat managed to translate as he waved one pistol at the clerk, who was now cowering behind his horse. 'What is he? An assassin? Thought you'd get rid of me, did you, you bitch? Or was he to hand me over to the law so I would hang?'

It must be Louis Beaufoy.

She reached the base of the market cross and Michael's slumped body. He was unconscious, blood flowing from a shoulder wound, a dead weight she could hardly shift as she crouched down, got her hands under his arms and dragged him until they were both sheltered by the battered old steps of the square base.

Cat lifted her skirts, took hold of her petticoat and yanked it hard. The kind of handkerchief a lady took to a dance would not deal with the blood from so much as a scratch. The fine linen came free and she tore it, wincing at the noise, then started to stuff it under Michael's shirt. She was so intent on what she was doing that the arrival by her side of two young men took her my surprise. One of them was Ben, the other the grocer's apprentice.

'Carry him back, find a doctor,' she whispered. *'Quietly.'*

They nodded, lifted Michael between them and began to move slowly back towards the Arms. Cat saw the crowd was watching silently, realising the need not to panic Beaufoy into action. Some moved forward and helped with Michael for the last few yards and she saw Helen gesturing at her to come back.

Cat turned away. *Where is Quinn?*

'Je n'ai jamais envoyé personne après toi,' Madelaine was shouting.

I never sent anyone after you, Cat translated in her head.

'I never want to see you again.'

'Où est mon fils?'

'Pierre? Where you will never find him! You are no fit father for him. *Cochon!*'

Beaufoy raised his left hand, the pistol in it steady,

the barrel long and gleaming dully in the flickering light. *'Dites-moi!'*

Cat wondered furiously if she could rush at him, collide with him from the back and knock his aim away from Madelaine. She stood up, uncertain whether that was more or less dangerous for her friend. She began to move forward, praying that Madelaine did not betray her approach.

Then she saw Quinn in the shadows in front of her shop, his arm raised, another duelling pistol in his grip.

'Tell me.'

Everything seemed to happen at once. The fireworks burst into life over their heads, exploding in showers of sparks, there was a shot and Beaufoy's arm jerked up. He fired wildly and a window smashed, glass showering down on Madelaine as Quinn ran towards her, caught her in his arms and bundled her into the passage between the new hotel and her shop.

He spun back to face Beaufoy, but the man was already running for the curricle, blood dripping from his left hand as he went.

The clerk, finding his courage, stepped out to confront him, was hit in the face with a pistol butt and went down, spooking his horse, which shied away towards Cat.

Beaufoy scrambled into the vehicle, dragged the

horses' heads around and drove them flat out towards the Oxford road.

Cat caught the nervous horse by the bridle, then Quinn was at her side. 'Caitlin. Thank God, if he had turned and seen you...' He snatched the reins, swung into the saddle and sent the horse after the curricle.

She stood staring after him, trying to puzzle out what he had just said, but there was so much noise, so much confusion, that she could hardly think straight.

She ran, her thin evening slippers slipping on the cobbles, and found herself jostled on all sides. It was as though something had released the watching crowd from their thrall. In a mass they rushed towards the exit from the marketplace that led down to the river and the bridge.

They were too late to see the collision, but they all heard it, the splintering crash, the screams of the horses.

Cat stayed long enough to see Quinn, tall on horseback, unscathed, then she turned and made her way back to find Madelaine, limping now as she became aware of her bruised feet.

Her friend was out in the square and she had the clerk by the arm and was shaking him. 'Who are you? How did you lead him here?'

'I did not know he had seen me,' the man was protesting. 'I had no idea he was following.'

'You are the Duke's man, aren't you?' Cat demanded, that at least making sense. 'How could you be so careless?' Reaction to the fear was making her feel sick and angry. And what had Quinn called her? Surely… 'Madelaine, are you hurt?'

'Non.' Her friend was shaking as Cat put her arm around her. She held out a hand and stared at it, as though puzzled by the spots of blood. 'Just a little cut from the glass. But Michael? He shot him. Peter?'

'Peter is safe where you left him at the almshouses. Michael is inside the Harland Arms and they will have found the doctor by now. Come, let us go and find him. Phoebe will need you too.'

'Yes. Yes, of course.' Madelaine turned away, then looked back. 'Louis? Where has he gone?'

'He drove too fast down the hill to the bridge. I think he must be dead, that was a terrible crash. Or if he is not, then he soon will be when the law catches up with him. He killed a man in London, my dear. I am so sorry it had to end like this.'

'Dead. I loved him once and he was Peter's father,' Madelaine said bleakly, then ran towards the Arms.

Overhead the fireworks exploded one last time, and silence fell.

'Cat?'

She looked up to find Quinn dismounting. 'Is he—?'

'Dead, yes. Thrown from the carriage head first into the stone wall. His neck was broken. Kinder than the hangman's noose and a mercy he did not deserve.' He turned to the clerk. 'Foster, how the hell did he get here?'

'I tracked him down in a lodging house in Southwark, sir,' the man said miserably. 'I thought I had bribed the man who gave me the address enough to stay silent, but he must have told Beaufoy after all, and he followed me in his turn. I am very sorry, Your Grace.'

'They told me that you were competent, experienced, and now this. A man has been injured, perhaps seriously. A woman has been put in grave danger, and others might have been hurt.' He glanced at Cat, his expression grim.

'Yes, Your Grace.'

'You had best go and write it all down for the Coroner.' He turned away from the man, effectively dismissing him. 'How is Dangerfield, Cat? That was a brave and foolish thing you did.'

'He might have bled to death otherwise,' she said and walked with him back towards the Harland Arms. She realised that she was shaking. That too was reaction, of course.

They reached the point where she had caught the horse. Everything seemed to be happening again inside her head, repeating like the scenery in theatres that was on rollers.

Quinn had taken the reins from her and finally what he had said came back clearly. *Caitlin. Thank God...*

'Caitlin,' she said, stopping dead. 'You called me Caitlin.'

'I did?' Quinn stopped too and stared at her.

Of course, he was about to say she had misheard, that was the obvious explanation. In all that chaos and noise and fear she could easily have done so, she realised. It had been so confusing. Then she saw Quinn's face.

'You know who I am,' she said, and her voice cracked. Anger, betrayal. 'That man, that...spy of yours. I remember him. He came to my shop, pretended he wanted to buy linen. But he was investigating me, wasn't he? He was working out who I was. No wonder you could produce someone to find Beaufoy so quickly—you had him to hand. How *could* you?'

'Cat—Caitlin—I care about you. I wanted to find out what had gone wrong for you in the past and try and put it right for you. I knew this was not where you belonged. This evening, the boat on the river, I was going to ask you to marry me.'

Cat realised that that she was angry. Furiously angry.

'I belong *here*. But you would not accept that, would you? Not allow that a woman can make decisions about her own life. So then you discovered that I was an earl's daughter. A lady. What had passed between us did not matter if I was just a shopkeeper, did it? But a gentleman does not kiss a lady on a ballroom floor, or in a vicarage parlour, come to that. When that happens a gentleman marries her.'

She was storming at him now, but almost in a whisper.

'My father is very wealthy, very well-connected, my bloodlines are excellent, so I am not ineligible to marry a duke, am I? Doing the gentlemanly thing will not be too much of a sacrifice on your part. Oh, and you won't have to bother with all that tiresome business of doing the Season and finding a bride, so that is a benefit for you.'

She could see, even in that fitful light, that Quinn had gone white around the lips, but he held his tongue. *Wise man.*

'Of course,' she continued bitterly, 'there is the little matter of explaining where I have been all this time, but you are good at deception, you will think of something, I am certain.'

Chapter Seventeen

Quinn found himself staring at Cat's back as she limped away from him towards the Harland Arms. Was she hurt? He strode after her, caught her arm.

'Cat, where are you going?'

'To see how Michael is, to look after Madelaine and Phoebe. Go away, I do not want to talk to you. Go and sort out the wreckage or something else useful.'

The only wreckage he was concerned about was the splintered mess that had been his plans for their future. 'Cat,' he began, then realised that talking now, here, was hopeless. It would have to be in the morning. But he could at least help her now with her friends. He stepped into the roadway as a blast on a horn made him look sharply to his right, then stride across to pull Cat onto the pavement beside the Arms as the Mail came skidding to a halt.

'What the devil are you doing here at this time of night?' he demanded of the driver as ostlers ran out to the horses' heads.

The man leaned down, took the pewter mug of ale someone was holding up for him and drank it down in one long swallow. Then he answered Quinn. 'The bridge at Whimbrels Cross is down. Big oak fell on it. Proper mess it is, we've been miles out of our way and I'm hours behind on the waybill.'

'Well, you're not going any further tonight,' Quinn told him. 'Not for an hour or so. There's been a crash at the bridge. Dead body, dead horse, broken curricle jammed across it.'

'That does it. Get me a riding horse, a good one.' The guard was climbing down from his perch at the back, mailbags slung over his shoulder. He landed on the ground, reached up for his shotgun and headed towards the stable-yard. 'The Mails must get through. They'll have to clear enough for me to pass.'

Passengers were climbing out of the coach complaining, voices raised in question. Inn staff hurried out, promising refreshments and rooms, sweeping them inside, making the best of the unexpected windfall of customers.

Behind them a peremptory blast of another horn sounded and a private travelling carriage turned into the yard, making the Mail passengers jump aside.

'That'll be more of them,' the driver said as he jammed his whip into its holder and started to climb down, the wide skirts of his many-caped greatcoat swirling around his legs. 'It wasn't just us who got diverted at the Cross.' He stomped off to have a word with the ostlers as they led the weary team though the arch and into the yard.

Quinn followed them. How was he going to make this right with Cat? Was it even possible? He could see why she was so angry—she assumed his intention to propose only arose when he decided her status was high enough for him.

And he supposed it had… Only his feelings for her before he discovered who she was had been so… But a duke could not marry a draper, not even if he loved her.

Oh, yes I could, he thought. *Whatever she was, somehow I would have made it possible because I love her and I don't care whose daughter she is.*

And that was enough to floor a man. Love. He had known he liked her a great deal, he knew he desired her and he had sensed that life with Cat would make him happy, but the word love had not entered his head. Had it? He certainly hadn't used it to her, that was certain. So what was she to think?

He reached the inn's internal courtyard, hardly aware of where he was. He had to find Cat, help her friends, then make certain that the bridge was cleared, the Coroner informed, Beaufoy's body in the hands of the undertaker—

'You mean we have to stop here tonight?' The accents might have been those of any well-bred lady annoyed to find her plans disrupted, but Quinn was suddenly alert. He knew that voice.

'They told me this was a very second-rate establishment, but I see it appears to have had some attention paid to it recently. I suppose it will have to do, because I am not prepared to spend any more time on the road. Come along, do wake up, Horace.'

The lady who had been standing in the doorway of the carriage, her hand on her groom's arm, stepped down into the yard and stared around her from beneath the brim of a fashionable bonnet. 'James, make haste and summon someone, I am not standing here all night.'

Another groom ran for the entrance to the inn and stood aside to let someone come out. To Quinn's horror he saw it was Cat. She looked strained and weary, her eyes on the ground in front of her as though she needed to check every step she took.

He was halfway across the yard to intercept her, not daring to run and draw attention to her, when she came face to face with the lady from the carriage. He saw her veer to the side, murmuring an automatic apology, and then freeze.

The two women faced each other, then, *'Caitlin?'*

As if released by her name, Cat spun around and took to her heels, running towards the marketplace, sparing Quinn one withering glance as she passed.

'After her! Catch her, you fool!' Lady Bowland cried.

The footman sprinted after Cat and crashed into Quinn who contrived to blunder into his path. The man picked himself up and ran for the archway, but was back a moment later.

'She vanished, my lady.'

'Good heavens, Lady Bowland. I do apologise for impeding your man.' Quinn took a slightly unsteady step towards Cat's mother. 'Chasing a pickpocket was he? Afraid I've had a trifle to drink, don't you know. We've been celebrating in the town.' He smiled at the Countess and at the Earl, who had descended from the carriage and was staring about him in the bemused fashion of a man who had been sound asleep and wasn't quite certain where he was, or why.

'Harland? What on *earth* are you doing here?' Lady Bowland snapped, then appeared to recollect that she was addressing a duke and managed a wintery smile. 'I mean, what a surprise to meet you here.'

'Well, this *is* the Harland Arms and my house is just a few miles away. We had an assembly here tonight. Do let me show you in, you will find the place has been greatly improved recently. Oh, you have never been here before?' He kept up a gentle flow of inconsequential talk until he had them both safely inside. 'Now, may I send for the constable for you? Did the thief take anything?'

'It was not a thief,' the countess began. 'It was my... That is to say, it is someone I thought I recognised. I cannot imagine why she ran away.'

'My dear, that was—'

'No one of any importance.' The look she sent the Earl had him blinking at her, but he subsided. 'You would recommend this place for the night then, Harland?'

'I would. Not that there is anything else in Duke's Forde fit for a lady.' He should invite them back to Harland Park, of course, but he had too much to do, and to worry about, that night to cope with them. 'Ah, here is Mrs Longford, the landlady. Mrs Longford, Lord and Lady Bowland find themselves stranded after a very trying journey. I have been assuring them that they will find nothing lacking in your hospitality.'

'Indeed not, Your Grace.' Despite having just dealt with a large assembly, a wounded man and the displaced Mail coach passengers, Mrs Longford exuded welcome and competence. 'Do come this way, my lady, my lord. I have just the suite of rooms for you. May I offer any refreshment?'

'I will leave you in safe hands and bid you goodnight.' Quinn walked away before he could become any more involved. He needed space to think, and he was not going to get it now, not with the accident to deal with, the need to ensure that Michael Dangerfield and Madame Arnaud were all right. Cat would have reached home by now and she would be safe there, at least until morning, and he was certain that the last person—after her parents—that she wanted to see at this moment was him.

What was she thinking? That not only had he pried into her past but that he had betrayed her whereabouts to her parents? That he had arranged their arrival just after his planned proposal, smugly confident that she would agree to anything he said, because he was a duke?

His heart told him to go to her now, explain, excuse, somehow make it all right. His head told him that she was exhausted, anxious and shocked and that neither of them was in any state for a conversation about trust and emotions and feelings. And the sense of duty that he had somehow inherited with the title told him that what he must do now was to see to the welfare of this town and its people, all of them. His own selfish concerns must wait.

Cat ran and did not stop until she was in the deep shadow of Church Lane. She flattened herself against the wall and looked towards the Harland Arms. The footman chasing her stood by the market cross, shaking his head in frustration as he peered around. She was safe here. He could not see her and, if he started towards her, she was only yards from the gate that led into the passageway behind the gardens.

She saw him give up and walk back to the inn, then almost cried out as she turned and took a step. Her dancing slippers must be in shreds, her feet felt as though they had been pounded with hammers.

It took five minutes to limp slowly down to the gate and along to her own garden entrance. Michael's house was in darkness except for the attic windows where his journeyman and apprentice had their beds. Michael was in a bedchamber at the inn with Phoebe and Madelaine and Peter was staying at the almshouses for the night, where a small army of substitute grandparents would be doting on him.

Her own back door opened as she let the gate bang closed behind her.

'Mrs Brandon? Ma'am?' Helen and Ben came down the path, took her, one at each arm, and steered her into the kitchen as though she was a frail old lady.

I feel like a frail old lady.

Everything hurt. Her feet, her knees where she had dropped down beside Michael's bleeding body, her head... And her heart.

Quinn. How could you? I trusted you. I love you. Loved *you*, she corrected fiercely, but even as she did so, she knew it was a lie. He had betrayed her, broken her heart, but still she loved him.

'Oh, your poor feet, ma'am.' Helen was crouched down beside the chair. 'Ben, fetch me a bowl of warm water and some of that soft muslin and a towel.'

'Call me Cat,' Cat said. 'Both of you.' They were her friends as much as her employees and they were loyal. Loyalty was precious. Rare.

Helen looked up, startled, but with a smile. 'Yes, ma'am. I mean, Cat. Thank you. Only in private, of course.'

'Of course,' Ben echoed, setting a pan of water down by her feet and hurrying off for the cloths.

When he returned, Helen shooed him out and began to peel off Cat's ruined shoes and stockings, making distressed little tutting sounds. 'They are bruised.' She got up, fetched the salt crock and sprinkled some into the water. 'There now, try that.'

Cat gave a small moan of relief at the caress of the warm water. It would be easy to slip into sleep sitting there. Sleep, oblivion where she would not have to think about Quinn, about her parents and what her discovery would mean. But she had not survived that first betrayal by refusing to face it, she told herself and somehow, she had to survive this.

'Ben,' she called. 'Come back. I must tell you both this. There is a couple staying at the Arms tonight,' she said, opening her eyes and sitting up straight in the chair. 'A Lord and Lady Bowland. They are looking for me, but they do not know my name, nor that I own this shop, only what I look like. It is very important that they do not find me.'

Bless them, they must have been full of questions, but neither asked why, only nodded solemnly.

'I shall have to stay out of sight until they give up and go away, which means you will have to run the shop yourselves, which I know you are both very capable of doing. I am only sorry to give you more work.'

Helen, who was dabbing her feet dry on a linen towel, made a dismissive noise. 'We will manage, ma'am. Cat. But what if people ask where you are?'

'I don't like to ask you to lie for me,' Cat began.

'Lying to confuse enemies is no sin,' Ben said. 'We could say you've gone to London to talk to the silk merchants. All the ladies in the town know you are buying special silks, so nobody would wonder at it. You will be staying here, though, won't you? We can ask you if there are any questions?'

'I will stay in the town, but I think I should move next door to Madame Arnaud's house. Just in case.'

In case Quinn betrays who I am and they come here. And why wouldn't he? It was a miracle they are not hammering on the door right now. I suppose they think I have nowhere to run to.

'But His Grace will protect you, surely?' Helen asked as she stood up and tossed the stained cloths into the laundry hamper.

'No. It seems he will not,' Cat said. 'I am afraid you must give him no reason to think I am still in the town.' She ignored their shocked expressions and added, 'If you will fetch me some fresh stockings and shoes I will go next door now. I know where Madelaine puts her back door key.'

Helen came back, not just with the shoes and stockings but with a valise. 'I have packed your nightgown and wrapper, some slippers, a change of linen and your hair and tooth brushes,' she explained as Cat put on her stockings and slid her feet cautiously into shoes.

'They are taking Mr Dangerfield into his house,' Ben called from the shop, where he had tactfully withdrawn. 'And Madame Arnaud and Miss Phoebe are with him.'

'Can you go out and tell Madame Arnaud that I am in her spare room, Ben? Make sure nobody else hears. Ask her not to say anything and that I will explain when I see her.'

The shop bell tinkled as he let himself out and Cat carried the valise to the back door. 'Thank you, Helen.'

'We will keep you safe, Cat, never fear.'

The bed in Madelaine's little spare room was made up with clean linen, cool as Cat slipped between the sheets. She had pinned a note to her friend's bedchamber door: *I'll explain in the morning. Let no one know I am here. C.*

She did not expect to sleep. Her feet were sore, her head ached and her heart hurt. There was so much to think about, so much to fear. Yet somehow, as her head touched the pillow oblivion took her.

* * *

'Cat?'

Cat came up out of the depths, blinking into the morning light to find Madelaine standing in the bedchamber doorway.

For a moment she could not remember where she was, and then it all came flooding back and she scrambled to sit up. 'Madelaine, I am so sorry I interfered. I never meant to bring Louis down on you, only to perhaps put your mind at rest. How is Michael?'

Madelaine came into the room and sank down on the end of the bed. She looked weary, but not distressed. 'The doctor says he will be all right. He has a slight fever, but that is to be expected, apparently. The bullet went right through and nothing serious inside has been hurt. I think you saved his life, Cat.'

'If I had not pried—'

'You are my friend. You did it with the best of intentions.'

'That is such a damning thing to say!'

They smiled at each other tentatively, then Madelaine said, 'I am free now. Safe. But I do not know how I feel. I did not want him dead, just…gone forever. You said he killed a man in London?'

'Louis was cheating at cards, there was an argument and he stabbed his accuser. There will be an inquest, I suppose.'

'Yes,' Madelaine said bleakly. 'I do not want to acknowledge that I was his wife, but how will I explain why he was confronting me, why he shot Michael?'

'Speak to the Duke, he and his man will come up with some explanation, it is the least they can do.'

There was a little silence, then Madelaine said, 'Is something wrong between you? He was asking for you, but in the shop they just said you had gone to London, and yet, here you are.'

'It is a long story and a great secret. *Was* a great secret. I will tell you everything, but please do not tell anyone else.'

'I promise. Come down to my parlour. We will drink chocolate and talk.'

Chapter Eighteen

Quinn spent the night in the Harland Arms and woke at dawn after a snatched few hours of sleep, feeling as though elves were working on his brain with tiny hammers. Two cups of strong coffee were some help, but only made the horrors of the night before more painfully clear.

Cat believed he had betrayed her to her parents, had intended to propose marriage to her only because of her true identity and, to crown it all, blamed him for the attack on Madame Arnaud and the wounding of Michael Dangerfield.

It was clear she wanted to avoid Lord and Lady Bowland at all costs, and somehow he had to get to the bottom of that. But first he had to find Cat and try to explain. Somehow.

The shop was closed, of course, and it was not going to help his cause to go waking the household at that hour. He watched the Mail finally leaving with its complement of grumbling travellers, so the broken parapet of the bridge must have been made safe and the wreckage cleared. He drank more coffee and watched the inn coming to life around him until eight o'clock struck, the strange *bong* at the end jarring his nerves. He really ought to see about getting a clock mender to deal with that.

I'll add it to the list...

There was no sign of life in any of the three shops as he walked across the marketplace, then down Church Street and along the alleyway at the rear so he could go to the back door.

It was opened by Ben, the shopman, who, like everyone else who had been at the assembly, was looking somewhat the worse for wear.

'Mrs Brandon is not at home, Your Grace,' he said politely, standing four-square in the doorway. He was a skinny youth, however, and Quinn could see past him to where Helen sat at the breakfast table. It was laid for two.

'Of course, she will be still resting after last night,' he began.

'No, Your Grace. I mean that Mrs Brandon is away from home at the moment. I cannot say exactly when she will return.'

'Where has she gone?'

'London.' It was said with no hesitation but Quinn was certain it was an untruth. The London-bound stage had not gone through yet and how else would she have left? The young man was not used to lying: there was colour up over his cheekbones and he was staring over Quinn's shoulder, not meeting his gaze.

London? Rubbish. She was upstairs, he was certain of it.

'Thank you.' He turned, went down the path and then, on the other side of the closed gate, stood and stared at the three houses as though he could see through their walls.

They had been built as one block, like a short terrace, and he knew that most builders saved on brick by never taking the party walls in the attics right up to the roof. It was usually left to the householders to ensure the security of their homes by boarding, or bricking up, the gaps. But in many cases they just didn't bother because they never penetrated to the cobwebbed spaces and did not realise, or perhaps had nefarious reasons for wanting to move secretly between dwellings. It was worth a try.

Madame Arnaud would probably greet him with a rolling pin in hand, so he went instead to Dangerfield's gate and walked up the path to their back door.

His knock was answered by Dangerfield's journeyman, who had no hesitation in opening the door wide to reveal the apprentice and the maid of all work at the kitchen table. The young men had been eating their breakfast and the girl was loading a tray.

'How is your master?' he asked when they had all finished their awkward bobs and curtseys.

'He had a good night, I think, Your Grace. Miss Phoebe's gone to her bed and Madame Arnaud's left as well,' the journeyman said. 'I was just going to take a tray up and sit with him, if he can manage a little breakfast.'

'I'll come up with you,' Quinn said. 'Just to see for myself.'

He followed the young man up the stairs, opened the door he indicated and went in after him. Dangerfield was pale and looked to be in some discomfort, but he was fully conscious and able to sit up against the pillows.

'Your Grace!'

'Do not disturb yourself. I only wanted to see how you were doing. I'll leave you in peace now.' Quinn backed out, closed the door and walked briskly down four steps, then tiptoed up and eased open the other door on the landing. All he could see in the bed was the top of Phoebe's head on the pillow.

He crept out and up the stairs to the next floor, keeping to the outside of the treads to reduce creaking. The journeyman and apprentice shared a room, the only space on that floor. A narrow stair led up to what must be the attic.

It was dark, with no window. Quinn groped his way cautiously through the cluttered space until his outstretched hand met brick, scraping his knuckles. He followed the wall, which must be the chimney and found, as he expected, a gap, a triangular space in the eaves.

Finally, somehow managing not to sneeze or fall over anything, he was in the attic of Cat's house. There were things stored up there, but it was more orderly, he discovered as he inched forward, hands outstretched. The door, to his relief, was unfastened. He had not come equipped for lock-picking.

It opened with a creak that sounded loud to his straining ears, but there was no reaction from below, so he crept down the stairs and found Ben's room. On the floor below he guessed the room at the back was Helen's, and a quick glance showed the gown he recognised from the previous night draped over a chair. He could hear her talking to Ben in the kitchen, although he could not make out her words.

So the remaining bedchamber must be Cat's. He did not knock, but eased it open.

The room was empty.

Cat and Madelaine talked themselves out and sat at the kitchen table, drinking coffee and making a breakfast out of the shop's unsold pastries from the day before.

Madelaine had been understanding about Cat's reasons for asking the Duke to trace Louis, and Cat knew she had been forgiven. It was hard for her friend to know how to feel about her husband's death, she thought. She had loved the man once, he was the father of her child and yet he had become a nightmare. But this was real life and no fairy godmother was going to appear to magic him harmlessly away. At least, as Madelaine had said, she could truthfully tell Peter that his father had died in an accident and not on the gallows.

'You will want to collect Peter and call on Michael,' Cat said eventually, chasing the last crumb around her plate with one fingertip.

'Peter will be fine where he is, and I want to be feeling a little calmer before I see him,' Madelaine said. 'And Michael told me to go and rest and not fuss over him, so I shall take him at his word until at least midday. They will send for me if there is any cause for concern.' She drew a long breath and smiled. 'It is a shock, and it may be many days before I can really believe that I am free, but it is as though I can see the future clear and bright at last.'

Then the smile faded as she looked at Cat. 'But for you, I worry. What will happen now? What will your parents do? What do you want them to do?'

'Nothing,' Cat said. 'Nothing except drive away and come to believe they were mistaken in who they saw last night.'

'And the Duke?'

Cat shrugged. 'I never want to set eyes on that man again.' Then she saw Madelaine's eyes widen and her mouth open in a soundless *Oh*. 'What is it?'

She twisted around to look behind her at the kitchen door, which stood open and in it, framed like a full-length portrait, stood Quinn.

'How did you get in here?' she demanded. 'We locked the doors.'

'Through the attics from Dangerfield's place,' he said, walking into the room. 'You were not at home and we need to talk, Cat. May I sit down?'

'No, you may not.'

'Yes, Your Grace,' Madelaine stood up, put a clean cup and saucer on the table and gestured to the coffee-pot. 'That is fresh. I will be upstairs, Cat, if you need me.'

'I need you to help me throw him out,' Cat said furiously, on her feet and quite prepared to use the coffee-pot as a weapon if necessary.

'Talk first.' Madeline paused in the doorway. 'It helped us.' Then she was gone and Quinn sat down.

Behind her was the door to the shop and that led only to the marketplace. Besides, the outer door was locked and she had no idea where the key was. Quinn was between her and escape through the garden, and she doubted very much whether she could get past him if he wanted to stop her.

Cat sat down. 'Well? What have you to say for yourself?'

'That I believed that you had been badly treated by your family in the past and that if I knew the truth, then I might be able to make things better. You did the same for Madame Arnaud.'

'I did no such thing and you know it. I needed information to establish whether she was free to marry and was safe from that abusive man. If your agent had not been so careless, we would have known the truth about him. We knew what we were dealing with. You know nothing about me, about what happened. You have no idea what you have stirred up.'

'Then tell me.' Quinn reached across the table and took her hand.

Cat snatched up the pastry fork and poised it over his exposed wrist. 'Let me go or I swear I will use this.'

Quinn released her, sat back, raised both hands in a gesture of surrender.

'You wanted me but you knew I would never agree to be your mistress,' Cat said flatly. 'Then you began to suspect that my birth was better than it appeared and decided that if it was good enough, then you could marry me.'

'You wanted me too,' Quinn said. 'Do not deny it.'

'Why should I?' she flung at him. 'I want many things I cannot or should not have. That does not mean that I poke and pry and betray someone's secrets to get them.'

'I have not betrayed you.' Quinn was on his feet now. 'I told no one about you, only my agent, Foster.'

'The how did my parents get here, so conveniently after you had planned to propose marriage to me, I wonder?' It was an effort to keep her voice steady, to stay where she was as he loomed over her from across the narrow table.

'Coincidence.'

'Oh, for goodness sake. Do you expect me to believe that? There is no reason for them to travel in this direction, no reason for them to stop in Duke's Forde. That is one reason why I have settled here.'

'I do not know where they were going, but they were delayed, as was the Mail, by a broken bridge further back. That is why they stopped, because it was so late. I give you my word of honour that I have told them nothing about you and that I had no idea that they would be here.'

'I do not believe you,' she said coldly as she stood up.

Quinn went white and she knew she should not have said that, but it was too late to take back the mortal insult to his honour now. If a man had said those words to him, it would end in a duel.

'I am going home. If Lord and Lady Bowland drive away this morning with no attempt to find me, then perhaps I might believe you. As it is, I can only assume that the shock of finding yourself a duke has addled your brain and given you an exalted idea of what you are entitled to do.'

It was quite an effective line to exit on, she thought as she swept out, head up. As soon as the door was shut behind her she ran, out of the back door, down the path and into her own garden. She took the back door key from its hiding place, let herself in and locked the door behind her.

There were no footsteps following, no voice raised to call her back. It seemed that she had effectively killed any desire Quinn might have for her. Now she had to wait and see whether she was wrong about him.

Ben and Helen came through from the shop when they heard the door and she managed a bright smile for them. 'Just opening up? Excellent. I will be in the office if you need me.'

She could only hope they did not, because all she wanted to do was sit and sob.

I love him. I love him and he is just like all the rest at heart—he believes a lady can have no will of her own, no existence beyond a suitable marriage and, if she is so deluded as to refuse to accept that, then, for her own good, a gentleman can go behind her back, betray her wishes, order her life to suit himself and his standards of what is right and proper.

Chapter Nineteen

The midday meal came and went with no interruptions. After the excitement of the previous evening it seemed that few ladies were shopping and Helen, taking her luncheon with Cat, reported small sales of sewing silks, mending thread and a pair of silk stockings to replace those worn out by dancing.

But Cat had hardly sat down behind her desk again when raised voices sent her hurrying to put her ear against the door.

'Mrs Brandon has gone to London,' Ben was saying, his voice raised as though he was repeating himself.

'Stuff and nonsense. There is no such person as Mrs Brandon, and the person pretending to be her was at the inn late last night.' That was, unmistakably, her mother's voice.

'I assure you, madam—'

'That is *my lady*, to you, young man. Tell us where this Mrs Brandon is or I will summon the constable.'

That was too much for Cat. She could not lurk in her office while her staff were abused and threatened. What could her parents do to her, after all? Drag her back in chains?

She opened the door. 'There is no call to browbeat and bully my staff. Come in here, if you please.'

For a horrible moment she thought they were going to refuse and make a scene in the middle of the shop, although, by some mercy, there were no customers. Then, tight-lipped, her mother swept past Ben and through the door, her father after her.

Cat closed the door and took her seat behind her desk. It felt like retreating behind battlements. 'Please, Mama, Papa, will you not sit down?'

Her mother subsided onto a chair to the right of the door in a rustle of dark crimson silk, her father seemed torn between taking a seat and looming menacingly, but finally sat down too, on the one on the other side.

'Well, Caitlin, what have you to say for yourself?' he demanded.

Cat found that now the worst had happened and they had discovered her, she could speak quite steadily. 'I see no reason to say anything. I left home some years ago, have married and am widowed. I am of full age and of independent means and no longer your concern, although I imagine I have not been from the moment you read my letter.'

'Unnatural creature,' her mother pronounced in

throbbing tones. 'You ran off with that disgraceful young man to the everlasting shame of the family.'

'As nobody else knows about it, I do not see what shame there is to the family,' Cat observed. 'I agree, it was a shocking mistake to make—I was sadly deceived in Wykeham's character, but I was rapidly enlightened.'

'You were ruined,' her father began.

'Exactly,' she said, almost smiling at the shock on his face at her admitting it. 'I saw no point in returning home, so I found myself respectable employment, a most respectable husband and now I run a profitable and highly respectable business.'

'Respectable? You are in trade!'

'Indeed I am. Do tell me, out of interest, how did you account for my absence? A nervous collapse and a retreat to seclusion in the country?'

'Exactly. And now we have to find some way of explaining your reappearance in polite Society,' her mother said with a frown. 'Especially now.'

Cat stared at them. 'You want me to do *what*?'

Her father gestured around him. 'All this must be disposed of and you must return to London.'

'I will do no such thing. Why on earth should I? There is nothing to connect me to you now. The only person who knows my true identity is my closest friend—'

And the Duke of Harland.

'That cur Wykeham has written his memoirs,' Lord Bowland said between gritted teeth. 'He is calling it *Memoirs of a Rake* and he is approaching the families of all the ladies named in it with the amount of money that will ensure the removal of their name before publication.'

'That is extortion, or blackmail, surely,' Cat said furiously. 'It is criminal.' Then she thought it through. 'But to prosecute him will ensure the widest possible publicity for the book. However, he has no idea who, or where I am, so he cannot harm me.'

'It is not you we are concerned about,' her mother snapped. 'You brought this on yourself, and if it only affected you, then that would simply be justice. But it will reflect on us, on your sister and her family, on your brother. We have already agreed to pay his price.'

'In that case–'

'But now he is asking for more.'

Of course he is. That is what blackmailers do.

'Call his bluff. He has no proof.'

'You vanished from London at the same time as he left. He says he has jewellery that can be identified as yours.'

'Which he stole. He can be hanged for that.'

'But it will all come out,' her father said. 'We cannot risk it. Your reappearance, restored to health, would ensure that no shadow of suspicion falls on you and, more importantly, no scandal touches your family.'

Cat was not certain whether they had taken leave of their senses or she had. How on earth could her reappearance years later prove anything, except that she was alive?

'You are not thinking clearly. There is so much that could go wrong with that plan, even if I was prepared to return to London. I vanish mysteriously, am not heard of for eight years and then suddenly reappear—how do we explain that?'

'Oh, but you have not vanished mysteriously.' Her mother settled back more comfortably in her chair, relaxing a little now her first outrage was spent. 'We made no secret of your poor health and where you had gone. You were such a shy little thing, nobody was at all surprised. At first we spoke of you frequently, and talked about how you were doing—your interest in gardening, your watercolours—and then your relapses in health, just when we were hoping you will return. After about the first year, people stopped asking after you and we stopped mentioning you.

'We thought we would give it ten years, just to be on the safe side, and then announce that, sadly, you had passed away. Dear Anna's children will still be too young to have their come-outs affected by the mourning period, you see.'

'And where have I been all this time?'

'At Sundley Manor. You recall? Your dear Papa inherited it from Aunt Philomena. It is in North Norfolk, absolutely miles from anywhere anyone of importance actually goes.'

Of all the cold-blooded... I was to die was I? At a convenient time, of course.

'Then kill me off now. If Wykeham tries anything, he will appear to be taking advantage of a family's grief and—' She broke off at the sound of raised voices in the shop. One was Helen's, the other, she realised with horror, was Quinn's.

The door swung open, almost hitting her father in his chair, and Quinn strode into the room, looking neither right nor left, all his focus on Cat behind the desk.

'Your parents are here,' he said. 'Someone at the Arms recognised you from their description of your gown last night and told them your name.'

'Quinn,' she began, but he had reached the desk, was leaning towards her over it, his hands spread either side of the blotter, unaware that they were not alone.

'Cat, marry me and I will make all this go away. I will make it all right, I promise.'

'And I am most willing to give my blessing to the match,' her father said.

Quinn spun round and found himself facing Lord and Lady Bowland. Both were beaming and the Earl was holding out his hand.

'Delighted, Duke. Delighted.'

Lady Bowland seemed to be beyond words.

He looked at Cat and saw the expression on her face. 'I think that congratulations are premature until Lady Caitlin decides whether she will accept me.'

'No,' Cat said. All the colour seemed to have left her face, making her eyes huge. He saw her swallow hard. 'No, I do not.'

Then she fainted, slipping from the chair to the floor.

She began to come to herself as he knelt beside her, lifting her in his arms. 'Put me down,' she murmured.

'You fainted.'

'I never faint.' She began to struggle. 'Put me down.'

'Lady Bowland, perhaps you would be so good as to summon Lady Caitlin's female assistant from the shop?' He lowered Cat back onto her chair as her mother hurried out. 'And then perhaps it would be best if we left her to recover in tranquillity.'

Beside him he heard her mutter bitterly, 'Tranquillity?'

He almost welcomed it—the Cat he knew was back. That faint had alarmed him even more than her refusal had. He needed to persuade her, that was all, and he couldn't do it with her parents hovering.

Helen came in, shot him a look that was hardly respectful, and went to Cat's side.

Quinn ushered the Bowlands out. 'May I invite you to Harland Park?' he said as they began to cross the marketplace. 'Last night I fear I was too involved with the accident to act the host, but I imagine you will find it more comfortable than the inn. Or perhaps you were travelling on a matter of urgency and must proceed?'

'No, not at all,' Bowland said. 'An elderly relative has recently moved to Oxford and we were intending to visit, that was all. This is of far greater importance. I have to say, I could never of dreamed of a more happy resolution to Caitlin's, er, problem.'

They clearly had had absolutely no idea where their daughter had been living for, what, eight years? What was the matter with them? Why hadn't they searched for her? Bowland could afford a regiment of Runners. It was clearly going to take some diplomacy to prevent them harrying and bullying Cat into marrying him—she was more than likely to refuse just because they demanded it.

She did not trust him. That hurt badly, as did the fact that she even refused to accept his word of honour. What had she said? *If Lord and Lady Bowland drive away this morning with no attempt to find me, then perhaps I might believe you.*

And they had not driven away. Instead they had discovered where she was, had gone to the shop, had clearly distressed her so much that she had fainted.

'How kind. We would be delighted to accept your hospitality,' Lady Bowland said.

Quinn wondered how long it was going to take before she started asking questions—how did he know who Cat was? Why had he said nothing about her when he met the Bowlands at the Langley's house party near Aylesbury? Had his arrival there been the accident it had seemed?

For the present it seemed that the miracle of finding a nobleman willing to marry their lost daughter—and a duke at that—had driven any such thoughts from either parent's head.

He needed to get back and talk to Cat, alone. But he could hardly send her parents off to Harland Park and not go himself to welcome them.

Hell and damnation. What on earth can Cat be thinking?

He lied to me. But that's what men do.

No, not all men, Cat thought, trying to be fair despite her aching head. Aristocrats told you what they thought you wanted to hear so they could get what they wanted or thought you should do. Men like her William, or Michael Dangerfield, were far more honest than so-called gentlemen.

More to stop Helen fussing than for any other reason, she had agreed to rest on her bed and sip tea with the curtains drawn. Now all she had to entertain her were her own churning thoughts.

Blaine Wykeham had charmed and deceived to seduce her and steal from her. Quinn Falconer had decided that a well-bred wife whom he desired physically, and who he had found to be intelligent, would be a convenient bride, saving him trouble and "saving" her from the life she was perfectly content living.

He had even had the gall to look hurt and insulted when she had refused to take his word of honour.

Cat put down her teacup, went to the window and drew back the curtains. She was not an invalid despite that faint, and she was not going to act like one. She would go downstairs, go into the shop, carry on as though nothing had happened.

If she refused to marry Quinn, then nothing and no one could force her and her parents could say nothing without revealing that their account of her whereabouts had been a downright fabrication. She just had to be strong and keep saying no, and eventually they would give up and go away.

Would Quinn? Probably not. Harland Park was his main seat, he had a vested interest in the town now and he would not abandon it. And where was he now? Plotting with her parents, she supposed. They must be in seventh heaven.

If only I could stop loving him.

Chapter Twenty

The next morning Cat decided to tell Helen and Ben who she really was and what had happened to her. She told Madelaine too. As she had expected they were all supportive, even though none of them could hide their shock, and it took Helen and Ben some time to begin to relax in her presence. Madelaine merely said that she had always guessed that Cat had a secret and that it was safe with her.

Cat tried not to be jealous of the air of contentment that hung around her friend. She was beginning to emerge from the first shock of Louis's reappearance and death and had dared to look into the future and see happiness ahead.

Cat told herself that she had nothing to be envious of. She had never had any hope of a life with Quinn, not even in her dreams.

Liar, the awkward little voice of her conscience nagged.

Perhaps she had dreamt, just a little. But now she

had no desire to fantasise about a man she could not trust. Not now she knew that he had gone behind her back, had searched out her identity for no good reason other than masculine arrogance and a belief that he knew best, or might find himself a convenient wife, and had betrayed her to her parents.

'More coffee? A lemon tart?' Madelaine prompted.

'No, thank you.' It seemed there were some things that even a lemon tart could not make better. 'I had best go back to the shop.'

Cat forced herself to stroll next door and not run, head down, for shelter. Where were her parents? Quinn? Why hadn't they descended again to browbeat her into doing their will? It was unnerving.

The church clock struck eleven and *clunk* as Helen came back from an errand. 'May I speak with you, my— I mean, ma'am. In private.'

Cat took her into the office. 'What is wrong?'

'Nothing's wrong, exactly, but it wasn't the Duke who told Lord and Lady Bowland who you were, it was Mrs Longford. She mentioned it to me when I was over there just now. She said she hoped that Lady Bowland had found you, but she thought she must have done, because your gown was so distinctive that she was sure she had given them the correct name.'

'Oh.' Cat felt sick. She had accused Quinn of betraying her, had refused to take his word that he had not done so. No wonder he had looked as though she had struck him. She'd refused to accept his word of honour, she had insulted him deeply. And she must apologise.

She still did not think she could forgive him for setting his agent to discover the truth about her, but that did not mean she had the right to ignore the fact that she had reacted unjustly.

'Thank you for telling me, Helen.'

She waited until the door closed, then pulled a fresh sheet of writing paper towards her and picked up her pen, dipped it in the ink and wrote,

Your Grace,
I find that I have wronged you by accusing you of betraying me to Lord and Lady Bowland. I accept that their presence in Duke's Forde was accidental and that you did not tell them who I was once they had seen me. Furthermore, I refused to accept your word that you had not done so, thus impugning your honour.
    I offer no excuse for this, but tender my heartfelt apologies for the insult.
Sincerely,
Cat Brandon.

It was stiff and it was formal, but it said what had to be said. Still, she would not apologise for her anger over his investigations behind her back.

She stared at the drying ink. So, this was how a friendship ended. And how a love affair never began. With a sigh Cat began to fold the sheet. There was a knock on the door.

'Come in.'

'Cat, we need to talk,' Quinn said as she looked up with a gasp. He closed the door behind him and, uninvited, took the chair on the other side of the desk.

'I have just written you a letter.' Miraculously her voice was steady although her breath felt tight in her chest. She handed him the sheet.

Quinn took it, opened it fully and read. 'Thank you,' he said. There was a long silence, then, 'You had a shock and you saw the life that you had built over so many years torn open. I understand your anger. And your fear.'

'Fear?' she queried sharply.

'Of the unknown, of what would happen next. You knew that I had pried into your secrets, you had no way of knowing what else I had done.'

'You…you accept my apology, then?'

'I do. It is honourable and courageous of you, although I sense I am not yet absolved. Cat, if I can forgive your angry, unjust accusations, can you not forgive a friend who only delved into your secrets to try and help you? To see if past wrongs could be righted?'

'Why should you want my forgiveness? What is

the point? We had a friendship and now we have… nothing,' she said, fighting to keep the misery out of her voice.

'Cat, I want to be friends again. Friends and more,' Quinn said and she lifted her gaze from her blotter and looked at him properly for the first time since he had entered her office.

There were dark shadows under his eyes, and he looked as though he had slept badly, if at all.

'I said that I want to marry you, Cat. I meant it.'

'You do, now that you know who I am,' she retorted. 'Before you were attracted to me, but were too honourable to attempt to seduce me. You liked me enough to be friends. Now you know I am the daughter of an earl and have realised how convenient it is to find a wife you are already on terms with, whose character you know something of. You can be a knight errant, save me from my scandalous past and gain a wife without risk or effort.'

'You really are the most stiff-necked, stubborn, proud woman I have ever encountered,' Quinn said, pushing back his chair with a screech of wood on wood. 'I wanted to make you mine, Cat, before I knew who you really were. But the Cat I *did* know then, the Cat I know now, is the product of her birth, her upbringing and her adventures since she left home, even if I was not aware of it then. If you had been born a merchant's daughter, a vicar's child, then you would not be the person you are now, and I would not have felt like this for you. You might have been a perfectly pleasant person, but not my Cat.'

'That is either a very clever way of twisting the facts or something profound and I do not know which,' she said.

My Cat... She so wanted to believe him.

'I forgive you for investigating my past,' she said carefully. 'But how can I marry you? Even if I wanted to, that is.'

'We can work it out,' Quinn said. 'If you want to.'

'And if I want to stay as I am?' Even as she spoke, Cat wondered why she was arguing, but it felt as though she was two people, two wills, pushing against each other. *You love him, say yes,* one argued. *It is too much of a risk*, the other protested.

'What is to stop me continuing just as I am?' she wondered aloud. 'My parents have no desire to cause a scandal, I trust you not to tell anyone. And besides, Blaine Wykeham, the man I eloped with, has written his memoirs and is blackmailing my parents.'

'You eloped?'

'I naively fell in love with a scoundrel who abandoned me after one night—fortunately before marrying me, if he had ever had that intention. He took my money and my jewellery. Duke's Forde is where I ran out of money for the stage.

'My parents have already paid him to remove all

mention of me from the book, now he is demanding more. But he has no idea where I am.'

'He will be dealt with,' Quinn said dangerously.

'You are not going to challenge him, are you?'

'Duels are only for gentlemen,' Quinn said grimly. 'No, I will ruin him. And his publisher with him if he refuses to destroy the book and hand over the manuscript. That you may leave with me to deal with, whatever you decide.'

You are not a coward, Cat, she told herself. *You made the right decisions after Blaine abandoned you. Make the brave choice now. Choose happiness.*

'Will you kiss me, Quinn?' she asked before she lost her nerve. Surely she would be able to tell how he felt about her, what her true feelings were for him, if they kissed?

'If you will come out from behind your fortifications, I would be only too happy to, Cat.' He pushed his chair right back against the door and came to her, holding out his hands as she stepped away from the desk.

This was the moment she must decide, because once she was committed, there was no going back. She did not make promises lightly and this one was for life. A very different life than she had lived for almost ten years. Would a kiss tell her the truth?

She walked into Quinn's arms as though she belonged there, and he gathered her in without any urgency and yet with a certainty that seemed to say that he knew this was right too.

His body felt solid and safe against hers, and they stood together for a while, not moving or speaking. When they had been this close before, they had been dancing, or locked in an urgent, dangerous kiss. Now Cat found herself, eyes shut, relaxing against his strength, her head resting against his shoulder, his heart beating against her breast, learning him with all her senses.

When, at last, she tipped back her head to look up at him, she saw his eyes had been closed too. He bent to kiss her and she moved with him, eager now, remembering the taste of him, the feel of his mouth against hers, the heat.

She parted for him as his tongue touched her lips, felt again the shock of how unfamiliar he was after the two men she had known before, the first so urgent, so careless of her, the other, her husband, so politely respectful.

Quinn was not polite, but he was careful, caring, even as he gathered her in closer, his body demanding, yet controlled, his tongue exploring, igniting the heat and the need in her.

Cat found her arms were twined around his neck and she was on tiptoe. *I could climb him like a tree, I could pull him to the floor here and now, I could... I could take him upstairs to my bed.*

Quinn broke the kiss and they stood, his forehead against hers, both of them panting a little.

'I think we had better stop,' Quinn said. 'The desire to take you on this floor, on your desk, against the wall, is becoming somewhat hard to ignore.'

The temptation to simply turn and lead the way upstairs was almost overwhelming, but some little flicker of caution remained. Once they had lain together the die was irrevocably cast, there would be no going back from there.

And then another thought struck her. 'Quinn, I have never become pregnant. What if I cannot give you an heir?'

He kept her in the circle of his arms as he listened to her. 'You had a lucky escape with Wykeham. With your husband…he was a widower, I think?' She nodded. 'And without children by his first wife? Well, there you are. And he was not a man in the best of health, you said? Um, was he a very…demanding husband?'

Cat could feel herself blushing. 'Er, no, not very.'

'Then there is no reason to suppose that you cannot conceive a child with someone else, don't you think?'

She nodded.

'Does that question mean you have made a decision?'

He had never said he loved her, but she was certain

that he cared for her, liked her, desired her. And she loved him. That was enough, surely?

'Yes, Quinn. I will marry you.'

'Certain?' There was a smile in his voice, but also a trace of anxiety.

'Certain,' she replied and looked up at him, suddenly completely sure.

Chapter Twenty-One

'I think we should go and break the news to your parents before anyone else,' Quinn said. 'They are at Harland Park.'

'They are? Isn't that somewhat awkward for you?'

'I could hardly abandon them at the inn once I knew about their dreadful journey, and I thought the further away from you the better, at least while we came to an agreement on what we were going to do.'

'Yes, I can see that.' Cat stepped back and began to rearrange his neckcloth which had suffered from the enthusiasm of their embrace. It felt like a very wifely thing to be doing, and she found she was blushing all over again. 'I had better go and change into something more suitable.' She waved a hand vaguely at her sensible day dress, one of those she wore to work in the shop.

'I agree, it would probably reassure Lady Bowland if you appear as conventional as possible, at least until we are married,' Quinn said with a grin. 'Do you realise how happy you have made me, Cat?'

'I hope I will. I hope I will be a good duchess,' she said as she went to the door to the stairs. 'I won't be long.'

From draper to duchess. What was she thinking? Yes, she had been raised to be the wife of a man of high position, but a duke had never entered Mama's head, she was certain. It had never entered hers, even in dreams.

But Quinn had been in her dreams ever since she had seen him through the honeysuckle…

She stopped at the head of the stairs, then ran down again and looked into the office. 'Please, could you ask Helen to come up to me?' She couldn't change into the walking dress she had in mind without help.

Helen joined her after a few minutes. She stared at the smart, and very new, outfit Cat had laid out on the bed. 'You are going out?'

Cat took a deep breath. Telling someone was going to make this real. 'I am going with the Duke to Harland Park to tell my parents that we are to be married.'

Helen sat down on the end of the bed as though her legs had given way. 'You will be a *duchess*.'

'Yes, but I don't want you and Ben to worry about what might happen afterwards. I thought you could take over as joint managers of the shop and run it for me. On an increased wage, of course, to reflect the extra responsibility. But we can talk about it together, the three of us, and you must say what would be best for you and I will make that happen.'

'Manager?' Helen's eyes were wide. 'Oh, ma'am. Cat. Thank you!'

'I will speak to Ben on my way out and then have a longer discussion with you this evening when I am clearer about what our plans are and how long everything will take. And this is a secret—again, I have no idea how we are going to manage the news.'

'Goodness, yes.' Helen was fanning herself with one hand and clearly had no idea she was doing so. 'What a stir this will cause in Duke's Forde.'

'I had much rather it didn't,' Cat said grimly. Telling Helen she was going to marry Quinn—making her the first person to know—felt a bit like taking a step on a ladder and hearing the rung below drop off. There was no way back, not now she had promised Helen such an opportunity.

When she went downstairs, the shop was empty, so she told Ben her news quickly, obtained his somewhat stunned promise not to say anything and went outside to find Quinn waiting for her in his smart phaeton with a tiger in livery at its head.

Quinn got down to help her up, took the reins, and the lad ran round and jumped up onto his perch as the carriage moved off. There would be no chance of talking about any of the things that were clamouring to be spoken of with him right behind them.

It was not until they reached the front steps of Harland Park, after a drive in near silence, that Cat was free to speak.

'I told Helen and Ben,' she said. 'I have said they will be joint managers if they wish. Quinn, there is so much to untangle!'

'A positive cat's cradle of a tangle,' he agreed as they mounted the steps. 'But it is a question of finding the end of the piece of string and patiently working our way along it.'

'And Blaine Wykeham. I am so worried about him and his wretched book.'

'I have had some thoughts about that,' Quinn said as the front door opened and the butler bowed them inside. 'But all in due time.'

'Your Grace, madam.'

'Whiting.' Quinn handed his hat and gloves to the footman, who hastened forward at a gesture from the butler. 'Where are Lord and Lady Bowland?'

'In the Blue Salon, Your Grace.'

'Have tea sent through, and then we do not wish to be disturbed.'

'Your Grace.'

'Right, let us begin untangling,' Quinn said to her and guided her to the door on the right.

It opened onto a very elegant drawing room with

blue moiré silk on the walls and furniture in a darker shade of the same colour. Her father stood up as they entered and her mother, seated on a gilt-legged sofa, gave a little cry at the sight of Cat on Quinn's arm.

He guided her to a seat and took another so, when her father sat down again on the sofa, they formed a tringle with a low table in the middle.

'Tea is being sent up,' Quinn said. 'We can then talk undisturbed.'

Her mother made an obvious effort to stifle the questions on her lips and said instead, 'What a charming walking dress, Caitlin.'

'Thank you. I employ several skilled seamstresses to make up designs for my clients based on the latest fashion plates.'

Her mother winced at the mention of clients but said nothing as footmen brought in the tea tray and plates of small cakes.

When the door was closed behind them, Quinn said, 'Lady Caitlin has done me the honour of accepting my hand in marriage. I believe this would be acceptable to you?'

Her father opened his mouth, closed it again and nodded.

'Although, of course as she is of age and a widow, consent is not needed.

'What is required, however, is a way of tying up the loose ends and to do that we must all work together.

According to what Society believes, Lady Caitlin has been living retired since June 1809, when in fact she has been living here, lately as Mrs Brandon, her married name.'

'Apparently I have been residing at Sundley Manor,' Cat said, suddenly seeing a way around at least part of the conundrum. 'Which is in Norfolk. Quinn, you have a house in Norfolk, have you not?'

'I have. Willington Hall. It was my great uncle's preferred residence.'

'How far apart are they?' Cat asked.

Everyone looked blank, then Quinn got up. 'I will find a map.'

While he was gone, Cat poured tea, passed cakes and made no attempt to break the silence. Clearly, her parents were at a loss over how to deal with her.

Quinn returned with a map of Norfolk, which he placed on the table, pushing aside a plate of scones. 'There,' he said after a moment, pointing. 'Sundley Manor is fifteen miles north of Willington and lies between it and Holt. I think that it is perfectly feasible that we could have met in Norfolk. We will work on that a little, make certain we have a consistent story to tell. I suspect we encountered each other on one of my visits to my great-uncle, became close and now, with my mourning over, we can announce our marriage.'

'I meanwhile, have grown out of my shyness and

fear of large gatherings, and am ready to rejoin Society,' Cat said.

'Excellent. Now then, Duke's Forde presents a different problem. This is my principal country seat. Unless I stop coming here, or you stay away, there is the risk you will be recognised.'

Her mother gave a faint moan. *'Trade.'*

'You know, people see what they expect to see,' Cat said thoughtfully. 'They are used to Mrs Brandon in her modest, sensible clothes, running a drapery. Will they recognise the Duchess of Harland in her far more fashionable gowns, her new hairstyle, if they have no reason to make the connection? Especially if it is some time between me leaving the town and returning here to Harland Park as the Duchess. It means I will have to restrict my appearances in the town, I suppose, which is a pity.

'Madelaine knows the truth, as do Helen and Ben. I trust Michael Dangerfield and, if he is to marry Madelaine, then it will be necessary to tell him. I think too, that I will tell the Vicar and his wife, whose discretion I can trust. That just leaves the staff here. Mr Yorke has met me as Mrs Brandon, so has Mr Turnbull. Then there is that little maid who sat with us the first time I came here and your tiger and the grooms in the stable yard.'

'Milly has left to live with her ailing mother in Oxford,' Quinn said. 'Yorke and Turnbull are both completely trustworthy. As for Garnett, my tiger, and the grooms, they have all been with me a long time, since before I inherited. They are not gossips and, I suspect, that if I say nothing about it, they will just accept you without question. If anything does get out, from whatever source, then we react with complete indifference. Blank incomprehension is far better than denials.'

Quinn grinned at Cat. 'It is taking me a while to become used to being a duke, but the extent of my influence is, finally, beginning to dawn on me. If whispers begin, we simply ignore them. If anything is said, we look incredulous and, if anyone spreads rumours maliciously, then they are dealt with.'

Cat thought this was probably not the time to ask exactly how they would be *dealt with*. The way Quinn listened to her thoughts, then came back with his, as though they were playing a two-handed game, delighted her. It felt like a partnership and not at all what she had feared marriage to an aristocratic husband would be like.

Early days, that little inner voice murmured. She ignored it.

'That is all very reassuring. But what about that swine, Wykeham?' her father demanded.

'I agree that he is the main danger,' Quinn said. 'How did he approach you? In person?'

'No, by letter. I would have wrung the dastard's neck for him if he had shown his face with that story.'

'And did he give you any evidence that this book of memoirs exists? A printed page from it, or even a manuscript section? The name of a publisher?'

'No.' Her father looked puzzled. 'Why, would you expect him to?'

'If I was attempting to extort money in that way, I would certainly include evidence to ensure the maximum certainty that I could do what I was threatening,' Quinn said. 'Tell me about Wykeham's reputation. I can't recall hearing anything about him and, obviously, his name cannot have been so black that he was not received, or your daughter would never have met him.'

'He is the great-nephew of the Bishop of Wessex and is shunned by the family, but apparently they did not make his misdeeds known because it reflected on them,' Lady Bowland said bitterly. 'Thus exposing innocent girls to his wiles. We only discovered this after he and Caitlin eloped, and I heard whispers about him leaving London and learning of several young ladies in some distress because he had been courting them too.'

'And have you heard anything of him since?' Quinn asked.

They shook their heads and Cat said, 'But if he has written a book of shocking memoirs to scandalise and blackmail Society, where *are* all these awful misdeeds? Who are these other well-bred ladies he has seduced? Where has he been?'

'I wouldn't be surprised if he hasn't been living off his wits in various towns and cities a safe distance from London,' Quinn said. 'Perhaps he is losing his youthful looks and is finding it harder to seduce merchants' daughters or charm his way out of gambling frauds.'

'Or possibly his family have cut off an allowance,' Lord Bowland said, suddenly looking much more alert. 'So he decides to try and extract money from the one *ton* affair that he was responsible for and which he knows was kept secret. By gad, I would like to get my hands on him!'

'Horsewhip, sir?' Quinn asked. 'I will hold your coat. We need to discover his whereabouts and deal with him. I will put my enquiry agent on to it. Where did you send the money?'

'Hendry and Cromford's bank in Dover. And he was using an accommodation address in the town.'

'Then that's the place to start. Let me have the details and I will set my man to work. Useful that Wykeham's on the coast—sending him off to the Continent seems a good solution.'

'He might come back,' Lady Bowland said nervously.

'Not if he is scared enough.' Quinn's smile was chilling. 'But to speak of more pleasant matters. I suggest that Lady Caitlin, having dealt with her affairs here, travels to Sundley Manor and then to London, where she can re-emerge into Society and everything will proceed from there.'

Her parents greeted that plan with enthusiasm, and Cat sat back, sipped her cooling tea and tried to think about all the practical things she must do before she could leave. Instead she found all she could do was look at Quinn.

This was the man she was going to marry, the man who would make her a duchess. That, strangely, was the least of her worries. It might take her a while to find her feet again in Society—not that she had had much of a place there before—but its ways would soon come back to her and a lot would be excused to the betrothed of a duke. To her face, at least. The mamas of hopeful young ladies would be sending her dagger-looks behind her back, she was sure.

No, it was Quinn himself who was making her so uneasy. Most *ton* marriages were not love matches, in fact such a thing was thought a trifle vulgar and definitely unsophisticated. But Cat wanted love. She had eloped out of love and had been betrayed. She had married for affection and security and had been… comfortable. But always she had yearned, had dreamt, that there was the right man for her somewhere and, if she found him, he would feel the same for her.

But Quinn had never told her he loved her and he'd

had plenty of opportunities. He liked her, desired her, saw her as a friend. All of those things were wonderful to find in a husband, and she should be truly thankful, but still she felt that cold little ache deep inside.

One thing was certain, he must never know how she felt. How dreadful to have him pity her, be kind to her. Or perhaps distance himself from her because he feared she might be clingy and embarrassingly needy. The possibilities grew in her mind as she thought about them to the point where she almost jumped to her feet and declared she could not, would not, do it.

With an effort of self-control Cat made herself sit still, kept the smile on her lips, found herself pouring tea and passing cakes. She could do this. She had faced ruin and fought her way to a contented, productive life. She could use that strength to make a happy marriage, and one day, perhaps, Quinn might find he loved her.

One day.

Chapter Twenty-Two

Quinn excused himself, saying that he would find his agent, Foster, who was in the house, and set him on Blaine Wykeham's trail while Cat talked to her parents. Then he would drive her back to Duke's Forde.

Foster was clearly braced for an ignominious dismissal after the horrors of Louis Beaufoy's arrival and death but, now Quinn had had a chance to think it through, he could see it was not the man's fault and told him so.

He gave Foster all the information he had about Wykeham and saw, as he was speaking, Lord Bowland strolling up and down on the terrace. He had probably fled from feminine discussions about weddings, Quinn thought, which reminded him that negotiations about marriage settlements loomed on his own horizon. That would be simple enough, he had no desire to do anything but ensure Cat had a very generous settlement.

Leaving Foster scouring the reference books in the

library for details of the Bishop of Wessex's family and their residences, Quinn strolled back to the Blue Salon. The door was ajar and he stopped and listened, unwilling to break in on any intimate conversation between mother and daughter.

'Really, it is like something from a novel,' Lady Bowland was saying. 'So romantic. I never thought that love matches were sensible—there is so much else that must be considered than that in a suitable match—but really, for you to fall in love with a duke, Caitlin, quite makes up for all that has gone before.'

'I have not fallen in love, Mama,' Cat said sharply, just as he was about to move away and stop eavesdropping.

Quinn froze.

'I like the Duke very well and he is an attractive, intelligent man with many fine qualities. We are, I believe, friends. But to talk of love, as though I was some giddy eighteen-year-old, is ridiculous. I have had my fingers burned once by fancying myself in love, believe me. I have every intention of doing my utmost to be a good wife, the perfect duchess, but this talk of romance is embarrassing, Mama.'

It took an effort, as though pulling his feet out of deep mud, for Quinn to move, but he forced himself away from the door, across the hallway and let himself out of the front door. He closed it behind him and stood where he had with Cat, that first time she had come to Harland Park. This was the place where she had made him see how fortunate he was, understand just what he had here.

He hadn't meant to fall in love, hadn't expected it, but he had and, with Cat's friendship, her passionate responses to him, he had fallen into the trap of believing that she loved him too, that he only had to tell her of it when they were alone and with no risk of being disturbed and she would admit her feelings.

It was a mercy that he had not spoken. This hurt, but not as much as seeing her trying to be kind would have done, he knew that. Somehow he must keep his feelings hidden.

Cat emerged about ten minutes later, declaring that she must get back to the shop because she had so much to attend to. He noticed that she kissed her parents, so hopefully there was the beginning of a rapprochement. It would give rise to even more comment if Lady Caitlin was seen to be estranged from her family.

He left Garnett, his tiger, behind for the return journey, but he did not take advantage of their privacy to try and talk, there was too much to absorb.

They had reached the outskirts of the town when Cat suddenly said, 'I cannot do it.'

'You cannot marry me?' He reined in the pair, fortunately outside someone's orchard and not close to any observers.

'No, not that. I will marry you, but I will not lie about my past. The more we do that, the more we open ourselves up to rumour and scandal. And I want to be a good duchess, one who does her best for her tenants and employees and the local communities,' she added passionately. 'I cannot do that at arm's length. There is still so much to be done here—a school, for a start.'

Quinn took a deep breath. His instinct was to do whatever it took to protect Cat, but not if it made her unhappy. 'How do we tell the truth and not expose your parents' prevarications?'

'As they told everyone, we say I went to live at Sundley Manor, but after a year or so I became unhappy there and decided to travel a little. I arrived at Duke's Forde one afternoon and witnessed William's accident. I looked after him, we fell for each other and married. We can gloss over the fact that I was employed by him for a while first and refer to him as a merchant, I think.

'Such a misalliance naturally offended my parents, causing a breach between us. Then you came to Harland Park, we met and there we have it. Minimal untruths and enough of a mild scandal admitted to, to keep the gossips happy.'

'The fact that you are in trade is more than a mild scandal,' Quinn observed, although he did like the notion of keeping as close to the truth as was possible without admitting to her elopement with Blaine Wykeham. 'You may find yourself cold-shouldered.'

Cat shrugged. 'Only by people whose opinion I care nothing for. But I should have thought how it would affect you,' she added, sounding discouraged. 'I'm sorry.'

'No, you are quite correct. We can well do without acquaintances who would disparage us because of that. And I am a duke, something I am beginning to become used to. Offending me might prove awkward. Whether or not you will be received at Court, I do not know. We shall see.'

'If you are content that we tell virtually the whole truth, then I have to admit, I feel much better. I prefer to meet trouble head-on and not hide from it. Deception just leaves traps waiting to snare us.'

'I admire your courage, Cat, I have from when I first learned your story. You have a strong will as well as physical courage.' He clicked his tongue and the pair walked on.

'Perhaps I have Blaine Wykeham to thank for that after all. When I realised what had happened I knew I had two choices—either I gave in to despair and slunk back home or I faced up to what had happened and made a new life for myself.'

Quinn shifted his reins to his whip hand and reached out to lift Cat's right hand to his lips. 'My brave duchess.'

Her hand trembled in his, but she did not withdraw it. Should he tell her? Declare his love, despite knowing what her reaction would be? She would be kind about it, he was certain of that. Kind and affectionate and understanding, because that was the kind of woman she was. No, that would put an unfair burden on her shoulders and she had quite enough to bear as it was. And, he admitted to himself, he would feel humiliated at being the recipient of her kindly pity.

The usual lads were hanging around the market square and came running to hold his horses while he helped Cat down.

'When shall we meet again? How would it be if I send a carriage for you mid-morning tomorrow, and we can spend the day making plans? Stay for dinner—there will be a full moon and the carriage can bring you safely back afterwards.'

The church clock stuck one and a *clunk*.

'I am going to get that confounded thing repaired,' he said, glaring at the tower.

'Oh, no. Don't do that,' Cat protested. 'No other town has a church clock that both chimes and clunks! We would miss it. And yes, send for me tomorrow.'

She stood there, hesitating and looking suddenly vulnerable, and he lifted her hand to his lips again.

'*Au voir,* Cat.'

He drove away without looking back. *Love me, love my clock...* His heart felt as though it was likely to go *clunk* at any beat when he thought of her. *I will make you happy, Cat, I swear it and that will be enough for me. It must be...*

Was she asking too much of Quinn to reveal virtually all of her story? Cat wondered, her eyes on his back as he drove away. He could have said *No*, that they would adhere to the plan they had made with her parents, she supposed, but perhaps, like her, he thought this was safest in the long term.

He could hardly take back his offer now, of course, not unless she did something utterly outrageous. A gentleman, once he had offered marriage, could not honourably withdraw. A lady might do so, and perhaps she would have done if he had shown the slightest reluctance to do as she suggested.

But she knew Quinn well now, and he had been open with her in the way he had considered what she had suggested.

Cat fixed a smile on her face and entered the shop where she was promptly swept up into a discussion of the latest fashion in sleeves according to *La Belle Assemblée,* freshly delivered and being pored over by a group of eager ladies.

When they finally left, Cat locked the front door, put up the Closed sign and swept Ben and Helen into the kitchen.

'We eat and we plan,' she announced. Here, at least,

she was on firm ground, and she found her two assistants had been thinking and planning too.

'Madame Arnaud and Mr Dangerfield are getting married in a month's time,' Helen told her. 'She came to leave invitations for all of us this morning. And Mr Dangerfield and Phoebe are moving in to her house. Which means that there are two rooms that Ben could rent from Mr Dangerfield as an apartment, because there will just be his journeyman and apprentice living over the shop.

'Then if we take on a female apprentice, she can live here with me and that will all be perfectly respectable,' she finished, breathlessly. 'We haven't asked Mr Dangerfield yet, because obviously we couldn't reveal your news, and anyway, you might have changed your mind about us. It is a big responsibility.'

'It is,' Cat agreed. 'And one you are both well able to cope with. I have every confidence in you. Now, let's start thinking about the details.'

By the time that Quinn arrived to take her back to Harland Park the next day, virtually everything had been discussed, notes made and all the financial details outlined. There were lists everywhere of things to be decided and things to be done, and they still had to draft an advertisement for an apprentice, although Helen had several girls in mind.

'We can save the cost of advertising if I approach

them directly,' she had said, and Cat had to repress her smile over the instinct for economy now they would have control of the finances.

The stimulus of planning and a good night's sleep had restored her spirits considerably, and she was able to snatch up her bonnet and run out with a smile on her face when she saw the phaeton draw up outside.

The following two weeks saw Cat's smile replaced by pursed lips or a furrowed brow for much of the time. There was so much to do, to plan, to think about, and her mother's focus on her reintroduction into Society, her gowns and the wedding threatened to overwhelm everything else.

She broke the news to the Vicar and Mrs Newnham and to her regular customers and found, to her amazement, that none of them seemed very surprised and that she detected no criticism either.

'They are happy for you,' Madelaine said. 'You are part of the town and have been loyal to us—and they will be loyal to you, especially as everyone likes the Duke.'

Her parents went back to London after two weeks and Cat prepared to follow them after Madelaine and Michael's wedding, ten days later. The sun shone for it, the town was *en fête* and, instead of a wedding breakfast, there was a party at the Harland Arms.

Cat saw Helen dancing with James Turnbull and

looked up anxiously at Quinn beside her. 'That is beginning to look serious. Do you mind?'

'Why should I? She is intelligent, well-spoken, hard-working and confident. She can be nothing but an asset to him in his career. I can see that young Ben is soon going to find himself the sole manager of a draper's shop.'

He led her onto the dance floor for the next set, and Cat wondered why she was feeling rather flat. Perhaps it was Quinn's scrupulous restraint now they were betrothed. She had expected, hoped for, kisses, but he seemed to feel that a polite peck on the cheek was enough. No doubt he was already thinking ahead to how things must be once she entered Society again, she reassured herself. She must relearn how to go on within the strict bounds of acceptable behaviour.

Chapter Twenty-Three

'Upon my word! Lady Caitlin Montgomery, back in London. I hardly recognised you.' Lady Trent's expression was avid as she scanned Cat from head to toe. 'How you have changed.'

'It is Lady Caitlin Brandon now, Lady Trent.' Cat's smile was every bit as sweet and as false. 'And one does change in eight years, I am sure you'll agree.'

That little barb went home, Cat thought. There was only so much that powder and dye could do to disguise wrinkles and greying hair. Not that there was anything wrong with either, unless you were obsessed with appearances.

'Married? So that ridiculous rumour that you are to marry Harland is false.'

'No, it is quite correct. My first husband died some time ago.'

Around them in the large drawing room of the Trents' London house, heads turned slightly, ears pricking, Cat was sure. It was some time until the

Season began, but people were drifting back to London, and the more energetic hostesses were already beginning to entertain.

'Oh. Brandon? One of the Sussex Brandons, perhaps?'

'No, my husband was a merchant.' This reception, the first social occasion since her return to London was her opportunity to drop that little bombshell.

Lady Trent drew in a sharp breath.

'A short marriage, sadly, but a happy one,' Cat said, affecting not to notice the whispers around her. 'Do excuse me, I have just seen Lady Wilsborough, and I know Mama particularly wishes to speak to her. So lovely to talk.'

She drifted off into the throng, looking for the next person to drop a hint to about her past life. Ah yes, Miss Perrott, who had come out the same Season she had, and who was now married to Augustus Farely, a banker.

They greeted each other with delight—entirely assumed on Cat's part—and, as she expected, Mrs Farely had no hesitation in asking what had become of her.

'I became weary of country life, delightful though the Manor is, but I still did not feel strong enough for London's excitements, so I decided to travel and found myself in a delightful little town near Oxford.'

When she and her parents were finally seated in

the carriage, driving home again to Park Street, her mother seemed pleased.

'The word is spreading—first about dear Harland, of course, and then the little snippets we have been letting drop. It is clear nobody knows quite how to take it. You are not at all ashamed of your first marriage, so they assume he must have been exceedingly wealthy, which makes all the difference. And, of course, the fact that he is deceased,' she added.

Cat bit her tongue.

'And the way you look, of course, greatly helps,' Lady Bowland continued, undeterred by her daughter's silence. 'Such an excellent gown and everything in the best taste and fashion. Really, I would never have thought you would turn out to such advantage. Dear Anna was always the pretty one, but you have style.'

Cat rather thought that this was the first genuine compliment she had ever received from her mother. 'Thank you, Mama. It did go well, I thought.'

'And Harland's absence was helpful, I think. It allowed the first shock of your reappearance and the tale of what had been happening to be absorbed. When they next see you, it will be in his company, and that will allow everyone to see how well-suited you are.'

Lady Brandon fell silent and Cat thought she had dropped into a light doze.

'Have you heard anything from Wykeham, Papa?' she asked quietly.

'Nothing since I wrote to the accommodation address and demanded to see actual proof of this book of his. That was two weeks ago.'

'His bluff has been called, then,' Cat said with satisfaction. 'That will be the last we will hear of him, I am sure.'

The next day the news sheets were full of her return. The more reputable commented on the appearance of Lady C—B— at Lady Trent's reception. The more popular mentioned that Lady C—B— had been Lady C—M— and had been absent from Society for some years. The out-and-out gossip sheets referred to a merchant first husband and Cat's mysterious disappearance eight years before.

'It could be very much worse,' her mother decided after they had read them all. 'Provided nothing occurs to create more talk, then I believe all is safe.'

Because of the time of year, one could not expect invitations every day, and it was the end of the week before Cat found herself strolling on the lawns of the Marquis of Falmouth's estate at Richmond where the Marchioness had decided to hold a picnic.

As picnics went, it was magnificent and the weather

obliged with sunshine, warm breezes and a blue sky, a perfect late September day.

Lady Falmouth's idea of a picnic was about as rustic as Queen Marie Antoinette's concept of a milkmaid's cottage, Cat thought, viewing the lawns sloping down to the Thames. Long tables were set out to receive a veritable banquet, and groups of chairs placed so no guest had to recline on the ground unless they wished—there were rugs and heaps of cushions dotted about in the shade.

Discreet retiring tents had been set up for ladies and gentlemen so that nobody had to walk up to the house for any reason, and footmen were swooping on arrivals with trays laden with glasses of champagne, lemonade and other drinks.

Punts and rowing boats bobbed at the end of mooring lines beside a jetty, should any gentleman wish to demonstrate his prowess with the oars, she saw as she strolled down to look more closely.

She wondered if any proposals would occur in the intimacy of one of those little vessels. What would she have said if Quinn had proposed to her as he had planned on the night of the Duke's Forde assembly? *Yes*, she decided. And they would probably still have been on the river when her parents arrived and were taken in to spend the night. They would have moved on without ever knowing she was there and she would probably never have known that Quinn had investigated her past.

I would have had to tell him who I am, she thought. *Perhaps he relied on that so he never had to reveal what he had done, what he knew. Or am I being very unfair?*

Perhaps. Probably, she told herself firmly as she wandered along the riverbank. If only Quinn was rather more demonstrative. Those passionate kisses seemed a very long time in the past now. Was it because he was behaving as any conventional suitor would, now they were back in London? Or was it because that first violent attraction they had both felt had faded for him now she was no longer a novelty, a mystery?

It was very quiet down there. Cat looked around and saw that most people were still clustered at the top of the lawn, talking, and had not yet begun to explore. It was early yet, of course, about eleven o'clock, and the food would be unlikely to appear before two.

It was very pleasant to be alone, she realised, relishing the absence of people with whom one must make conversation but, at the same time, say nothing of any actual depth or interest. Nothing challenging, nothing that indicated that a lady might have opinions and ideas. Mama had been very firm about that—Cat had enough problems without appearing to be a bluestocking or an eccentric.

I shall be as eccentric as I like once I am a duchess, she thought rebelliously. *I wonder when Quinn will get here?*

They had not appeared together in public yet, and Mama had decided that this relatively informal occasion would be ideal.

A few people were beginning to drift down the slope, drawn by the picturesque river view, so Cat turned towards the weeping willows that lined the far end of the lawns, their drooping boughs making domes of privacy.

It was pleasantly cool in the dappled shade, and Cat decided to linger there for a few minutes before making her way up to find her mother, who was probably beginning to become anxious about where she had got to.

A pair of ducks swam up looking hopeful and she went down to the water's edge.

'I have nothing for you, I'm afraid,' she told them.

'But I hope you have something for me.'

Cat turned to find herself confronting a man. A complete stranger or…no, there was something familiar. Horribly familiar.

Blaine Wykeham was eight years older, and those eight years had left the marks of self-indulgence and hard living on his face and body. His stomach bulged where it was confined by a waistcoat that looked, to Cat, as though it had been sponged and cleaned far too often. He had the beginnings of a double chin and his face was flushed, his eyes had bags beneath them and the handsome young man she had fallen in love with looked forty at least.

His formal suit had been a good one once, but now would only just pass muster amongst the fashionable set gathered there that morning.

'Wykeham? What on earth are you doing here?' Cat demanded. 'I cannot believe you have been invited.'

Of all the banal things to say! She realised that her fists were clenched and that, if she'd had a weapon in them, she would have used it.

'No, but it was simple enough to stroll in. What I want, my dear Caitlin, is money. I am sure that if the whispers I hear are true, you will be very glad if I went away and kept silent about one night at a certain inn…'

'You mean the inn where you stole money and jewellery from me?'

And my innocence and my old life.

'And what happened there before I left,' he said.

'You'll get nothing from me, nor any more from my family,' she retorted. 'Although I can see by the look of you it is needed. What have you done? Drunk it all?'

Wykeham was on her before she could do more than raise one hand to slap his face. He seized that wrist, then the other, and pulled her close.

'You do not look like a gentleman any longer and

you certainly do not smell like one either,' she threw at him. 'No money even for laundry, Blaine?'

Her heart was banging against her ribs and her throat was dry, but she was so angry that she was conscious of fear only as a background sensation. Was she so close that she could not raise her knee? Or perhaps if she threw her weight to one side and got him off balance—

Suddenly he was gone. There was a thud and she saw he had been thrown back against the trunk of the tree and was clutching his head, half-stunned. She teetered, losing her balance herself now, and a hand clasped her wrist, pulled her away from the water's edge and against a large, solid and wonderfully familiar chest.

'Quinn. Thank heavens.'

'Are you unharmed?' He was staring down at her with an expression in his eyes that she had never seen before.

'Yes. Disgusted, but quite unhurt. Quinn, this is—'

'I know who it is. Foster has been following him for a week. He left Dover three days ago. By chance I met Foster as I was arriving here, so we advanced our plans a little. I am sorry we did not reach you before he made himself a nuisance. You had better return to your mother while I deal with this.' He gestured towards Wykeham.

'What are you going to do with him? Not the river?

Although he needs a good bath, drowning him might cause more problems than it solves.' Her forced laugh sounded somewhat hysterical to her own ears, and Cat made herself take a deep, calming breath.

'Foster is taking him to Bristol for a nice long sea voyage. To Jamaica. Very unhealthy place, the West Indies, so I hear.' He moved away from her, leaving her feeling cold, took hold of Wykeham's shoulder and gave a piercing whistle. 'You go before Foster and the grooms arrive, Cat. I'll see you shortly.'

'Very well.' She twitched at her Villager hat until it was sitting properly, gave her skirts a shake and pushed aside the dangling leaves. Foster and two large men emerged from the shrubbery and ducked under the willow, and she walked up the lawn towards the party, trying to work out how she felt.

Disgusted with Blaine Wykeham and appalled at the deterioration in him, certainly. No wonder he was desperate for funds, because he was not going to charm any innocent and romantic young ladies any longer. Very grateful to Quinn for coming to her rescue and dealing with Wykeham, of course. But he had been all business. He had held her, but only to prevent her falling in the Thames. He hadn't even kissed her cheek.

She had almost reached the first group of picnickers who were finding seats now, the ladies and more dignified gentlemen taking the chairs, the younger men reclining amidst the cushions like so many Turkish pashas.

Cat smiled, waved at the few people she recognised, and finally spotted Lady Bowland taking her place with several matrons of her own age under a great cedar tree.

'Mama,' she said, taking the chair next to her. 'I have just seen Harland, who was talking to that writer. You recall? The one whose fiction we thought far too highly priced? The Duke was equally unimpressed and has dealt with his importunities. Goodness knows how such a man got in here.'

Lady Bowland stared at her for a moment then went pale. 'Here?' she whispered.

'Harland is removing him,' Cat murmured back, then, unwilling to seem to be sharing secrets, added in normal conversational tones, 'He is leaving the country, I understand. The author, that is, not Harland.'

'Harland?' Lady Falminster sitting on the other side to her mother leant forward. 'You are acquainted with the Duke, Lady Caitlin?'

Cat was very conscious that word had spread about her first marriage and that everyone was treating her with a certain distance, presumably alert for her showing any regrettably mercantile behaviour.

'Oh, yes,' she said and did her best to look demure. 'Harland Park is close to where I have been living and the Duke involved himself very much in the social life of the town, as well as in various charitable matters.'

'I see.' Lady Falminster clearly did not *see* at all. Lady Caitlin Montgomery and a duke, yes. Lady Caitlin, widow of a merchant, and a duke, no, that did not fit with her expectations in any way.

At which point, just as the other ladies in the group were pricking up their ears and turning to look at Cat, Quinn appeared from the direction of the house. He strolled down the slope, stopping frequently to greet other guests and then, as he passed their tree, glanced across and immediately changed direction.

'Lady Falminster, Lady Bowland, Mrs Dorrington, Mrs Percival.' He bowed to all the older ladies and then turned to Cat. 'And Lady Caitlin. You are already much missed in Duke's Forde.'

Cat thought there was no mistaking, from his tone, who was missing her the most. She could almost feel the attention of the other ladies focusing on them.

'Your Grace,' she said, willing herself to blush.

'Can you spare Lady Caitlin to me, Lady Bowland?' Quinn asked. 'This is too lovely a day for a gentleman not to have an equally lovely lady on his arm.'

That really did make her blush, and she got to her feet, hardly hearing her mother's complaisant agreement.

Chapter Twenty-Four

'What an outrageous piece of flattery,' Cat scolded as they strolled away. 'Really, you will have all the gossips expecting you to go down on one knee and produce a large ring here and now.'

'I can do, if you would like me to,' Quinn said. 'I have the ring in my pocket.'

'You... You do?' He was teasing her, surely?

'I fetched it from Rundell, Bridge & Rundell this morning. Most of the family jewellery is in their vaults. Is your father here?'

'Papa? Yes, he is over there with Lord Falmouth, by the little pavilion where they seem to be serving ices.'

'Well, in that case, shall we go over? I will fetch you an ice, then be seen to take Lord Bowland to one side for an earnest discussion, then I will come back and, having obtained his consent, propose. I am quite happy to kneel if you would like that.'

'*Quinn*. For one thing we do not need Papa's permission, for another we know he is delighted that we intend to marry and thirdly, think what a stir we would cause!'

'Exactly. I find I have no patience for pretending to a lengthy public courtship. Now we are being open about your first marriage and the fact that we met at Duke's Forde, I see no need for complications. The egregious Mr Wykeham is off on his travels. Let's set the *ton* in a turmoil and make Lady Falmouth's picnic the talk of the town.'

It was daring, but Quinn's high spirits were infectious, and it was as though she had her friend back again and not the correct and formal gentleman of recent weeks.

'Yes,' she said. 'I am already weary of behaving myself as I ought and obeying all these rules. We are going to cause talk and controversy whatever we do, so let's manage it in our own way.'

Quinn escorted her to a table close to the little Chinese pavilion. He brought her a strawberry ice, much to the barely concealed interest of the occupants of the surrounding tables, and then strode off to detach Lord Brownlow from his conversation with Lord Falmouth.

Cat savoured her ice cream until, a few minutes later, Quinn returned.

'Lady Caitlin.'

'Your Grace.'

Quinn went down on one knee and produced a small green leather box which he opened with a flick of his thumbnail. Caitlin, already on the verge of laughing through sheer nerves almost asked him if he had removed a snuff box by mistake. Then she saw what was inside and all desire to laugh left her.

She raised her eyes from the emerald surrounded by diamonds that flashed in the sunlight and met Quinn's gaze. He was serious, intent, and the sound of gasps and whispers all around them faded away.

'Lady Caitlin, you know of my deep regard and affection for you. Will you do me the honour of becoming my wife?'

'Yes, I will. Gladly.'

Quinn took her hand, slipped on the ring and leaned forward and kissed her on the lips. 'You have made me the happiest of men.'

Cat wished she could be certain of that, but Quinn was standing up, holding out his hand to her and she let him lead her towards her father, who was beaming at them.

Around them the guests were unashamedly staring. And smiling, she realised with surprise. There was even a ripple of applause.

Her father kissed her, and the three of them began to walk towards the great cedar where her mother was still sitting.

Cat clung to Quinn's arm, trying to recover from what had happened. It had all been so fast. First Wykeham's appearance, then Quinn's flamboyant public gesture.

They had talked of weeks of courtship under the eyes of the *ton* but it seemed he could not wait. When she looked up and saw his expression, his smile, the look of fondness in his eyes, her spirits soared.

Perhaps he does love me after all.

Word was spreading fast, in that miraculous way that it did in this world. Little whispers, nods, gestures. Everywhere she looked Cat saw approval, or in the case of hopeful mamas with daughters to marry well, disappointment and some resentment. Gone were the reserved looks she had been receiving, the faint air of puzzlement over how to treat the daughter of an earl who had done a shocking thing and lowered herself to marry into trade and now reappeared, apparently untainted by any hint of vulgarity.

Then it hit her. This was why Quinn had acted as he had just now. Blaine Wykeham had been removed and now Quinn had played the duke to the hilt—unconventional, defying Society to criticise anything he did because of his high status. He had made his choice so publicly, so unconventionally that, what would have shocked in a viscount, enchanted and amused.

Nobody would think to criticise Cat now, she realised, or be so foolish as to probe into exactly what kind of merchant her late husband had been, as they might have done if their courtship had been prolonged and jealousy and curiosity had been given time to grow.

To cross a duchess—or a duke as in love with his new wife as Quinn appeared to be—would be social suicide.

How very clever of him, she thought bitterly, even as she acknowledged that he was protecting her at the same time, that it had been a brilliant tactic. Just not the romantic gesture all the witnesses would believe.

'Mama, look,' she said as they reached Lady Bowland, and held out her left hand where the great emerald glowed in the sunlight. If her voice was shaky, then who could be surprised?

'Oh, my dear! Harland, you have made me the happiest of mothers.'

'The delight and pleasure is all mine, ma'am. I hope I will be a good son-in-law to you.'

That was enough to send her mother off into floods of happy tears, while her husband patted her shoulder and said, 'There, there,' and her friends gathered round to make a great fuss of all of them.

Footmen arrived with champagne and Cat downed one glass and reached for another.

She smiled and smiled until her cheeks ached and told herself to stop her foolish daydreaming. She was marrying the man she loved, she would have a position in Society that all would envy and she would be, more importantly, in a position to do a great deal of good.

* * *

'That was a very clever idea,' Cat said when the fuss had all died down a little. Luncheon was being served and, by common consent, the happy couple had been left to a table for two, a little removed from the crowd. It was, of course, exceedingly visible.

'Thank you. It suddenly struck me that trying to be conventional only served to emphasise how very *un*conventional this is.'

Quinn recalled thinking in terms of "uns" at an early stage in his acquaintanceship with Cat—unwise, unsuitable, unfashionably tall, unfashionably intelligent and undoubtedly independent.

Now, he thought, she looked uncomfortable, although one would need to know her very well to notice it.

'Did I embarrass you?' he asked, noticing that she was picking at her food, chasing a morsel of cold chicken around her plate with the tines of her fork.

'No,' Cat said immediately. 'You took my breath away a trifle, but I could see at once how sensible it is to do the unconventional thing under the circumstances. And dukes, as you are beginning to discover, can get away with almost anything.'

She speared the chicken and ate it. 'I would like more champagne and then something sweet and indulgent. Something you can offer to me in little spoonfuls. It will make us look like a couple quite ridiculously in love.'

'Is love ridiculous, then?' There was suddenly a cold, hard lump inside him.

'Oh, terribly unfashionable and sentimental,' Cat said with a laugh. 'So much better to have liking and friendship as we have.'

And desire, he thought. He wanted her so much. If she didn't want him to say the words, would she accept him showing her just how much he loved her? Whenever they had kissed he was left in no doubt about her answering passion and that gave him hope.

'Your wish is my command, Your Grace-to-be.' Quinn stood up and made his way slowly up to the tables of food, taking his time and thinking of ice buckets, accounts ledgers and rain in an attempt to calm his inconveniently ever-excited body.

He returned with a footman bearing a bottle and the creamiest, most decadent desert he could see amongst an impressive array. It appeared to contain chocolate, strawberries, alcohol of some kind, and a great deal of cream.

The footman poured the wine and left.

'My goodness.' Cat eyed the bowl with unladylike interest.

Quinn had a sudden desire for her to look at him like that, followed by a vivid mental picture of two naked bodies spread with cream, and was thankful for the protection of the tablecloth.

'Strawberries? They must grow them under glass.'

'We could do that at Harland Park. And pineapples, perhaps.' He dipped a spoon into the mound of cream and raised it to her lips.

Cat opened her mouth and made a sound like a purr that went straight to the base of his spine.

'If you make noises like that, I will not be accountable for my actions,' he warned.

Cat took up the other spoon and offered him a taste.

'How much alcohol is there in this?' Quinn demanded, licking his lips. 'It is the most delicious thing I have tasted since the last time I kissed you.'

'Quinn.' Cat dropped the spoon.

'And I cannot wait to marry you, because I know perfectly well that if I kiss you now, my self-control is going to crumble.'

Her eyes were wide and, he could have sworn, surprised. Surely the effect she had on him was no revelation to her?

No, he realised, it was not surprise, it was something else. He stared back, but she dropped her gaze and he was left puzzled. Surely that hadn't been hurt? Or, no, disappointment?

He was imagining things. He gave himself a mental shake and dipped the spoon again. 'More?'

'No, thank you. It is delicious, but it is too rich. If

I am not careful I will end up slumbering the afternoon away.'

'Why not? This weather is holding fair, it is still warm and sunny. Look, they are laying out more rugs with cushions. Come and sit with me on that one over there. You may recline on piles of pillows and gently doze while I repel passing wasps and nosy guests.'

It was going to be utter agony to have her there, next to him, and be unable to so much as touch her, but the sleepy smile she gave him made it worth the pain.

Cat woke slowly, confused. There was daylight through her closed lids, she was lying on something very firm and she was beginning to feel a slight chill in the air.

She heard a murmur of voices and opened her eyes to find herself reclining against a pile of cushions and looking out over a sweeping lawn dotted with strolling couples and small groups, all dressed in the height of fashion.

'I was just going to wake you,' Quinn said beside her and she remembered where she was. 'It is becoming cool. Best put on that delightful hat and we will find your mama, who is doubtless equipped with shawls and wondering where you are.'

Cat looked down at her hands and there was the ring. So, no dream then. She was very publically betrothed to the Duke of Harland, Blaine Wykeham was banished and she should be very happy indeed.

Which she was, of course. Cat resumed her wide Villager hat and held up her hands for Quinn to pull her to her feet. They stood toe to toe for a moment, then he lifted her hands to his lips and kissed her fingertips.

'Come along, we had best brace ourselves for being the centre of attraction. No doubt everyone has decided we have had quite enough time billing and cooing together.'

'What a revolting expression,' she said with a laugh and tucked her hand into the crook of his elbow.

It is going to be all right, she told herself. *Quinn desires me, we are matched in that. We are still friends, we enjoy each other's company. Do not wish for the moon like that innocent girl peeping through the honeysuckle at a handsome young man so long ago. This is real life, not a dream.*

Even so, it felt unreal to be a source of pride to her parents, to be smiled upon and petted, with Mama basking in the congratulations of her friends and Papa beaming paternally.

As the air became cool and ladies shivered in their thin gowns, the picnic finally began to break up. Quinn rode back to the town house in their carriage.

'There is so much to plan,' Mama said. 'First we must fix upon a date for the wedding.'

'I shall obtain a special licence,' Quinn said. 'I would hope that Caitlin agrees to a date in the near future.'

'Oh, but we will need at least two months to prepare,' Mama protested. 'This is all so sudden.'

'I had thought two weeks,' he countered.

'That sounds perfect,' Cat said, ignoring her mother's murmurs of protest. 'Two weeks from tomorrow.'

Her mother shook her head as though despairing of Cat having so much as a pair of silk stockings in her trousseau with such appallingly short notice, but all she said was, 'And where do you wish the ceremony to take place? Our chapel at Bowland is very small, but, of course we could use the ballroom… Or St George's, Hanover Square. Or here? Or Harland Park? No?'

Cat realised that they must both have looked appalled at the thought. The idea of dozens of members of the *ton* descending on Duke's Forde when she hadn't even had her shop sign repainted and none of the local people could be relied upon not to talk enthusiastically about how wonderful it was that dear Mrs Brandon from the draper's shop should be marrying a duke, sent cold shivers down her spine.

'The town is still in a state with the building work,' Quinn said. 'I am proud enough of it not to want to show it off until everything is finished. I believe that the drawing room at my town house in Bedford Square will be ideal and will save you a great deal of trouble,

Lady Bowland. I will ask my secretary, James Turnbull, to make himself available to you. Perhaps he and your own secretary can liaise over the arrangements.'

'So kind,' her mother murmured.

Cat knew perfectly well that she would have no say in the arrangements. Mama would decide it all and Papa would pay for her trousseau—she knew better than to think that she would get away with ordering and paying for herself.

When Quinn stood up and said that he must leave and begin his own arrangements, she jumped up too. 'I will show you out,' she said, waving her father back to his seat. Mama, she could tell, was dying to begin making lists.

Once outside the drawing room door, Cat steered Quinn into the small morning room. 'You must tell me if there is anything you particularly want—or do not want,' she said, closing the door firmly behind them with a complete disregard for the proprieties. 'I know Mr Turnbull will manage every detail with Mama's secretary, but Mama does rather tend to, um...'

'Take the bit between her teeth?' he said.

'Yes,' Cat admitted. 'So, you will say, won't you?'

'I know exactly what I want,' Quinn said. 'May I kiss you, Cat?'

'I thought you would never ask,' she said demurely and walked into his arms.

It was a very different embrace from the ones they

had shared before. They would be married soon. They could take their time, taste and savour, begin to learn each other's bodies.

Cat shivered with anticipation as their mouths met and she pressed close to Quinn, curving into him, finding how they fitted together.

It doesn't matter that he doesn't love me, she told herself. *He desires me, that is enough. It has to be enough.*

Quinn's big hands cupped her behind, lifting her on tiptoe against his hardness, showing her how much he wanted her. He growled, deep in his chest when she started to nip at his lower lip.

With that part of her brain that was still able to form rational thoughts, she wondered whether she would please him in bed. Her prior experience with two men had not exactly prepared her for what she knew would be a very different experience. Blaine had simply been selfish and all he had required of her was that she submitted while he took his own pleasure. William had been very proper: both of them in nightshirts with the lights out. She realised with a shock that she had never seen a completely naked man before.

There is rather a lot of this one, she thought as one hand roved over her back, cradled her head, tilting it to give him access to the sensitive skin below her ear.

I love you, I love you. Freed from his kiss, her lips silently shaped the words.

Quinn eased her back until her feet were flat on the floor again and rested his forehead against hers. 'I am looking forward to a time when we do not have to stop just as this is becoming interesting,' he said ruefully.

'Mmm,' Cat said intelligently. Her powers of speech appeared to have deserted her.

'I had better leave,' Quinn said, not moving.

'Mmm.'

'Definitely, I must go,' he said after a minute, stepping back. 'I suspect we may be somewhat busy over the next two weeks, Cat, with a lot to think about and decide, but here is another decision for you—where would you like to go after we are married? Would you like a tour of all our relatives? Or to visit all my estates, of which there appear to be more than I had realised at first. Or somewhere else? It is late in the year for Brighton or another seaside resort, of course.'

'Harland Park,' Cat said, suddenly certain that was what she wanted. 'And then we can plan journeys to visit your other estates from there.'

'Certainly, that would suit me very well.'

Quinn had one hand on the door handle when she said, 'Quinn—'

'Yes?' He turned, smiling, but, she thought already with his mind on the next thing on his agenda.

'Nothing. Goodbye.'

Just, I love you. She had almost blurted it out. *I love you. Can you love me?*

But no, it wasn't safe to admit it because the answer was sure to be *No* and *Perhaps*. Or he would lie to spare her feelings.

The front door closed.

At least she was going home. Almost.

Chapter Twenty-Five

The Marchioness of Glandford, one of Cat's godmothers, held a reception in honour of the happy couple a week before the wedding.

As Cat's relatives from near and far, and many she had no recollection of ever having met, had descended on London in anticipation of a ducal wedding, this did remove some of the pressure from Lady Bowland to entertain them.

Cat was pleased to have another opportunity to meet and mingle amongst the *ton* after so many years away. She did not particularly enjoy the formality and the rituals, but as a duchess she would be expected to play a leading part in Society and she was determined not to let Quinn down.

As the guests of honour, Cat and Quinn stood beside the Marchioness in the receiving line, smiling and shaking hands and responding to the good wishes of the guests.

Cat, keeping up her social smile even though her

lips felt stiff and her hand was aching, was aware that not all the congratulations were sincere. Several young ladies regarded her with jealous eyes, and their mothers clearly felt aggrieved that she should appear from obscurity and land the biggest catch of the Season before it had even begun.

She was reminded, yet again, of the need to present an appearance of impeccable respectability however much it chafed. She had not fully appreciated what compromises her new position would impose.

Released at last from the line, Quinn led her into the principal reception room and, once she was circulating, took himself off in the opposite direction. Her mother had warned her that they should not appear to cling together. 'So unfashionable, dear, and, as this is in your honour, you must be certain to speak to everyone.'

So Cat kept smiling and talking of the same things over and over again as she moved around the rooms, thanking people for their felicitations, replying to questions as best she could: Yes, she had seen Harland Park; no, she was not familiar with the Duke's other estates; indeed it was a rush assembling a trousseau in just two weeks but how fortunate that with the Season not begun the modistes were able to oblige her without delay; yes, she did find London somewhat changed, which was very interesting.

At least she had no worries about her gown, which

was a delicious confection in amber silk with a plaited trim around the hem and cream Brussels lace at the neck and sleeves. One of the benefits of her age and widowed status was that she was spared the insipid pastels of the young ladies making their come-outs, she thought appreciatively.

Quinn, having enquired about colours, had retrieved a parure of emeralds from the jeweller's vault for her, and she was wearing, with some apprehension about their value, a small tiara, a necklace and earrings that matched her ring.

After half an hour she finally escaped the attentions of one of Quinn's elderly and unmarried cousins, who seemed determined to recount every occasion she had seen his late great-aunt wearing those jewels, by pretending that a hairpin was slipping and she must go to the retiring room.

The door to it was partly concealed behind a screen and, as she came out again, she had to wait as three ladies had stopped, effectively blocking the exit.

'Well, I call that most tactless of the Marchioness, inviting Lady Ansley,' one of them said.

'Perhaps she does not know she is the Duke's *chère amie*,' another said with a little titter. 'Dear Lady Glandford is somewhat above such things, is she not? I have never known her to so much as mention a crim con case.'

Cat, her heart thudding, slid sideways behind a potted palm.

'This is hardly a question of marital scandal, is it?' a third lady remarked. 'After all, Lady Ansley is a widow and, one must admit, usually very discreet. She is received everywhere, even at Court.'

'At least Harland appears to be careful too. I don't imagine his bride knows about the *affaire* either.'

'Hmm,' murmured the first speaker. 'It could be amusing. Lady Caitlin is hardly a naive little debutante, for all that she has been out of Society for years. That young woman looks as though she has a mind of her own. If she does find out, I'll wager Harland will discover he has a spitfire in his hands.'

Blinking back shocked tears, Cat slipped back into the retiring room which, fortunately, was empty except for the maids, busily tidying the dressing tables. She sat down at one, waved aside an offer of assistance, withdrew the little pot of rice powder and the small soft brush from her reticule and pretended to be studying her complexion closely in the glass.

So, Quinn had a mistress. Of course he did, she told herself harshly, that is what gentlemen did, and a wife had to be grateful if it was a well-bred widow and not a professional courtesan, or, much worse, he had a taste for picking up girls from the Haymarket or Covent Garden.

Nobody thought the worse of the men, provided

they were not debauching innocents, sleeping with other men's wives or flaunting lovers in public. Wives just pretended they knew nothing about it.

I am not going to cry. I was a fool not to expect this.

She put away the rice powder, blew her nose and stared at herself in the mirror until she was certain no untoward emotion showed on her face.

Could she accept it? Should she not tell Quinn now that she could not marry him? Pride and hurt almost had her on her feet ready to seek him out that moment and end this.

But was the affair still going on? Because if it was, then she could be certain that Quinn did not love her. If they had ended it, there was still that faint hope that there might be something in this marriage she could build on.

Cat left the retiring room. How was she going to discover who Lady Ansley was? She had no recollection of her from the receiving line, so she must have arrived after Cat had left it.

She scanned the room, then began to circulate again. *Not you, not you, too old, too young...*

Then she saw Quinn, who had stopped and was talking to an attractive blonde lady of about his own age. As she watched they drifted sideways behind one of the arrangements of palms and ferns that dotted the rooms, creating little conversation nooks where seats were set out.

Cat began to move in that direction. When she reached it, she stood close to the greenery and pretended to be searching for something in her reticule while she peered through the gaps. She could not hear what they were saying, but they were standing very close together and they were both smiling. As she watched the blonde put one hand flat against Quinn's chest and stroked his lapel.

Unless Quinn was in a liaison with more than one woman, then this must be Lady Ansley. Cat tried to study this rival dispassionately. She was beautiful, elegant and looked both intelligent and amusing. Of course Quinn wanted her for a lover and probably he loved her too. Why not marry her? Perhaps she was too independent, or he wanted a younger wife because she was more likely to give him a quiverful of children.

Quinn said something that made Lady Ansley laugh softly, and she went up on tiptoe to kiss him.

Cat turned away, the room blurring through the tears her pride would not let her shed.

Well, at least she knew what she was facing, and she would no longer have any foolish, romantic daydreams. She would not back out now. She had been foolishly naive not to imagine he had a mistress, and she had hurt and upset her parents enough. He had made her no promises of fidelity, no declarations of love. And there was all the good she could do as a duchess: she could not throw that away because of a wounded heart and hurt pride.

Cat took a glass of wine from a waiter passing by with a tray, fixed a smile on her lips and sailed into the crowd.

'Aunt Augusta, I am so glad you are able to be here for the wedding. Do tell me, are you still breeding those adorable spaniels?'

Most things healed in time and perhaps broken hearts did too.

Chapter Twenty-Six

'Wilt thou obey him and serve him, love, honour and keep him in sickness and in health; and forsaking all other, keep thee only unto him, for so long as you both shall live?'

The Bishop of Mulchester—of course, Quinn had a bishop in the family—waited for her answer and it felt to Cat as though the ranks of seated guests in the large drawing room held their breath.

'I will,' Cat said, trying to ignore several mental reservations. Love, keep and forsake all others? Yes. Serve and obey? Yes, when she agreed with him. As to honour? Not if he broke his own vow, was breaking it even as he made it.

Her father by her side gave her hand to Quinn. His felt warm and steady and his thumb brushed the base of hers for a moment.

She kept her eyes lowered and did not turn to look at him as he repeated after the Bishop, 'I Quentin Arthur

Henry Falconer, take thee, Caitlin Mary Louisa Montgomery, to my wedded wife, to have and to hold…'

I should have confronted him, told him what I knew, refused to marry him, she thought, angry with herself.

It is too late now, the weaker part of her, the part that loved him, wanted him, said. It had won out in the furious mental battles she had fought with herself ever since she had seen that kiss. *What does your pride matter?* the insidious little voice had asked. *It will not keep you warm in bed at night, it will not give you children. It will not give you the influence you need.*

Somehow she got through the rest of the service, said all the right words at the right time, allowed Quinn to slip the ring on her finger and had not clenched her hand into a tight fist.

The Bishop pronounced the blessing and she put back her veil, took her husband's arm and was led slowly down between the rows of guests, some beaming, some serious, a few, like her mother, in tears.

They took up their position at the door into the dining room where the wedding breakfast was waiting and greeted everyone as they came through. Cat called on all her years of experience dealing with customers and smiled and murmured thanks for the compliments.

Such a beautiful bride, such a lovely ceremony, such an auspicious beginning to a perfect marriage.

She was kissed by a number of new relatives whose

names she was just learning, was scrutinised sharply by a number of the older matrons, clearly on the lookout for imperfections in the new duchess, and remembered to call the Bishop, "My lord".

'Cousin Herbert,' he corrected her with a twinkle.

So that had gone well, she thought, taking her place beside Quinn in the centre of the long table.

She had said all the right words at the right time. She knew herself to be looking as well as she ever had in a gown of palest green with darker green ribbons in the elaborate hem, neckline and sleeves. She wore diamonds, borrowed from Mama, with the Montgomery tiara holding her veil in place and, beneath the rustling petticoats, a blue garter presented by her sister who had worn it at her own wedding.

'Something borrowed, something blue,' Anna had quoted. 'My goodness, Caitlin, you have surprised us all.' That was Anna: always a little sting in the tail of a compliment.

'Well, Your Grace?' Quinn said, and she realised he was speaking to her. Now she was the Duchess of Harland, with precedence over just about everyone except the royal family.

'Very well,' she replied and found her smile was quite genuine. She had married the man she loved, she had power, wealth and status most women could only dream of and she could use those to do good. The confused, desperate girl who had stumbled for the stagecoach into the market square of Duke's Forde could never have imagined such a fairy-tale end to her adventures.

She had flourished in her new world then, and she could do so again in this. Nothing is ever perfect and to yearn for it is foolish, Cat told herself. She put her hand over Quinn's and gave it a squeeze, then turned to the Bishop on her left and asked him about his family. 'I have so much to learn about all my new relatives,' she confided. 'I am so looking forward to married life with Quinn.'

They had to leave in the early afternoon for the long journey to Harland Park, Quinn had warned her, so she slipped upstairs when dessert had finished and was joined in her dressing room by her new personal maid, Linden, and her mother.

Linden—Miss Linden to all the other staff, such was her status now—dealt with the change of outfit efficiently and in silence. Mama chattered on, slightly flown with champagne and happiness, but Cat hardly heard a word of it. Her own head was spinning slightly as she stood still for Linden to undo the tiny buttons and then lift her wedding dress over her head.

'Do you like this walking dress, Mama?' she asked in an effort to focus her mother's thoughts.

'Delightful, dear. Is that the one from Mrs Bell?'

That led on to a lament about the other fashionable modistes they could have patronised if Quinn had not been in such a hurry to wed, and an acknowledgment that really, almost anything could be forgiven a duke.

Finally she was dressed again and made her way downstairs, leaving Linden to organise the last of her bags to be packed into the second carriage that she and Quinn's valet would occupy.

It took almost an hour of talking and kissing before they actually managed to leave. Cat fell back against the squabs of Quinn's luxurious travelling carriage—my *luxurious carriage*—and began to take off her bonnet.

'No, leave it,' Quinn said.

'But I will be much more comfortable on the journey if I take it off.'

'The journey is almost over. Look.'

Cat stared. They should have been making their way westwards towards the turnpike road but instead the carriage was drawing to a halt in some mews. 'Where are we?'

'Back at the town house. I thought you might find the journey tiring after everything else today but, if we told everyone we were staying, the party would have gone on for hours. They think we are on our way, when all the time we are climbing the back stairs to the peace and quiet of our rooms. We can leave after breakfast tomorrow.'

'That sounds much better,' Cat said with a sigh of relief. At the moment all she really wanted was to take off her stays and lie down on her bed. Too much bustle and noise, too much emotion, too much food and wine. Far too much to come to terms with. 'Who else knows?'

'Only Linden and my man Jessup, who are still in the house. When everyone has left, they will speak to the other staff and organise food and hot water for us.'

'That is quite brilliant of you.' Cat retied her bonnet ribbons. 'I am longing to collapse onto a bed.'

'Indeed,' Quinn said with some feeling.

'Oh! I'm sorry. I mean...'

'That you would like to rest before you can contemplate a little light supper and a bath and anything else?'

'Yes,' she agreed. 'Quinn, do you mind?'

'The alternative was hours on the road and arriving too tired for either of us to take any interest in anything,' Quinn said as they came to a halt and a groom opened the carriage door.

It lifted her spirits to be sneaking in through the back door and up the servants' stair, Cat realised. It was so much like a childish prank that she felt like giggling and nudging Quinn as they climbed.

Somehow Cat managed to resume her dignity as they emerged onto the landing to be received by a lady's maid and valet as though their employers creeping up the back stairs was perfectly normal.

'You had hardly any chance to look at your suite,' Quinn said. 'You must let me know how you would like it redecorated. I am just next door, should you need anything. Have a good rest.' He opened a door in her sitting room and went through, closing it behind him.

What do I need? You, of course. But first a rest, for her mind as much as her body.

Half an hour later Quinn stood at the interconnecting door and listened. Silence. There was a faint thread of worry beneath his happiness, fretting at him so he could not sleep, even though he had undressed and was wearing only a heavy silk banyan.

Something was wrong with Cat, although he could not put his finger on quite what it was. It was like looking at a very familiar, complex painting and suddenly becoming aware that some element had changed.

She was tired, that was all, he told himself. Weddings were emotional occasions and this one had held more stresses than most, he imagined.

He eased open the door and went in to the sitting room, then across it to the half-open bedchamber door. Cat, dressed in a flowing, and very bridal negligée, was curled on top of the covers, deeply asleep.

Quinn padded in bare feet across the carpet and lay down beside her, not touching, just listening to her breathing. After perhaps a minute he moved to drop a kiss on her temple. 'Love you.' Then he rolled back to his side of the bed, closed his eyes and slept.

* * *

Cat woke slowly, aware of being warm and comfortable and of the fact that the bed beneath her was gently moving up and down.

Under her cheek was the soft slide of silk, not linen, and when she opened her eyes she found she was looking at Quinn's chin. He was fast asleep and she had somehow moved across the bed and wrapped herself around him without waking him.

She shifted a little to look at his face and that woke him. Sleepy dark eyes regarded her and his mouth curved into a smile. 'I looked in to see how you were and could not resist joining you. How are you now?'

'Awake,' she said demurely. His closeness, the scent of warm male skin and the feel of his body beneath the robe were enough to send all her doubts and anxieties into some deep dark recess in her mind.

Just in case he had any concerns that she was still tired, she wriggled up against the pillows, leaned down and kissed the vee of skin that was visible at the neck of his robe. The tickle of coarse hair against her lips was delicious.

Quinn made a sound that was almost desperate and sat up abruptly. 'We are wearing altogether too much,' he said, shrugging out of his robe and casting it on the floor. 'How does this thing come off?'

Cat had not expected to be introduced to her first fully naked male body with quite so little warning, but her blushes were hidden by the frills and flounces of her negligee and nightgown which Quinn was disposing of ruthlessly. They went sailing through the air to join his robe on the floor and then they were looking at each other, both of them breathing hard.

'Is it too soon, Cat? Do you need more time?'

In answer she put her arms around his neck and fell back on the bed and, at last, his weight was over her and she could feel his body as it began to learn hers, lean muscle accommodating itself to soft curves as she shifted beneath him, cradling him so that his heat and hardness met her soft warmth.

Quinn was kissing her while one hand worked its way between their bodies, found the core of her. He would find her so ready for him, she knew, although it had been a long time since she had done this and a flicker of apprehension ran through her.

'Cat?' Had he sensed it?

'Yes,' she said. 'Oh, yes.'

The slow slide, the filling, the moment when she held her breath while he seated himself fully within her and then became still, looking down at her.

'Oh, Cat. Darling. At last.' He withdrew slowly, then thrust and she gasped, lost for a second, then found the rhythm that made them one entity, moving with him and under him, as he pushed them both up, and up, tighter and tighter into a knot of pleasure that was almost pain. One more thrust and she cried out and heard his answering cry as she spun away into the starlit darkness.

They lay together simply breathing and being for a while, then Quinn eased away, sat on the edge of the bed. 'I will go back to my rooms and ring for bathwater for us both,' he said, although he seemed in no hurry to move, running his hand down her flank and over the curve of her hip. 'Oh, my duchess. You are magnificent.'

The rest of the evening passed in a blur for Cat. After her bath, Linden dressed her in another robe she had no recollection of buying, but which was rather less provocative than the first one. Then they ate a light supper in Quinn's sitting room and retired to her bedchamber again.

Their lovemaking this time was slower, an exploration, a deliciously intimate discovery of each other.

As Cat lay against Quinn's chest afterwards, she acknowledged that the gentle pace had let her think and, wonderful as it had been, all the hurt and yearning came back. She wanted to talk to him but she did not know how to begin or what she actually wanted.

At last she moved away a little, curled up and pretended to sleep. She felt a touch on her hair—his hand or his lips?—and did not react, although she felt a little comforted. Tomorrow, she thought as she began to slide into genuine sleep. Tomorrow I will be more settled and I will be able to accept what we have. Because that was already wonderful.

Quinn woke alone in his own bed and let the memories of the previous day sift through his mind as he woke.

He had not thought he could love Cat more than he had before they married, now he realised that this feeling was going to keep growing, expanding, taking over his emotions. He had to do something, but where were the words when his wife had been so clear about her own feelings for him?

She had responded with such trust and passion to his lovemaking that perhaps that was the way to show her his feelings—make love to her until she could not fail to realise.

He got out of bed as the clocks in the house began to strike six, shrugged on his robe, and went across his sitting room to the connecting door. As he touched the handle it turned and he stepped back as the door opened to reveal Cat in the robe that she had worn over supper.

'Cat—'

'I have to talk to you,' she said, walking right into the room. 'I cannot stand this any longer.'

Quinn could feel the blood beginning to drain away from his head and put one hand on a chair back to steady himself. 'Cannot stand what?' *Our marriage?*

* * *

Quinn was as pale as she felt, but Cat made herself speak. 'It isn't honest of me to conceal that I know about Lady Ansley. I heard some talk at the reception and then I saw you together. I saw you kiss. I know that I am supposed to pretend I suspect nothing, or that I accept that this is just something that married men do, have a lover, but I cannot live that lie.'

There was a chair very close and she sank down on it when her legs gave way.

'Hell.' Quinn sat too, within touching distance, although he did not reach for her. 'Cat, we were lovers, for some years. We were fond of each other, we still are. But it is over. We have not been together since before I came to Duke's Forde and we agreed, as friends, to end it. I knew I would marry and I take my promises seriously, Cat. That night at the reception, she was wishing me good fortune, saying goodbye after what had been, for us, a pleasure, but a temporary one. An *affaire*, but not a love affair.'

Cat felt so dizzy that for a moment she did not recognise the feeling for what it was. Relief. 'I... I believe you. I am sorry that I doubted you, but...'

'The way it looked was damning. I understand, Cat. It would be a blow to your trust and to your pride.'

'My pride?' Relief was swamped in a wash of anger. *'My pride?'*

'I know you do not love me, Cat. You have a right—'

Now she was confused by the conviction with which he spoke. 'Why are you so certain of that? We have never spoken of our feelings in that way.'

'I overheard you talking to your mother. You were very definite.'

There was a bitterness in his voice that she recognised, understood. 'Mama can be insensitive and intrusive. I had no desire to lay out my vulnerabilities for her to pick over. I told her what she wanted, expected, to hear. I never meant to hurt you, because I do love you. I would never have married you if I did not.'

The colour was back in Quinn's face now, and those dark, intelligent eyes were watching her with something like hope in them. And yet he did not speak. Was she a fool to wish?

'Quinn, why were you at my door just now? Was it simply to wake me, join me in bed again?'

'It was to tell you that I love you,' he said, his voice strong and sure. 'That I have for an age. That I realised I had to have the courage to risk your rejection.'

How she ended up in his arms, she was never quite sure, but she was there, kissing him, crying, hugging and being hugged until the little chair gave an ominous creak and Quinn stood up with her still in his arms.

They did not break the kiss until they were on his bed in a tangle of limbs and clothing. The struggle to free themselves somehow allowed them space to breathe and to laugh and finally to lie back against the pillows facing each other, close enough for their breath to mingle.

'Back in July I decided to propose to you,' Quinn said, his smile rueful. 'I got myself dressed up in my best, took the shiniest carriage in the stables and took you to a nice romantic, secluded spot on the riverbank.'

'Oh! And I thought you were going off to propose to someone else—and I talked of nothing but Madelaine and how marriage was a trap for women. I am sorry.'

'So then I thought I must give you more time to realise you could trust me.'

'And then it was the night of the assembly, and everything went wrong because I could not trust you.'

'There is no blame here, Cat. I do not think that either of us found it easy to understand our own feelings, let alone each other's.'

'No. But we understand them now, I think,' she said as she leant forward for his kiss.

Quinn took her in his arms and they made love slowly, discovering each other all over again, whispering the emotions they had held back and guarded inside their hearts until the words broke free and joined as they reached a shuddering peak of pleasure together.

'I love you, oh, so much.'

'I love you, now and for eternity, my love.'

Epilogue

June 1822, Harland Park.

'Ouch,' Cat said mildly. 'You have very sharp elbows, young lady.'

She was certain this baby would be a girl and she was growing impatient waiting for her. Cat made a final note on the plan in front of her and stood up, balancing carefully to compensate for the bump, before rolling up the large sheet of paper and walking slowly out of her study and towards the Blue Salon.

'Is your Papa home yet?' She was certain that her conversations with the baby were heard, just as she was sure that music reached the child. 'He was very worried about that fire, you know. I do hope he hasn't worn himself out.'

One of the tenants had woken to find his rick yard ablaze, and Quinn, of course, had joined the firefighters. That had been eight hours ago, but she was not unduly concerned, because he had sent messages back to say all was under control and nobody was hurt.

She opened the door and stopped on the threshold at the sight of the Duke of Harland, flat out on the sofa, snoring gently, their three-year-old son sound asleep on his chest.

'His Grace came in a few minutes ago and his young lordship was being brought through the hall by his nurse and saw him,' Whiting, the butler, murmured.

'And with his boots on,' Cat said, smiling. 'Oh, well, the suite needed recovering, I suppose. Please send coffee in shortly, Whiting, and let the kitchen know breakfast will be required.'

'A bath first, ma'am?'

'No, food I think.' Marriage had taught her many things, amongst them the fact that food trumped hot water every time for the male of the species.

Cat lowered herself into an armchair within touching distance of her sleeping husband. Young Jocelyn Harvey Montgomery Falconer, Earl of Longmere, opened his eyes and beamed at her.

'Mama! Papa's asleep!'

'Not any more,' Quinn said without opening his eyes. 'Off you get, Joss.' He grunted as his son and heir levered himself up and then slid to the ground.

'Good morning, my love.' Quinn stood up, bent over the chair and kissed her thoroughly

'Good morning. Coffee is on its way, followed by food, followed I suspect, by an upholsterer.'

'Sorry.' He sat down again and ran one grubby hand through his hair. 'The buildings will have to be torn down.'

'There are some interesting plans for model farms in Ackermann's *Repository*,' Cat remarked. 'Now the school is finished, you have the builders free. And—'

'I thought you were supposed to be resting, not reading about agricultural improvement. Surely this baby is going to make an entrance at any moment?'

'Not before I appoint the teachers for the enlarged school,' Cat said anxiously as Joss scrambled up onto what was left of her lap and applied his ear to the bump. She laid one hand on his dark curls and closed her eyes in thankfulness for a moment. So much to love.

'And what is that?' Quinn pointed to the roll of plans.

'I asked Mr Abernathy to draw up a proposal for an infirmary. I should have guessed that the result is grand enough for St Thomas's in London.'

'I have no doubt you will end up with something suitable, you seem to have tamed the man,' Quinn said with a smile. 'The first school, its extension, the institute and reading room, the improved cottages for the labourers' families and now an infirmary, all exactly as you ordered. Never mind about model farms, Duke's Ford will soon be a model town.'

With any other man Cat knew that could well be a complaint: why wasn't she being a "proper" duchess? But from her husband Cat knew it was admiration for his partner.

It hadn't been easy at first. They were both strong-willed, both full of ideas. They had argued and fought until eventually they discovered the knack of working together, of being parents, of managing the estates and carrying out works that earned them the admiration—and from the more reactionary, criticism—of their peers.

'I hope so,' she said, reaching out so their fingers touched. 'After all, we have a model marriage, don't you think?'

'I do not have to think. I know that we do. And I know that I love you more than I ever thought possible and that you love me, and I will never cease to be thankful that you stepped down from that stagecoach onto the cobbles of Duke's Ford.'

'It was meant to be, Quinn. We were meant to find each other, my love,' she murmured as he went down on his knees and enveloped her, and their children, in his strong arms.

* * * * *

*If you enjoyed this story, be sure to read
Louise Allen's previous historical romances*

Becoming the Earl's Convenient Wife
How Not to Propose to a Duke
Tempted by Her Enemy Marquis
The Lady Who Said No to the Duke

MILLS & BOON®

Coming next month

DARING TO DREAM OF THE DUKE
Lauri Robinson

Book 1 in Brides for Sworn Bachelors

There was something in Michael's eyes, the way he was looking at her, that was stealing the air from her lungs. Making it hard to breathe and impossible to look away. It felt as if time stopped. As if the world forgot to keep turning.

She had the strangest sensation that he wanted to kiss her. Or maybe those were her thoughts. For that was exactly what she wanted. With every part of her body.

His finger was still beneath her chin, and his thumb was caressing her cheek and sending a thrilling heat through her face, down her neck. Her lips were tingling, her heart was pounding, and the rest of her had the greatest desire to rise on her toes so her face was closer to his.

She'd never wanted something so badly. So completely. An unusual excitement was growing stronger and stronger at the mere idea of kissing him. Of his lips touching hers. She could imagine that it would be better than dancing with him. Better than anything she'd ever known.

Just as she was giving in, about to rise onto her toes, a piercing sense of reality struck. This was Michael. The one man she'd always dreamed of kissing and the one man she couldn't kiss. Couldn't ever let him know about the dreams she'd had for years. He'd merely been being kind to her this weekend, watching out for her, because as Nora had mentioned that first day, he thought of her as another sister. Someone he had to protect. Nora had said that would never change, and he certainly hadn't done anything to make Rosemary believe otherwise.

She'd been the one wishing it would change, and she shouldn't have. It wouldn't matter what she wore—he would never see her as a woman he could be interested in for something more than friendship.

Coming to her senses, she jerked her head backwards, and knowing that wasn't enough, she took a step backwards, too, all the while struggling to catch her breath.

The hand that had been touching her face fell to Michael's side, and it suddenly felt like she'd lost something precious.

He stared at her for yet another stilled moment, and she wished with all her might that she could read his mind. She couldn't, so all she could do was hope that he hadn't realized how badly she'd wanted him to kiss her.

Continue reading

DARING TO DREAM OF THE DUKE
Lauri Robinson

Available next month
millsandboon.co.uk

Copyright © 2026 Lauri Robinson

COMING SOON!

We really hope you enjoyed reading this book. If you're looking for more romance be sure to head to the shops when new books are available on

Thursday 26th March

To see which titles are coming soon, please visit
millsandboon.co.uk/nextmonth

MILLS & BOON

FOUR BRAND NEW BOOKS FROM
MILLS & BOON MODERN

Indulge in desire, drama, and breathtaking romance – where passion knows no bounds!

OUT NOW

Eight Modern stories published every month, find them all at:
millsandboon.co.uk

LET'S TALK
Romance

For exclusive extracts, competitions and special offers, find us online:

- **f** MillsandBoon
- **X** @MillsandBoon
- **⊙** @MillsandBoonUK
- **♪** @MillsandBoonUK

Get in touch on 01413 063 232

For all the latest titles coming soon, visit
millsandboon.co.uk/nextmonth